A FRESH START

SUGAR SPRINGS
BOOK 4

ALEXA ASTON

OLIVERHEBERBOOKS

0 9 8 7 6 5 4 3 2 1

❀ Created with Vellum

PROLOGUE

HOUSTON—LATE DECEMBER

D eb Busby couldn't help but smile at her date.

Tonight was going so well.

She hadn't had a date in several months, and this one was the best she'd had since moving back to her hometown four years ago. She had been reluctant to go out with Anita's brother, fearing if the evening fell flat that it might affect her relationship with her co-worker at the veterinary clinic where they both worked. Anita had pushed for Deb to go on the date, though, saying Jerry needed to get out after his divorce last year. He was new to Houston, having been transferred from his Boston firm a month ago.

Deb liked everything about Jerry.

He was nice-looking without being too handsome. Unlike many men, he could carry on a conversation with ease. They both had a love of sports. She had played volleyball and run track in high school, even winning an athletic scholarship to college. Jerry had also run track and played basketball. This evening had been like pulling the layers from an onion, slowly discovering things about one another. Deb hoped there would be a second date.

The server came to their table in the corner of the restaurant and asked if they needed anything else.

"No, just the check, thank you," Jerry said.

When the server handed over the bill, he gave her his credit card, and she left to process it.

Jerry gazed across the table. "I will admit that I wasn't happy that Anita insisted on setting us up. I've only had one other blind date in my life, and it was a total disaster." He smiled at her. "This evening has been a pleasant surprise, though. I hope we can do this again soon, Deb."

A flutter filled her chest. "Yes, I'd like to see you again. I was a little nervous about tonight myself. I was afraid if we didn't have anything in common, it might affect my friendship with Anita."

"We really haven't talked about your work. How long have you been at Dr. Wallman's practice?"

"Four years. After I graduated from vet school, I spent three years as research assistant for my favorite professor in College Station. I learned a lot, but I really wanted to roll up my sleeves and practice veterinary medicine. I wanted to be closer to my parents since I'm an only child, so I moved back to Houston. I was lucky Dr. Wallman had an opening at his practice."

The server returned with Jerry's credit card, and he signed for their dinner and stood, going to her chair and pulling it back, helping Deb to her feet.

They walked through the now-empty restaurant, having spent three hours over dinner. She realized they were the last patrons to leave. The time had flown by. When they reached the parking lot next to the restaurant, only a few cars remained in it.

Suddenly, an expletive flew from Jerry's mouth, taking her aback since he'd been so polite all evening. She glanced and saw both tires on the left side of his car were flat. A chill filled her, and she quickly looked over her shoulder.

Standing across the street watching them was Cris Calder.

She whipped her head around, nausea filling her. Up until

now, she'd thought Calder persistent but harmless. This changed everything.

Jerry was kneeling beside the left rear tire. "Slashed. Who would do this? I thought this was a safe part of town."

Deb glanced across the street again, but Calder had vanished. She looked back at her date. "This is all my fault," she blurted out.

A quizzical look crossed his face. "You're telling me you sneaked out here when you went to the restroom and slashed my tires?"

"No," she said quietly. "But I think I know who did."

Frowning, he pushed to his feet. "Tell me," he said harshly, all signs of friendliness gone. She knew what she would reveal would send Jerry packing.

"I had dinner with a guy about two months ago. He brought in his beagle, who had been struck by a car. The poor little fellow had broken a leg but was otherwise okay." She swallowed painfully. "The client was so grateful that he asked if he could take me to dinner as a thank you. I met him at a steakhouse."

Deb fell silent, discouraged that the pleasant evening was quickly unraveling—and she had no way to set things right.

"And?" prompted Jerry.

"He was... off. He seemed charming one minute and then... I don't know. He just gave off a vibe that made me feel really uncomfortable. At the end of the night, I thanked him for dinner. He insisted on walking me to my car. He tried to kiss me, and I pulled away. I was totally surprised. Told him this hadn't been a date. That he'd said that he was thankful I had saved his pup, and that's why we'd shared a meal. He grabbed my arms and insisted it was a date and that he wanted to marry me."

She shivered, being taken back to that night. To the pressure Calder had used, so much that it had left bruises on her arms.

"I totally freaked out. Started struggling to get away. If another couple hadn't come upon us on the way to their car, I'm not sure what would have happened. The guy asked if I was all right. Calder released me. I jumped into my car and locked the doors and sped out of the parking lot as quickly as possible."

Her date glared at her. "So, you go out with a guy two months ago, and now you go out with me—and think this first guy is the one who slashed my tires?"

She nodded timidly. "He's been sending me letters. A few emails. Leaving little presents at my door. You're the first man I've gone out with in several months. I'm afraid... I'm afraid he's stalking me."

Her date made a noise, letting Deb know how disgusted he was. "I can't believe you let us go out when you have some psycho stalking you. Sorry. I didn't sign up for this. I'll call you an Uber, but I don't want to see you again, Deb."

"I understand," she said quietly. "I'll call my own ride share. You need to handle the damage to your car. Please send me the bill for any towing fees and the expense of putting on new tires."

"Your damn right I will," Jerry said, anger sparking in his eyes.

Deb moved away from him, bringing up her ride share app and calling for a driver. A car was only four minutes away. She looked around nervously the entire time. Fortunately, she didn't spy Cris Calder anywhere. Deb did think to zoom in and take a picture of one of Jerry's slashed tires, wanting to document the incident.

Getting into the car when it arrived, she knew she needed to go to the police after this latest incident. She had tried to convince herself it was nothing, but things were escalating. She had thought she could handle it, but she decided it was time to get a restraining order. Quickly, she Googled how to apply for one in Texas and saw an attorney would need to file for it on her behalf. Still, she would go to the police tomorrow to see if she also needed to file an official report there, as well. It would be hard, though, because she didn't really have any physical proof that Calder had ruined Jerry's tires.

The driver pulled into her apartment complex, and Deb thanked him, asking if he would wait until she got inside before leaving. He agreed, and she hurried up the sidewalk, spooked that Calder would pop out at any minute. Placing her key in the door, she unlocked it and waved at the driver, hurrying inside and locking the door behind her.

Deb got ready for bed, but it took a long time for sleep to come. When it finally did, she had a nightmare about Cris Calder chasing her with a knife.

She awoke with a start, her heart racing, and saw it was four-thirty. No sense in trying to go back to sleep. It would be impossible the way adrenaline was pouring through her body now. Instead, she made a cup of coffee and sipped on it as she dressed for the gym.

Cautiously, she opened her door, only to look down to find another gift from her stalker. She brought in the vase of flowers, the stuffed teddy bear, and the note, taking pictures of all three before throwing all but the letter in the trash.

Deb raced to her car and reached the gym by five, putting her body through a punishing workout. She preferred running the streets of her Houston neighborhood but no longer felt safe doing so.

After leaving the gym, she returned home to shower. This week, she was working from ten in the morning until seven in the evening. All the vets at Dr. Wallman's large practice worked the same shift hours each week and then rotated the next week. Deb preferred the early shift, which began at seven, since she was a morning person, but it worked in her favor today not having to be at work until mid-morning. She Googled and found the nearest police station, driving to it. She explained to the sergeant at the desk that she wanted to speak to someone regarding a stalker, and he told her to have a seat.

Less than five minutes later, a man appeared, introducing

himself as Detective Nix. He led her back to a small conference room and asked her to tell him about the man bothering her.

Deb explained how she had first encountered Cris Calder and that she willingly had gone out with him for a celebratory meal.

"He didn't call it a date when he asked me to go, and I never thought of it as one," she told the detective. "At the end of the night, however, he told me he was going to marry me."

She relayed all that had happened over the last two months and showed the detective pictures on her phone of various gifts Calder had left at her doorstep. Deb handed over this morning's note and watched as he read it.

"I believe he's escalating," she confided. "He followed my date and me to a restaurant last night. I'm pretty busy, and this was the first date I'd had since I'd gone to dinner with Mr. Calder." She swallowed. "When Jerry and I came out of the restaurant, two of his tires had been slashed. I saw Cris Calder standing across the street. He was only in sight a few seconds. Just long enough to let me know he was the one responsible for the damage."

"But you have no proof that this Calder is the one who damaged the tires," Nix pointed out.

"I really liked the man I saw last night, Detective Nix, but when I let him know I had a problem with a guy, he quickly cut me loose. I'm worried about myself. My safety. I looked up restraining orders online, and I want to apply for one."

The detective walked her through the process and said, "The courts are pretty backed up right now. Dr. Busby, I'm afraid it could take weeks before this goes through once your attorney files for it. Do you have a friend or family member you might be able to stay with in the meantime?"

"My parents live in town. I could stay with them. Thank you for helping me, Detective Nix. I appreciate your time."

Deb went to her SUV and got into it, sitting behind the wheel to gather her thoughts. She realized her entire body was trembling in fear.

She couldn't expose her parents to such a threat, especially since she believed Calder's irrational behavior toward her was escalating. Her dad was in Stage Four of pancreatic cancer. He had abandoned all treatments last week, saying with the little time he had left, he didn't want to be so sick from them. Her mom was hanging on by a thread. Deb refused to bring her problems into their lives now.

She got control of herself and dialed her parents' phone number. Her mom answered on the second ring.

"Good morning, Deb, dear. How are you?"

Lying through her teeth, she replied, "I'm fine, Mom. How's Dad this morning?"

She could hear the worry in her mother's voice as her mom said, "Today is not a good day, honey. I'm not sure how many more days he has left, to be honest."

"You know I said I can take off and give you some relief."

"Oh, baby, you already come over several nights a week after work and spell me. No, your dad wouldn't want you to miss any work over him."

She wanted to be there for both her parents, but she was now afraid, not knowing if she should go to their house. What if Cris Calder had followed her there on one of her many visits? She didn't want to put them in any kind of danger.

"Does Dad feel like talking?"

"No, he's resting now. Why don't you call later? He might feel up to talking a few minutes then."

"Okay, Mom. I love you. Bye."

Deb scrolled through her contacts and found Winston Pym's name. He had served as her parents' attorney for many decades and now acted as hers, as well.

She called, and his receptionist put her through.

"Deb, how have you been? I haven't seen you since last Christmas at your parents' open house."

"I'm fine, Winston. Actually, I'm not fine. That's why I'm calling. I have a bit of a problem. A man is stalking me. I went to the police station just now, and they recommended that I file a restraining order against him."

Briefly, she walked the attorney through the situation, and he responded with sympathy.

"I'm sorry this has happened to you, Deb. Especially at a time like this. With what your dad is going through and all."

"They don't know about this, Winston. I want to keep it that way. I don't want either of them worrying about me."

He got some information from her and said, "I'll file for the restraining order this morning, Deb, but the courts are moving like molasses these days."

"Detective Nix warned me about that. He said it could take several weeks before a judge would schedule a hearing for me to attend."

"That's true. Once it does, the order will be in effect for two years. We'll have to refile at the end of that period if you feel it's necessary to extend it."

"Let's hope it's over long before then. Thank you, Winston. For handling this matter and keeping things confidential."

"I'm just sorry you're experiencing this at such a trying time, Deb. I'll see that paperwork is filed today and email you an update once it's been done."

She thanked him and started the car, heading to work. When she pulled into the parking lot, horror filled her. Over one hundred yard signs were scattered in the grass, surrounding the building.

Every one of them said in capital letters, *MARRY ME, DEB*.

The side of the clinic had also been vandalized, spray-painted in bright red with the same phrase, over and over. Two men with long brushes were scrubbing the words from the brick. Sick to her stomach, she entered the animal hospital.

Immediately, Anita gave her an ugly look. Whether it was

because of the scene outside or that she had spoken to her brother, Deb didn't know.

"Dr. Wallman wants to see you immediately, Dr. Busby," Anita said frostily.

Deb went to the office and knocked on the vet's door. He called for her to come in, and she pushed the door open.

"Have a seat, Dr. Busby," he said sternly.

She closed the door behind her and took a chair. He always called her Deb behind closed doors. His choice of words had her steeling herself for whatever he might say.

Trying to head things off, she said, "I am so sorry, Dr. Wallman. I went to the police just this morning, and my attorney is filing for a restraining order against Cris Calder as we speak."

"You've always done good work. You are nurturing and knowledgeable, and I will be happy to provide a reference for you, but this situation has gotten out of hand. Mr. Calder's obsession with you is affecting my practice. Why, he's even emailed me repeatedly, asking me to provide him with information about what you like. It's becoming too disruptive. I can't have my clinic in disarray over this situation."

"You're... firing me? When I'm the injured party?" she asked in disbelief.

The vet cleared his throat. "I can either let you go—or you can choose to resign. We can do this whichever way you want so that it reflects on your résumé accordingly."

She rose. "I'll resign then, Dr. Wallman, and I would appreciate the reference you mentioned. May I at least finish out the week? The day?"

The vet shook his head. "No. I don't think that's wise. Clear out your desk at once. Anita has already placed a box on your desk for your convenience."

He stood, handing her a sheet of paper he took from his desk. "This is a copy of the recommendation I will send to any prospective employer who might request it." A pained look crossed his face. "I'm sorry it's come to this, Deb."

"I'm sorry, as well," she replied. "I've really enjoyed my time working at your practice."

As if sleepwalking, Deb went to her office, where she found a cardboard box sitting on top of her desk.

She opened drawers and took a few items, placing them in the box, and then removed her diplomas from where they hung on the wall. Her bachelor's degree in biomedical sciences. Her DVM from Texas A&M's School of Veterinarian Medicine. She swallowed the lump which had formed in her throat, hating that her time here was over. She felt at loose ends. Threatened, fearful —for herself—and anyone around her.

Deb didn't bother saying goodbye to her colleagues. She doubted she would ever speak to anyone at the clinic again, despite four years of having worked here. She had done nothing wrong, yet she felt like the pariah as she carried the box to her car. Opening the back of the SUV, she placed the box inside and closed the hatch.

When she turned, she found Cris Calder at her elbow.

Enraged, Deb pushed him with both hands, hard in his chest, causing him to stumble back.

"Don't ever come near me again," she snapped. "I never want to see or hear from you. Ever. You've cost me my job, all because of your sick games."

Calder smiled benignly. "If you would just marry me, Deb, you could see how happy you and I could be. I'd like four children. If you're agreeable, that is. Two boys and two girls."

Anger rippled through her. "You think you can just put in an order and have kids of the gender you want magically pop out? You are batshit crazy. I have applied for a restraining order against you, Calder. You aren't allowed to communicate with me by phone, email, or letter. Or social media. You'll have to keep your distance from me and not follow me. I never want to see you again!"

She hurried to the driver's door and opened it.

As she got in, he said, "You don't mean it, Deb. I know you love me. We're meant to be together."

Glaring at him, she said, "Even if you were the last person on earth, I wouldn't have anything to do with you. Get out of my life."

Slamming her car door, she started the engine and pulled out of the parking lot, her tires screeching. She drove three blocks and pulled into a Target parking lot, her hands trembling so that she gripped the wheel for support.

Deb had lost the job she loved and the friends she had at the clinic. She no longer felt safe in her own home. And she doubted her dad would last another week. A sob burst from her, followed by more wrenching sobs. She cried until she felt sick at her stomach and no more tears came.

She went home and packed a bag, hurrying back to her car. Driving aimlessly for half an hour, her eyes watching the rearview mirror the entire time, she felt assured that Cris Calder wasn't following her. She began heading toward her parents' house and the moment she saw a Holiday Inn Express, Deb pulled in. She went inside, furtively looked around her, and booked a room for a week, telling the desk clerk she might wish to extend her visit.

The clerk handed over a key card, and Deb took the elevator up to the fourth floor. The corridor was empty. She found her room and unlocked the door, bolting every lock once she was inside. Collapsing into the chair at the desk, Deb wondered how her life had gone off the rails so quickly. At least she was freed from work now and could spend whatever little time her dad had left with him. That was the only upside to losing her job.

She sat in the chair, paralyzed, not moving for a few hours, everything a jumble. The only thing that brought her out of her thoughts was when her cell rang. She didn't recognize the number and for a moment, almost didn't answer it. But it might be from a line at Winston's law office. Or even Detective Nix, following up to see if she had filed for the restraining order.

Answering it, Deb said, "Hello?" trying to sound confident and assured.

"Is this Deborah Busby?" a voice asked.

"Yes, it is," she replied, tapping down the nerves that raced through her.

"Ms. Busby, when was the last time you spoke to your parents?"

Glancing at her watch, she said, "I talked with my mother about three hours ago. Maybe less," she said guardedly. "What is this about?"

"I see you have a Houston area code, Ms. Busby. Are you in town currently?"

"Who *is* this?" she demanded.

A slight hesitation came, and then the voice said, "I apologize for not identifying myself sooner, ma'am. This is Detective Paulson of the Houston Police Department."

"Oh, are you partners with Detective Nix?" she asked, feeling relieved. "I met with him earlier this morning."

"No, ma'am, I'm not. May I ask why you met with the detective?"

"I've had someone I know... stalking me. Detective Nix suggested I apply to the court for a restraining order. My attorney is doing so today." Deb paused. "Wait. What is this about? If you don't know Detective Nix, then why are you calling?"

"Because your cell number was listed as your mother's emergency contact, ma'am," Detective Paulson said.

"Oh! Has something happened to my dad? Has he been taken to the hospital? He's on hospice now. He shouldn't be revived. Did Mom lose her phone? What's going on?"

"I'm sorry to tell you this, Ms. Busby, but your parents were murdered. I'm at the scene now. I'll let the ME know when you spoke to your—"

"My parents are *dead*? Murdered?" she asked, her voice rising in hysteria. "I'll be right there."

"You can't have access to the scene, Ms. Busby. It would be better if we met at the station." He paused. "And you'll have to make the ID for us, as well, to confirm it's them."

"But who... why..." Her voice trailed off.

Then realization dawned on her.

"You need to arrest Cris Calder, Detective. He's my stalker. He's the one who killed my parents."

1

DALLAS—A YEAR LATER

Former detective Gideon Ross took one last look at his Dallas apartment. He had lived in it for nine years, ever since his divorce from Melinda. He had never had a friend over. Never brought a woman here. It was a holding space. One where he'd slept for four or five hours a night, showered, and left for long days of police work. He had never cooked a meal in its kitchen because he'd never had any pots or pans, much less a plate to put the food on. He'd never seen a single episode of TV here because he didn't own a television.

He closed the door on the life he was leaving behind and locked it. Heading downstairs, he dropped the keys into the slot of the manager's office.

He was free of Dallas. Of his old life.

And ready to start a new one in Sugar Springs.

Waiting in the car for him was Walker Cox, his best friend since preschool. They had both attended SMU together, Walker because he was smart and his attorney dad could afford the pricey tuition, and Gideon because he won a football scholarship. Walker had followed in his father's footsteps, earning a law degree from SMU, while Gideon had gone through the police academy and become a patrolman and then detective. His friend had left his high-powered law firm six months ago and returned to their childhood home in East Texas to take over his dad's practice. Campbell Cox had decided it was time to retire.

Thanks to another retirement, a new job awaited Gideon, as well. Police Chief Roscoe Hamilton, a good friend of Campbell's, was turning in his badge after decades in law enforcement. Gideon was Hamilton's handpicked choice to take his place as head of the Sugar Springs force. Inspired by the Coxes, who had been gone for months on a cruise after their retirements, the Hamiltons had a world cruise of almost one hundred days planned. Roscoe told Gideon that he liked not having to pack and unpack over the three months they would be gone, making stops in over thirty countries and going on excursions in cities as varied as Sydney, Dubai, and Barcelona. After cruising, the Hamiltons would join Roscoe's brother in a planned retirement community close to Fort Worth, where they would be near their grandkids.

While Gideon liked Roscoe, he was glad the former chief wouldn't remain in town, hanging over his shoulder, offering unsolicited advice and second-guessing Gideon's every move. He would be able to run the police department his way.

He had put off accepting the job when Roscoe had first asked him to take the reins back in October, when Gideon had come into town for the high school's homecoming game. He was working on a task force trying to catch a serial killer and wanted to see that case through. The chief had agreed to put a hold on retirement until Gideon was available to replace him. In a twist of fate, the serial killer had turned out to be an ex-boyfriend of Walker's fiancée, Rory Addison.

The case was now closed, and Walker and Rory had wed over the Christmas holidays. He had been best man at their wedding and would now see the couple frequently, living in the same small town.

Opening the door, he got into the passenger's seat. "Keys are turned in. Let's roll."

Walker indicated two coffees sitting in the cup holder. "I walked over to the convenience store while you were doing a last check." He tossed a sealed plastic bag to Gideon. "Rory made blueberry muffins this morning. She didn't know if anything would be open on New Year's Day for us to grab a bite to eat."

He opened the bag, handing a muffin to Walker and pulling out one for himself. "Must be nice to have a wife who thinks about things like that." Gideon bit into the muffin.

His friend laughed. "It's nice to have a wife I'm crazy about. Marriage to Rory is incredible, Gid. I never knew it could be like this." He grinned. "All we need to do now is find you the right woman."

"Nope. Been down the marriage rabbit hole before, Walker. I did my five years with Melinda."

Walker snorted. "Melinda was a stuck-up snob. Typical, spoiled rich girl whose daddy gave her everything and more. She loved dating a football player in college, especially one who garnered all the awards you did."

"Yeah, one who tore up his knee and couldn't make it in the pros."

Walker frowned. "You made it to the cut just before the fifty-three man roster was set, Gid. You put yourself through hell, rehabbing your knee. You came this close to a pro career."

"I was still cut," he said flatly. "So, no glamorous life for my wife, as I raked in millions."

Walker glanced over. "Melinda was never good enough for you. She fell in love with the idea of being the wife of a famous athlete. I don't think she ever really loved you."

His friend's words stung, but Gideon realized they were true. "I agree. My ex enjoyed being treated like royalty because I was an All-American player. She thought that would continue when I moved on to the NFL. And when that didn't pan out, she never got that I had a servant's heart. It's part of my makeup."

"Your character and attitude destined you to serve others in the community. I'm just glad you'll be doing it now in Sugar Springs." Walker hesitated a moment and then added, "I do think you can find someone who could be the partner Melinda never was, Gid."

He shook his head. "I'm not looking to settle down. My focus will be on my new job and making certain Sugar Springs is safe. Move on, Walker. You've beaten this topic like a dead horse."

His friend talked about mutual friends and acquaintances after that, both from Sugar Springs and their days at SMU. Walker elaborated on Rory's new venture into designing skating wear for athletes and how they hoped to start a family soon, despite being newlyweds.

As they approached Sugar Springs ninety minutes later, Gideon said, "Thanks for getting up early on New Year's Day and picking me up."

Walker laughed. "Your car was so ancient, it might not have made the trip here. I can't believe someone actually paid you a few hundred dollars for it."

"At least I'll have the police chief's SUV now. Roscoe said it's only a year old. Just one of the perks of the job."

"The best perk is that you're now the boss. You can run things like you want. Hey, text Rory that we're close. She was going to have Cole meet us at the apartment."

Gideon did, thankful that Rory had arranged for him to meet up with Cole Johnson, the football coach at the high school. Rory had gone through new teacher training with Cole and liked the coach quite a bit. Cole had also gotten married during the Christmas break from school, and he was looking to sublet his apartment since his new wife already owned a house in Sugar Springs.

They pulled into the parking lot of the apartment complex a

few minutes later, which was located close to the high school. As they got out, he spotted Cole, who was a few inches over six feet, with broad shoulders and a solid build. Johnson, who was about four years younger, had played tight end for the Texas Longhorns and had had a stellar career. He had also suffered an injury which had ended his athletic days, but he had chosen to go into coaching. The Sugar Springs position was his first head job, though, after a decade as an assistant.

Cole approached them, offering his hand. "I'd recognize Gideon Ross anywhere. You were one of my idols when I was in high school. That winning touchdown pass you caught against Notre Dame? Priceless."

The two shook hands, and Cole greeted Walker. "Nice to see you again, Walker. Let's go look at the apartment."

The coach led them down the sidewalk and unlocked the door to a first-floor unit. They stepped inside, and Gideon saw the only furniture was two lawn chairs in the living room, which was a decent size. The kitchen was small and had a breakfast bar. The bedroom did have bed, though.

Cole laughed. "You're welcome to the chairs and bed, which is new, by the way. I've got some kitchen items. Not much. A few things still in the pantry. I'm sure Rory told you that I just got married. I've moved in with my wife and her son."

"It's all I need," he said. "How long does your lease run?"

"Through the end of July, so if you're willing to sublet it until then, I'm happy for you to take it over," Cole said. "Unless you also get married and need to sub-sublet it," he joked.

"Hey, I've got one divorce behind me from almost a decade ago. I've been pretty much married to my job ever since. I've figured out marriage and me don't mix," he said.

Walker and Cole looked at each other—and died laughing.

Gideon figured both men, being newlyweds, were smitten with their wives and thought every man should be married.

"I'll take it—and everything in it," he told the coach.

"Although I'm definitely going to get some furniture and a TV. I'm hoping I'll actually have time to watch a few games."

"I live at the fieldhouse," Cole said. "I didn't spend much time here. Glad you can take over my lease, Gideon."

They went outside, and Cole turned the keys over to Gideon. They decided Cole would continue to pay the monthly rent to the manager, while Gideon would then pay Cole. It would give him a good chunk of time to familiarize himself with Sugar Springs again and locate and purchase a house. He'd told himself now that he would have regular hours, he would also get a dog. He hadn't had one since he was a kid and wanted the companionship a pet would bring him.

He offered the coach his hand. "Thanks for helping me out, Cole. This saves me from having to find a place to live. Like you, I'm sure I'll be spending most of my time at the station. Maybe we can get together and talk football sometime, though."

"I'd like that," Cole said. "I'd love for you to meet Nova and Leo, too."

"It's New Year's Day," Walker pointed out. "There are bowl games starting soon. Why don't you and Nova come over to the house and watch a couple with us? Rory's made a huge pot of chili and has all kinds of dips and chips waiting. Gid had promised to come spend the day with us."

"Let me check with her," Cole said.

"Do that while we're carrying in Gid's stuff," Walker said. "He travels light so it won't take us long."

They brought in Gideon's clothes and the few boxes he had packed.

When they returned outside, Cole said, "Nova is in. My wife knew nothing about football when we first met, but Leo and I have been teaching her all about the game. She's really become a big fan."

"Leo's invited, too," Walker said, turning to Gideon and adding, "Leo plays wide receiver for the high school."

He wondered about Cole Johnson marrying a woman old enough to have a son that age but figured it was none of his business.

"Leo is over at the Fletchers' house with his friends all day. Nova baked a few dozen cookies and sent them along with him. I'll stop by and pick her up, and then we'll head to your place, Walker."

Walker drove Gideon to his house, where Rory flung her arms around him.

"It's so good to have you in Sugar Springs for good, Gideon," she told him. "Ready for a day of football?"

"Cole and Nova Johnson are coming over to join us," Walker said, petting Comet, their Irish setter.

"Oh, that's great," Rory said. "I've only met her once. It'll be nice to get to know her. Cole is a terrific guy. The kids love him."

"Yeah. He's bequeathed me a couple of lawn chairs and the bed at his apartment," Gideon said drily. "All his worldly belongings before marriage."

She laughed. "Sounds like your soulmate. A man who travels lightly."

The Johnsons arrived soon after, and Rory said, "Come to the kitchen. Let's get everyone something to eat and drink."

They spent the rest of the day watching football and talking. Gideon saw the camaraderie between the couples and chalked it up to them all being newlyweds. He admitted to himself that he was a little envious. It had been so long since he'd had any physical closeness with a woman.

Cole and Nova left after the second bowl game ended. Gideon saw the couple had had enough social time and were ready to be alone. Rory insisted that Gideon stay at least one night with them.

"You have no bed. No groceries to speak of. Knowing you, you didn't even bring shampoo or towels. We can take care of that tomorrow," she said. "It'll be Friday, so stores will be open. We'll stock your fridge and pantry. Maybe even go into Tyler and get you some more furniture."

Walker laughed. "Don't try to stop her when she's on a roll, Gid. Rory is a force of nature. Just go with it."

"I don't report for work until Monday, so I do have time for a little shopping," he said, glad he'd have a woman to help him pick out a few things. His Dallas apartment had come furnished, with cheap items. He'd had no say when he and Melinda had bought furniture. He hadn't been able to afford what was to her taste, so her parents had stepped in and paid for an interior decorator to furnish the condo they'd purchased.

Gideon said goodnight to his friends, going to the guestroom.

As he drifted off to sleep, he thought he was starting act three. The first act consisted of his life in Sugar Springs. The second act had been his time spent in Dallas. This third act was his return home.

He hoped to make it a good one.

2

HOUSTON—EARLY FEBRUARY

The alarm went off, and Deb silenced it, rising from the bed. Jake lifted his head in anticipation and then leaped to the floor, excited that it was time for their morning exercise.

As Deb readied for her daily run, she was grateful she could do so, no longer afraid to be pounding the pavement, thinking that Cris Calder would be stalking her.

Hopefully, today would be the day the murderer got his just punishment. His trial had ended yesterday afternoon about half-past two. Deb had not missed a single day of testimony, sitting in the first row, directly behind Calder and his legal team, her presence a constant reminder to him of what he had done to her parents.

The prosecutor's case had been a strong one, and Deb hoped the jury would come to its decision before today was out.

Because she was ready to finally start a new life.

She had sold her childhood home, which she had inherited, months ago. Although she had to disclose that two murders had occurred within it, market inventory was low, and the house had sold quickly for above its listing price. She had not wanted anything from inside the house and had an agent hold an estate sale, where everything from furniture and linens to kitchenware and art on the walls had been sold. The only thing Deb had kept was a slow cooker her mother had made many meals in and her father's coin collection, two sweet reminders of those whom she would always love.

She hoped to begin again once this trial ended. She had been wearing a dark wig which reminded her of Catherine Zeta Jones' character in *Chicago*. The trial had garnered a huge amount of media attention, and she had wanted to hide from the world while still being in plain sight. The dark wig and glasses she wore every day were like pieces of armor she put on, girding herself against the press and Cris Calder.

Recently, Deb had also had Winston help her apply for a name change. It was fairly easy to accomplish in Texas. She was over eighteen and had no felony charges against her. Her choice of name wasn't vulgar, and she showed good cause why she was requesting the change. She'd had her fingerprints taken and paid for the required FBI background check before filing the papers with the court clerk and then attended her hearing. A very sympathetic judge signed the order, and Deb had then filed that order with the clerk. Thankfully, no journalists had gotten wind of her actions, and she believed she would be able to shed not only the wig and glasses but her old name and rise like a phoenix from the ashes with a new moniker, looking like her old self.

Once she received the official paperwork stating her new name, she'd taken care of official documents and seeing the change reflected in items such as her Social Security card and car registration. She'd gotten a new driver's license but hadn't yet applied for a passport. She'd never journeyed outside the country, and travel was definitely on her bucket list.

When the verdict came in, she would go exclusively by her new identity and hopefully, start in a different place away from Houston, trying to forget—if not erase—her past.

She finished dressing and brushed her teeth, pulling the dark ski cap over her blonde hair, not bothering to wear the wig at five-thirty on a dark, February morning.

"Ready to go, Jake?" she asked, and the beagle scampered to her.

Deb snapped the leash onto the dog's collar, and they set out from the Airbnb which she had rented ever since the sale of her parents' house.

As she ran the streets of the quiet neighborhood, she couldn't help but glance over her shoulder every now and then. Running had always been a joy, but ever since Cris Calder terrorized her, she would veer from dark shadows and startle at an unexpected noise behind her. Sometimes she thought she would never be able to put the trauma behind her.

While running, she wondered if she would be able to land a job as a vet anytime soon. She preferred a large city because of its anonymity, but she would be willing to relocate to a small town's practice if the opportunity arose. She had already received a second copy of her bachelor's and DVM diplomas from A&M, with her new name displayed on it, and that was the name she used now as she applied for open positions.

The only person who knew her new name besides Winston was Dr. Wallman. She had contacted her former employer, asking to see him away from the office, and he had agreed to meet with her. Over coffee, she had shared with him that she was starting a new life with a name change, trying to escape the horrors of her past. Deb asked Wallman if he would be willing to continue to provide a job reference for her under her new moniker.

He had quickly agreed, expressing sympathy for her situation. The vet had also promised not to share her new name or where she eventually would practice.

She tugged on Jake's leash, having him turn left to return home when he would have preferred to keep going straight.

Beagles were easygoing, loving, and curious dogs. The breed needed lots of playtime, though. Because of that, she took Jake on her run each morning and tried to walk him for half an hour at night.

She had come to love Jake, despite where he came from. Jake had been Cris Calder's dog, the one he had brought to Deb with the broken leg. When Calder was arrested for the murders of her parents, he had asked to meet with Deb before giving the police a statement. She had done so reluctantly. Two detectives had been in the room with her, both who guaranteed her safety.

Her stalker had been led in, handcuffed, and those cuffs had been attached to some apparatus on the table which prevented him from moving too far. Calder had not expressed any remorse for his actions, nor had he apologized for killing her parents to punish her. Instead, his one concern had been the year-old beagle. The accused prisoner had asked Deb to take the dog and keep him until after the trial, when he said they could be parents to the pup and their other human children. His words had chilled her, but surprisingly, she had agreed to take the beagle—and didn't plan on giving him back if the jury were crazy enough to let Calder walk.

Deb had renamed the pup, though. Jake had taken to his new name and environment quickly, and she had fallen in love with her new pet. She had never believed in the sins of the fathers being visited on their children, and she looked at the innocent beagle as a lifeline. She had ceased contact with all her old friends and acquaintances, cutting ties with everyone and everything she had known in preparation for her future as someone else. Consequently, Jake had become her only companion and confidant, and she knew she might have gone off the deep end had she not had the dog's company.

Deb reached her rental and went inside, turning on the TV to listen to the morning news shows. She fed Jake and as she ate breakfast, she skimmed her phone. She skipped over any article about the Calder trial, only hoping she would receive justice today.

After showering and dressing, she drove to the Harris County criminal courthouse and parked. She went through the security line and took her usual seat in court. The courtroom was empty now since the trial was not in session, but she planned to sit here all day, waiting for the verdict to come in, wanting to see Calder led away in handcuffs. Of course, there would be a separate sentencing phase if he was found guilty. Deb wasn't sure if she would attend that or not. Winston had said she might be asked to testify as to how her parents' murders had affected her, and she was reluctant to take the stand, afraid she would break down. More than anything, she wanted Calder to know she was strong. That, despite everything, he hadn't broken her.

She was aware of a few others entering the room, journalists hanging out, waiting for the verdict, as well. One approached her, but Deb waved the woman away. She had given no quotes to the press during the entire trial and would continue to maintain her silence even after the jury had come to its decision.

Her scalp itched dreadfully. She was tired of wearing the wig and dark glasses, but she had been featured on the news repeatedly. When she shed her old skin and name, she wanted to emerge as her new self. No one would associate the buttery blond with a new name with the dark-haired woman from the sensational murder trial.

More people started coming in, including the prosecutor, who made her way over to Deb and took a seat next to her.

"I was just notified. The jury has reached a decision. The judge should be here in about fifteen minutes."

The woman reached and took Deb's hand, squeezing it. "We built a strong case, Deb. I'm hoping for a guilty verdict."

"I know you've done your best. I'm grateful for all the hours you and your team have put in on my parents' behalf. No matter what happens, you have honored them."

The defense attorneys came and took their chairs in front of Deb, and others began filling the empty seats around her. Officers brought in Calder, and Deb avoided making eye contact with him. Within a quarter-hour, the courtroom was full once again. Winston joined her, claiming the spot next to her, and she was grateful for his presence.

The bailiff called, "All rise," and the courtroom came to its feet.

Once the judge was seated, everyone followed suit, and he said, "Bring in the members of the jury, please."

As they filed into the jury box and took their seats, Deb studied them for any sign as to what their decision might be. Most of them kept their focus in their laps, and she took that as a good sign. Typically, juries didn't like to look at someone they had just found to be guilty.

She watched as the judge opened a piece of paper, seeing what the verdict was. He handed it to the bailiff, who returned it to the jury's foreman.

"Have you reached a verdict?" the judge asked.

A woman rose. "We have, your honor."

Deb listened and wanted to jump for joy when she heard the guilty verdict for second-degree murder in both instances. The prosecutor had explained to her before the trial that second-degree murder was murder with malicious intent—but not premeditated—and that the mens rea of the defendant was intent to kill by inflicting serious bodily harm. The attorney had said because of the time frame when Deb had spoken to Calder and when he had reached her parents' house, it would be difficult to prove his actions were premeditated. Instead, they had been spur of the moment, meant to hurt Deb, and she had agreed that she would rather Calder be found guilty of second-degree murder than not guilty of first-degree.

The lead defense attorney informed the judge that they were waiving the sentencing hearing, saying Mr. Calder wished to be

sentenced immediately and did not want to present any miti-
gating circumstances which might delay this process.

"This is highly unusual," the judge said. "I am, however, ready
to sentence Mr. Calder if he so desires."

Deb watched Cris Calder as the judge sentenced him to
twenty years for each guilty charge, specifying the sentences were
not to run concurrently. That meant that Calder would be locked
away for forty years, and she breathed a sigh of relief.

The judge asked the court officers to escort the defendant
from the courtroom.

As they reached him, Calder turned. Smiling at her, he said,
"I'll be out before you know it, my love. I'll be the best behaved
inmate they've ever seen. And when I'm released? I know you'll
be waiting for me. I'll find you. We can finally be married. I'll
never stop loving you, Deb."

Horror filled her as those around her began to buzz at
Calder's words. She saw several people held cell phones pointed
at the murderer and must have recorded his parting words to her.
As Calder was led away, they immediately turned on her,
demanding she make a statement.

"Get me out of here, Winston," she said, panic filling her.

The gruff attorney told everyone, "Back off," and led her from
the courtroom to a narrow hall. They entered a small conference
room off it.

"I'll text my driver and have him meet us at the back entrance.
It doesn't mean there won't be any reporters waiting there, but
he'll have the door open, and we can quickly slide in and make
our escape."

Deb nodded numbly, almost feeling as if she had left her
body and was observing everything around her.

Winston's phone chimed, and he said, "He'll be there. We can
use the service stairs."

They hurried down the staircase, and he took her arm as he

opened the exterior door. Sure enough, a few reporters waited for them, and they began barking questions at her.

Fortunately, Winston's driver had the rear door open and stood by it like a guard dog. In only a few steps, they made it to the car. Deb threw herself into the back seat. Winston followed, and the driver slammed the door, quickly sliding behind the wheel and driving away.

Winston ordered, "Just circle the streets of downtown for a few minutes." He turned to her. "I'm sorry Calder addressed you."

"That's why I wanted to change my name," she said, her body trembling. "I don't understand why he's obsessed with me, but I don't think I will ever be safe from him. That's why Deb Busby has to cease to exist."

"Have you taken another job yet?"

"No, but I have several résumés out. I'm hoping to land a new one soon and leave Houston far behind. Whatever happens, I'll let you know where I end up, Winston. You've been a good friend to me."

After another ten minutes, Deb thought it was safe to return to the courthouse and told the driver where her car was parked. He dropped her at it, and she hurried into the vehicle, locking the doors and driving back to the Airbnb.

Jake greeted her enthusiastically, and she changed her clothes, leaving on the dark wig and glasses as she took the dog for a walk. The exercise helped. She could feel the tension melting from her body with each passing minute, relieved to know Cris Calder would be behind bars for a very long time.

She returned home, and Jake curled up on the sofa next to her, exhausted by the long walk. Deb reached for her new cell phone and scrolled through her email, hoping she might have a response from a prospective employer. That hadn't happened— but she did have a voicemail. Since the only people who had this number were those who had seen it on her résumé, she listened to the message, her heart pounding in her chest.

"Hi, this is Dr. Richard Bisch in Sugar Springs, Texas. We're a small town of about thirty thousand in East Texas, about twenty to thirty minutes outside of Tyler. I was very impressed by your résumé and recommendation from Dr. Wallman. We went to vet school together at A&M, and I called him to ask about you. Please give me a call as soon as you can."

Though her hands shook, Deb touched the phone number and heard it ringing.

"Hello?"

For the first time, Deb said her new name aloud.

"Dr. Bisch? This is Hope Keller returning your call."

Deb had chosen her new name with care. She hoped with her new identity and different location that she would be able to start over. One of her childhood heroes had been Helen Keller. She had been in awe of Keller being both blind and deaf—and yet she had learned to accomplish the impossible, even graduating from college and becoming a political activist and lecturer.

"Ah, Hope. Thanks for returning my call. Dr. Wallman thinks quite highly of you. He says you have an intuitive, nurturing spirit when it comes to animals. You also graduated in the top two percent of your class, which isn't easy at A&M, with the stiff competition. Tell me a little about yourself."

She focused on her professional life, describing in detail the research she had completed once she had graduated from vet school and then her years at Dr. Wallman's practice.

"Your experience and age tell me you would be an ideal candidate to take over my practice," Dr. Bisch said. "My goal is to retire by the end of summer." He chuckled. "Actually, I'm not retiring. I'm only fifty-one. I've been offered a faculty position as a professor at A&M's vet school, though. I would love the opportunity to work with students who will become future vets, and I have a few decades of practical experience to back up what I teach. A&M would like me to start in August with the fall semester. I'd prefer to see you in action before I make a final decision, though. Maybe a brief trial period where we get to know one another. See if you like the town. If we mutually agree after a month, I'd be happy to sell the practice to you and stay on as long as you need me to do so."

Though she had not seen herself in a small town, she thought it would be nice to be a part of a community where many people knew one another. She had not anticipated his offer of selling the practice outright, but with the sale of her parents' house, it would be possible for her to take on that responsibility. Excitement filled her at the prospect of running her own clinic.

"That sounds good, Dr. Bisch. When would you like me to begin?"

"As soon as possible, Hope. If things work out like I believe they will, my wife and I can get to College Station sooner than later and settle in before I start my teaching duties."

"I can be there tomorrow," she said, ready to cut ties with her old life.

He told her he would text her the address of his practice, and they arranged for her to be in Sugar Springs by noon so that he might show her around and then take her to lunch.

Deb hung up, thrilled at the prospect of starting over.

No.

Hope hung up. *Hope* would make the fresh start in Sugar Springs.

Deborah Busby no longer existed.

3

Hope passed a Walmart and thought it would be convenient for one-stop shopping if she did decide to move to Sugar Springs. The drive from Houston had been a quiet one. Though it was early February and not the best time of year for nature to show off, she could see the potential beauty in East Texas as she drew near her destination.

She spotted the sign declaring she was entering Sugar Springs, population 32,001. She wondered once again about Dr Bisch's practice. Though Sugar Springs was larger than she'd thought and she assumed he would see mostly pets, being close to the country she hoped she might be asked to make a few house calls upon larger animals, such as cows or horses. That possibility intrigued her.

She could understand why Dr. Bisch was so protective of his practice and thought the idea of a trial run before he sold her his practice was a wise move. If he didn't like her particular way of practicing veterinary medicine—or if she disliked life in a small town—it would give them both an out without having made a commitment.

After her conversation with the vet yesterday, Hope had

headed straight to her bank, where she'd met with her financial adviser regarding this matter. Marc Saunders had worked with her ever since she had inherited her parents' entire estate. He believed that she had more than enough to purchase Bisch's practice, but he also told her to be sure and run the numbers by him before she orally agreed to anything much less signed any legal documents regarding a sale. She would also make certain that Winston was part of any legal transaction. The attorney had always had her best interest at heart.

Since she had a little time to kill, Hope asked Jake, "How would you like to drive around town, buddy? We can familiarize ourselves with what this place has to offer."

She drove through some of the residential neighborhoods, seeing the yards and lawns were well kept, before she passed by the high school and football stadium. Last night, she had searched online for everything she could find about Sugar Springs and had seen where the Knights' football coach was in his first year as head coach. He had taken his team deep into the playoffs and possibly would have gone farther if two of his star players had not been injured in an accident the day before the semifinals game. She wondered what it would be like, going to small town high school football games, where a good portion of the town turned out. Of course, she would want to support the volleyball team, having spent a good portion of her life on the court.

Passing the public library, it surprised her how large it was for a town of this size. She also drove by the headquarters of the police and fire departments, too, thinking the crime rate must be lower in a rural town with a small population.

A few blocks later, she found herself in the heart of Sugar Springs, on the town square, and parked a moment so she could study the shops along it. She spied several boutiques, along with a pizza parlor, sports bar, and diner called Ida Lou's. She wondered if there really were an Ida Lou or if someone had thought to use the name because it had small-town charm.

One store that intrigued her was called Playful Painting, and she got out of her car, walking toward it. It wasn't open, but Hope peered into the window and saw displays of pottery in all shapes and sizes on shelves. A large sign in the front window had pictures of people painting, and she supposed the owner must give some kind of group lessons. Hope had enjoyed sketching as a child, but she had never really pursued any kind of art. Maybe she might take a lesson or two from the Playful Painting proprietor. It would be something fun and different, possibly a way to relax after putting in a long day at the clinic.

She checked her watch and returned to the car so she could head toward her appointment at Sugar Springs Veterinary Clinic. She found it easily, parking and placing Jake's leash on him before making her way inside the one-story building.

The receptionist greeted her, giving Hope a friendly smile, asking, "Are you Dr. Keller?"

It took her aback, hearing her new name come from this woman's lips, since it was the first time anyone had addressed her this way in person.

Stepping up to the counter, where a fluffy white cat stretched out, she said, "Yes, I am Dr. Keller, and this is my dog, Jake. I suppose Dr. Bisch told you to expect me."

The woman, who had bits of gray in her hair and wore glasses, laughed. "I'm Sally—and married to Dr. Bisch," she said. "I also keep his books and try to keep all his patients straight."

She stood and came from behind the counter, offering her hand to Hope, and they shook. Sally also knelt and petted Jake. "My, what a handsome fellow you are, Jake Keller."

"Your husband tells me that you'll be heading to College Station soon."

Rising, Sally said, "Yes. We actually met while we were students at A&M. Richard was a senior, and I was a fish, what

Aggies call a freshman student. We dated the entire time he was in vet school there and married after I earned my bachelor's degree. Since he had one more year before he received his DVM, I worked at the university in the registrar's office."

Curious, Hope asked, "How did you wind up in Sugar Springs? Was it home to either of you?"

"We actually made a detour, living in Dallas for a few years. Richard was from there and went to work at the clinic of a family friend from his church in Highland Park. Then he was contacted by one of his professors from vet school, who told him about the opening here. The Sugar Springs vet was ready to retire, and my father had recently passed away, leaving me a healthy inheritance. We used it to invest in the clinic and have been here ever since. We had a two-year-old when we arrived. I was pregnant at the time and had one more baby. Raising our children in Sugar Springs was a wonderful experience. Both kids became Aggies, and they both live in the Houston area now. It will be nice to be closer to them."

A stout, dark-haired woman wearing scrubs appeared and greeted Hope.

"You must be the new vet," she said. "I'm Shirley Lovell. I've been working as a vet tech at the clinic for twenty-eight years. My nephew Randy is our other tech. He's been here eight years."

"Yes, I'm Hope Keller. It's very nice to meet you, Shirley."

"Same," the older woman replied. "I look forward to working with you." She turned to Sally. "I'm leaving on lunch break. Randy's finishing up with a grooming, and then he'll be gone, too." Glancing back at Hope, she added, "I'll talk with you later, Dr. Keller."

The vet tech left the clinic, and Sally said, "Let me take you to Richard. He's in his office, catching up on some paperwork. If you want to slip off your coat, you can hang it here."

"Do you have a place I can leave Jake?" she asked.

"Oh, he can stay with Sam." Sally indicated the cat who lazed on the counter. "We can hook his leash here. There aren't any clients with pets that will be coming out."

"Jake is extremely well-behaved," she told the receptionist. "Even if they did, he wouldn't stir."

They attached the beagle's leash, and then Sally led them through a door and down a hallway. They reached the end. The door was open, and Hope saw Dr. Bisch sitting at his desk. He was bald and wore glasses. He glanced up and smiled, standing.

"You have to be Dr. Keller." He came from behind his desk and shook her hand enthusiastically. "Did you have any trouble finding the place?"

"No, my map app was right on target. I even had time to drive around and see a bit of the town before I came here."

"Excellent. Let me show you the place," he said, pride evident in his voice.

Sally said, "I'm going to run a few errands, honey, and pick up some lunch for myself. Do you need me to bring back anything for you two?"

"No," her husband said. "I thought I would take Dr. Keller to Ida's Lou's for lunch."

The vet took her on a tour of the clinic, showing her the examination rooms and where supplies and medicines were stored. She was pleased at the good-sized room where surgeries took place. Another room was designated for grooming, and he said that Randy usually handled that task. A very large room lined with cages housed animals who were boarded, though Dr. Bisch said they had no animals staying overnight at this time.

They returned to the front reception room, and she noticed a glass window. Peering inside, she saw two tortoise shell cats lying close together.

"Sometimes, I take on a few small animals if the humane society is full," the clinic owner shared. "These two came from a widow who just passed recently. They're from the same litter. Two years old and in good health. People usually want a kitten or puppy when they're adopting, though. Hopefully, we'll find someone who wants them soon. Together, if possible."

"Where is the humane society located?" she asked.

"Oh, about a mile and a half from here. You ready to grab a bite to eat?"

"I am hungry."

"Let me get my jacket," he said. "Be right back."

Hope studied the reception area while he was gone. While functional, it looked extremely dated. If she took over this practice, she would be making a few changes, based upon what she had seen. She didn't want to share this just yet with Dr. Bisch, however.

She petted Jake, telling him she would be back soon, and collected her coat from where it hung, slipping into it as the vet returned.

"We'll drive today. It's only a few blocks to the town square. I walk to lunch when the weather is nice. Today's got a nasty wind, though."

As they drove the short distance, he told her, "I probably eat lunch at Ida Lou's three or four times a week. I'll mix it up sometimes and try something else, but my heart belongs at the diner. Sometimes, I grab something to go at the Dairy Queen if I'm heading out on a call."

"So, you do make house calls for larger animals?"

"I do, but not that often. There's another vet, Dr. Paulson, who lives about seven miles outside of Sugar Springs. He handles most of the large animal health issues in the county and beyond. Every now and then, though, I'm called out when his schedule is full, especially if it's an emergency. Have you treated many large animals?"

"Mostly ones while I was in vet school," she told him. "College Station was a great mix of household pets and large farm animals. I would be interested, though, in the challenge of seeing a few cases with animals beyond pets."

He parked, and they entered the diner.

"Why, Richard, who have we here?" said a woman with snow-white hair and sparkling blue eyes.

"This here is Dr. Hope Keller, Ida Lou. She knows I'm a frequent flyer at your diner. Dr. Keller may be taking over my practice."

"Is that so?" the woman said as she led them to an open booth, handing them menus after they took a seat.

"Richard, honey, you're much too young to retire," Ida Lou admonished. "Are we losing you back to the big city after all these years?"

The vet explained the new job opportunity he had waiting for him at the university vet school in College Station, and Ida Lou told him how much he and Sally would be missed.

"You need time to look over the menu?" the diner owner asked.

Hope looked to Dr. Bisch. "You tell me what's good."

He chuckled. "Everything." Turning back to Ida Lou, he said, "We'll take two blue plate specials. Rolls and cornbread, please. Iced tea for me."

Hope spoke up. "I'll take water with lemon. Thank you."

"Your food will be right out," Ida Lou promised, heading toward the kitchen.

She looked around the diner, which was about three-quarters full.

"I suppose you know just about everyone in here," she said.

He grinned. "Yup. That's what a small town is all about. Of course, a true small town has about two thousand in it, counting the chickens and pigs. I like the size of Sugar Springs, though. It has enough places to shop, and it's full of good people. Sally and I will really miss living here."

Ida Lou returned with a tray carrying their drinks and meals. Setting their plates in front of them, she said, "You better like fried chicken and mashed potatoes, Dr. Keller. Black-eyed peas came on the blue plate today, but I gave you a corn on the cob, too."

For the next half-hour as they ate, Dr. Bisch told her more about Sugar Springs, in general, and his practice, in particular.

"What makes you want to make a change, Dr. Keller?" the vet asked. "I hope you don't mind me calling you Hope. You said you were from Houston and that you'd worked at Dr. Wallman's clinic for four years."

"Please, call me Hope." She stuck as close to the truth as possible, saying. "I lost both my parents a year ago. I was an only child, and it was pretty hard to deal with. My dad had pancreatic cancer, and it was difficult watching him slip away so quickly." She swallowed. "Mom's death was.... unexpected. Without any siblings or close family nearby, I just decided that I needed a big change."

"From Houston to Sugar Springs will definitely be that," Dr. Bisch said. "Dr. Wallman was really high on you. That's why I called you before contacting any other applicant. And you were cool as a cucumber when I sprang on you that I'd be selling the practice. I hadn't mentioned that in my ad."

She smiled. "I'll admit that it did throw me for a moment. I hadn't considered purchasing an existing practice, but I do have the means to do so since my parents' death. I've met with my financial adviser, and he's crunched the numbers. Depending upon what you plan to sell the practice for, I believe I would be able to swing it." She paused and then added, "I think I would enjoy being my own boss."

Ida Lou brought them the bill, and they both reached for it.

"Please, let me get it," Hope said.

"Not a chance, honey," the vet replied. "You're my guest."

He took out his credit card and told Hope, "Sugar Springs does have a lot to offer. It's a great, tight-knit community. You haven't mentioned a husband or children, so I'm assuming you're single."

"I am. I worked long hours at Dr. Wallman's clinic. It didn't give me much time for dating."

"Well, maybe you can find yourself a fellow here in Sugar Springs."

She chuckled. "Getting married is the last thing on my mind now, Dr. Bisch. I just want to immerse myself in your clinic and see if it will be a good fit for me. If not, I will explore some other options."

"I'm sure you have some, but I hope you'll take to Sugar Springs. And call me Richard, please. Let me pay the bill and we can head back. I'll let you roll up your sleeves and get started this afternoon."

"I would like that, as long as you can point me toward a hotel at the end of the day."

"Why, I didn't even think about you needing somewhere to stay. We don't have any hotels in Sugar Springs, I'm afraid. We do have a few bed and breakfast places scattered about. I can recommend one, in particular, run by Ida Lou's older sister. Maybe we should let you get settled this afternoon and then start fresh first thing tomorrow morning."

They left their booth and as they walked to the register, the vet said, "Let me check with Ida Lou about the B&B while I pay. She can give Lizzy Lou a call and see if she's got an opening."

The register was close to the door, so she said, "Thank you. I think I'll head outside instead of hovering and blocking customers coming in."

She turned and opened the door. As she stepped outside, someone came around the corner fast, crashing into her. For a moment, she thought she might fall, but strong hands clasped her elbows, steadying her.

Raising her face, she looked up into mesmerizing gray eyes, which left her speechless. Blinking, she took in the handsome face, raven hair, and high cheekbones of the man who held onto her.

"Pardon me, ma'am," he said, his voice a low rumble. "I wasn't watching where I was going. You'd think a cop would know better."

Hope glanced and saw he wore a khaki uniform and short, bomber jacket. A patch on the left side of the jacket told her he was with the Sugar Springs Police Department. She gazed up at him again, searching for words. She had never been struck dumb, but his good looks—as much as slamming into him—had her tongue-tied.

Releasing his hold on her, he offered his hand. "Gideon Ross. I'm the police chief in town. Again, I'm sorry I ran into you like that." He paused. "Maybe I could make it up to you? Buy you a slice of an Ida Lou pie—unless you're already too full."

"Good news, Hope. Lizzy Lou has an open spot."

She turned and saw Dr. Bisch approaching. "Oh, I see you've met Chief Ross. He's only been in town, what, a month? Chief, this is Dr. Keller."

He nodded politely to her. "Dr. Keller. Nice to meet you."

"Dr. Keller worked in Houston at a practice one of my friends runs. She's thinking about buying me out," the vet declared.

Ross looked down at her. "Is that so?"

"I might," she said meekly, speaking for the first time, her heart hammering wildly against her ribs.

"We were headed back to the clinic," Dr. Bisch said. "Then Hope will be staying at Lizzy Lou's while she's in town. We'll let her get unpacked, and then she'll start tomorrow. We're letting her test the waters to see if a small-town practice is for her or not."

"It was nice meeting you, Chief Ross," she managed to say.

"Nice meeting you, Dr. Keller," he replied.

The police chief stepped aside, allowing her and Dr. Bisch to pass. The vet kept a running conversation going in the car, telling her all about the B&B, but Hope only listened with half an ear.

They arrived at the clinic and agreed that she would report at seven the following morning.

Returning to her car with Jake in tow, she put in the address the vet had provided to her and followed the directions to Lizzy Lou's. When she arrived, she saw a large SUV parked in front of the white-framed house. It was marked Sugar Springs Police Department.

Hope got out of her car—and Chief Ross exited the SUV.

He strode toward her. "If you're still interested in that slice of pie, Dr. Keller, maybe we could have it tonight. Over dinner."

"Are... are you asking me out, Chief?" she asked, so light-headed she was afraid she might faint. She dug her fingernails into her palms, trying to stay conscious.

He smiled lazily at her. "Well, I guess I am. So, what do you say?"

Her heart racing, Hope said, "I say yes, Chief. Yes to dinner." She grinned. "And definitely yes to pie."

4

Gideon grinned to himself as he drove away from Lizzy Lou's B&B.

When was the last time he had felt so lighthearted?

As he cruised the streets of Sugar Springs, he couldn't help but wonder what had come over him. He hadn't asked a woman on a date in... years?

And yet the sudden urge had come over him, so strong that he had gone out of his way to park in front of the B&B that Dr. Keller was checking into. Hell, he didn't even know her first name. What he did know was that she was new to town—and smelled heavenly.

He'd always been a sucker for vanilla. Dated a girl in high school for a couple of months who wore the scent. Vanilla seemed to warm on a woman's skin, making him want to glide his nose across it and drink her in. When he'd smacked into Dr. Keller, the first thing he'd picked up was that subtle smell of vanilla.

Who knew a scent would have him asking a stranger for a date.

Walker would be amused by that. In the month Gideon had

been chief of police in Sugar Springs, his friend and wife had subtly nudged him to try and date. Rory had offered to introduce him to a few single teachers at the high school. Gideon had turned down the offer, reiterating to his friends that he was here to keep the town safe, not play the dating game.

Asking Dr. Keller for a date came totally out of left field.

She was pretty without being drop-dead gorgeous. Shoulder-length blond hair and sky blue eyes. Lips tinted a soft pink, the bottom one full and tempting. Gideon guessed her to be five-eight, with a compact, athletic frame. He knew nothing about her, other than she was a veterinarian who might be taking over Dr. Bisch's practice. And she smelled incredible.

Yet something intrigued him about her. Enough that he had blurted out an offer of pie. When Dr. Bisch had interrupted their conversation, Gideon—the old Gideon—would've merely let it go. Either seen Dr. Keller around town or not. This new Gideon, one who had surprised him, had taken the initiative to follow up by meeting her at Lizzy Lou's B&B.

What if she thought he was a stalker?

He cursed under his breath. He'd never made much of an effort when it came to women. He was nice-looking, and they always fawned over him. Back in the day if he'd asked someone for a date, she always accepted. He'd played the field in high school, not wanting to be tied down to any one girl. By college, he was more focused on his athletic career and succeeding in his classes to want to hop from girl to girl. When Melinda had shown an interest in him, he'd settled into a relationship, dating her through most of college. She hadn't been too demanding and knew how important football was to him. It had been enough to take her to a few parties and let her hang on his arm.

It was only after playing football was no longer a possibility that things had soured between them. Gideon realized—too late —that he never should have married her. They came from worlds which were too different to mesh. He'd figured out she'd been a convenience to him. A habit. He'd cared for her but hadn't really loved her. And once he wasn't a superstar in the athletic world, one whom she'd pinned her hopes on, her true colors had come out. He quickly realized his wife was petty, snobbish, and they had very little in common other than their degrees from SMU. Still, he'd hung in for five miserable years until she'd finally been the one to sentence the marriage to death. Melinda had remarried a few months later, to a former ex who traveled in her family's social stratosphere and made oodles of money as an attorney.

Ever since then, women hadn't been a factor in his life. He'd had the occasional hookup with someone he met, never pursuing anything lasting. Gone on a few blind dates to please his colleagues' wives, but nothing had come of them. Gideon had simply been married to his job.

He pulled over and parked, wanting to think more about how out of character his action today had been.

Could he be hankering for a relationship at last?

He suspected that might be the case after being around Walker and Rory. His best friend had a quickie, six-month marriage years ago, but when he came back to their childhood city, Walker had made it clear to Gideon that he was ready to sink deep roots into the community, as his parents had. The fact he'd found Rory so quickly and they'd clicked was simply a bonus.

Seeing Walker and Rory together had called up feelings within Gideon that he'd never dealt with before. He could see they were more than lovers. They were best friends who had many things in common, but they respected the differences between them. They both had busy careers. They enjoyed spending time with one another, and yet they also had lives away from one another. At the end of the day, though, they came home and had each other.

That thought caused a wave of loneliness to wash over him.

Gideon had never had that kind of closeness with any woman, especially his wife. Melinda hadn't worked. Hadn't wanted to work. Instead, she'd spent all her time lunching with friends and participating in Junior League events. Or she was over at her parents' house constantly, letting them poison her relationship with Gideon. Her high-society parents hadn't taken to their only daughter marrying a small-town, lower-class athlete. Her dad had pretty much written Gideon off as a dumb jock from Hicksville. After Gideon had been let go from the Atlanta Falcons in their final roster cut and chosen to enter the police academy, Melinda's father had flat-out told him they would never make it as a couple. That his daughter deserved far better than a man who drove a squad car and made in a year what he made in a month at his investment firm.

His marriage had soured him on women. Besides, he'd made detective a year after it ended, and Gideon had a new mistress. His job. He put in more hours on cases than he ever did on the field. He didn't think he'd missed out.

Until he came back to Sugar Springs and saw how happy his best friend was.

Maybe that had floated in his subconscious, spurring him to ask out Dr. Whatever Her First Name Was Keller.

"Are you kidding me?" he asked himself aloud. "One date does not a marriage make. Get a grip on yourself, Gid. It's just a date. It probably won't lead to anything. She might not even stay and take over the vet clinic. This is a one and done. End of story."

He pushed aside all thoughts of Dr. Keller and dating. He told himself it was good to put himself out there again after so long a time. That maybe he would begin seeing women. It wouldn't hurt to have a bit of a social life.

Gideon drove back to the police station, heading straight to his office and shutting the door. He kept busy with paperwork for a few hours, thinking how much of that consumed his days. In a way, he did miss being out in the field, trying to put the pieces together and solve cases. At the same time, he was grateful for the regular hours he put in. For the most part, he worked eight-to-five during the week. On a few occasions, he'd been called out at night and twice on a weekend, but he'd been able to handle those problems quickly.

Glancing at his watch, he saw it was almost five o'clock now. He'd arranged with Dr. Keller to pick her up at Lizzy Lou's at six. If he left the station now, it would give him time to get home and grab a quick shower and put on civilian clothes instead of showing up in his uniform.

He told his secretary goodnight and headed to his SUV, anticipation keeping him on edge, a mixture of a little bit of excitement combined with a slight case of nerves. Gideon told himself either he'd have fun, or he wouldn't. He wasn't even considering the option of a second date at this point. It would be enough to be out with a woman, sharing a meal. The rest could sort itself out.

Arriving home, he stopped by his mailbox and picked up his mail, sorting through it as he walked to his apartment. He entered, glad that he had a sofa and rocker which reclined, as well as a coffee table and lamp, thanks to Rory helping him choose a few things for the apartment. She had also convinced him to splurge on an expensive mattress, replacing the one Cole had purchased, and that had proven to be the best choice. Ever since he'd begun sleeping on it, his back felt better, and he was more rested when he awoke each morning.

Walker had persuaded him on which TV to buy. It was fairly large, and his friend had brought over a six-pack of beer a few times for them to watch football or basketball games. Cole Johnson had joined them once, and he enjoyed the coach's sense of humor. It felt nice to actually make a new friend at thirty-six.

After he showered, Gideon dressed in a dark pair of slacks and a blue, button-down shirt. He'd thought jeans might be a little too casual. Not that he was taking Dr. Keller anywhere fancy. Sugar Springs didn't do fancy. He hated to take her to the diner again, since she'd already eaten lunch there, and decided he'd give her a few local options and allow her to choose.

He texted Dr. Keller to let her know he would be there soon and had learned she was in the garage apartment Lizzy Lou rented out sometimes. He drove to Lizzy Lou's and got out, walking up the stairs beside the garage. It had been forever since he'd had a date, and he sure hadn't picked one up since before his marriage. The few times he had gone out since his divorce, he'd met his date at a bar or restaurant. A sudden case of nerves overwhelmed him.

"Get a grip, Gid," he said under his breath, and he knocked on the door.

HOPE FINISHED PLACING the last of her things in the dresser drawer and looked around the garage apartment, which would be home for now. Lizzy Lou had two bedrooms in her house which she rented out, but she also had this garage apartment available. It had one large room with a small kitchenette and then a smaller room which served as the bedroom. The bathroom was functional but miniscule. Lizzy Lou told Hope that she would be happy to have her stay as long as she wished since it was a slow time of year for vacation rentals, and she had no bookings for the apartment at the moment.

The older woman had resembled her sister Ida Lou quite a bit, and she had been delighted that Jake was part of the package. In fact, the landlady had told Hope that she had lost her own dog a few months ago and still mourned him. Lizzy Lou wasn't ready to get another pet just yet, but she told Hope that she didn't mind having her drop off Jake at the house each morning before she left for the vet clinic. She said the dog would be good company for her, saying that she, too, had a beagle growing up and knew how sociable they could be.

When Hope protested, Lizzy Lou convinced her that she wasn't just being what she termed small-town nice, and that she really would enjoy having the dog with her in the house during the day. Her new landlady convinced Hope of her sincerity, and she promised she would drop off Jake tomorrow morning at six-thirty, which would leave her plenty of time to drive to the clinic and get settled in for the day's work.

Lizzy Lou had even given her a key to the main house, telling Hope that she would be in the kitchen at that time of morning and to simply come in without knocking.

Hope returned to the closet and skimmed its meager contents, wondering what she should wear on her date with Chief Gideon Ross. She couldn't believe she had been in town less than a day and was already going out with the hottest guy she'd ever laid eyes on. While she doubted a small town such as Sugar Springs had a thriving single male population near her age, it was nice to have been asked out by the police chief.

She wasn't going to read anything into his invitation, however. She believed he merely felt guilty for slamming into her and was trying to right the situation, being a good ambassador for his town. She couldn't help but wonder, though, how a man in his mid-thirties could already be a police chief of a town. Since she was someone who paid attention to details, she had noticed he wore no wedding ring even before he asked her out. A man that good-looking who wasn't married either was a player or had been married at one point. Hope wasn't interested in the former, and she had never gone out with a divorced man—excerpt her one date with Jerry—though dating someone who'd been divorced really wasn't an issue for her.

Tonight would simply be an exploration. A getting to know one another. She wasn't going to go into the date hoping for a second one—or more. She really wasn't ready to form any kind of attachment since she didn't know if she would be staying in Sugar Springs or not.

She mulled over whether she should even change clothes. She gathered Chief Ross also was a man who paid attention to details, due to his line of work, and he would notice if she were wearing something different. Still, Hope thought she should at least make the effort. Who knew? This might be her last date for a long time to come.

She didn't want to go as causal as jeans, but she certainly wasn't going to dress up, especially if he were taking her back to the diner, as she suspected. Ida Lou had a sharp set of eyes and her thumb on the pulse of this town. She didn't want Ida Lou or anyone else reading into the fact that Hope was going to share a piece of pie with Chief Ross.

Finally, she decided to leave on the black slacks she wore and paired them with a dusty rose sweater since it was still chilly, and the temperature seemed to be dropping even further.

Her cell dinged with a text message, and she went to the bed where it lay and picked it up.

> Should be there in another five minutes or less.
> Hope we're still on.

LEAVE it to a cop to confirm the date. She texted him back.

> I'll come down and be waiting at the bottom of the stairs.

HOPE WENT to retrieve her coat when her phone chimed again.

You will not wait outside. It's too damn cold. I can walk up a staircase and knock on your door, Dr. Keller.

SHE SMILED TO HERSELF. Handsome—and a gentleman.

Slipping into her coat, she then fed Jake. The dog knew something was up, however, and showed no interest in his dinner. Hope picked up her purse and pulled out her keys so she would have them and be able to lock the door when Chief Ross arrived.

A solid knock sounded on the door, and she told Jake, "Be good."

Walking to the door, she opened it, immediately noticing he had abandoned his police uniform for a nice shirt and dress pants, though he still wore the same bomber jacket. She was definitely glad she hadn't opted for jeans.

"Hi. Let me just lock up."

As she started to step out and pull the door to, Jake jumped from the sofa and rushed to the door, barking a few times. Hope knelt, petting the beagle, soothing him.

"It's okay, Jake. This is Chief Ross. He's a friend. Go back to the couch where your blankie is. I'll be home soon."

The dog merely stared at her in defiance.

"It might help him settle down if I came in and we talked a couple of minutes," the police chief said. "Just to set Jake's mind at ease."

"All right," she agreed, closing the door and walking over to the sofa, taking a seat.

Immediately, Jake jumped onto the center cushion as Chief Ross sat on the other side of the dog.

Offering his fingers for the beagle to smell, he said, "I like dogs, Jake. You look like you're very protective of Dr. Keller."

The beagle began sniffing the visitor's fingers and then visibly relaxed. Chief Ross began petting him.

"You don't have to keep calling me Dr. Keller," she said. "After all, this *is* a date. At least I was under the impression it was."

He smiled slowly at her, and it was as if the sun had broken through an opening in the clouds on a dismal day. His smile warmed her in a way she'd never experienced before.

"Well, I would like to call you something other than Dr. Keller, but I don't know your first name. When Dr. Bisch introduced us, he called you Dr. Keller."

She felt her cheeks heat. "I'm sorry about that. I'm Hope." Then she giggled, surprising herself, because she had never been a giggler.

"Want to clue me in on what's so funny?" he asked.

"I'm just thinking that you asked me out without even knowing all my name. Either you're very brave—or moderately desperate."

He burst out laughing. "Maybe a little of both," he admitted. He glanced to the dog and petted him again. "Do you think Jake is calm enough now for us to leave?"

"He'll be fine," she promised, leaning down and kissing the dog on the top of his head. "This time, be good," she warned. "Or else."

Before she could push herself from the couch, Gideon held out a hand to her. She took it and observed, "Someone must have drilled good manners into you. I'm assuming your mom?"

A dark shadow crossed his face. "Yeah. My mom was big on manners," he said brusquely, his entire demeanor changing in an instant. "Shall we?"

She'd already opened the door to something personal—and Gideon Ross had slammed it shut.

Hope suddenly felt as if things would be going downhill from here.

5

Gideon could have kicked himself. He felt the playful energy between Hope Keller and him dissipate in an instant. He shouldn't be so sensitive, especially after all these years.

They reached the bottom of the staircase, and Hope said, "I think I'm going to pass on that slice of pie, Chief Ross."

He turned and looked at her. "Don't give up on me," he said quietly, not bothering to disguise the pain in his voice.

Her brows shot up, and she looked at him inquisitively. "I... I just feel as if your heart isn't in this date anymore."

"It is," he quickly assured her. "I just reacted poorly to something you said."

"The comment about your mother?"

"Yes." He swallowed the lump forming in his throat. "I really do want to spend time with you, Hope, but I think I would like it to be something a little quieter. Anywhere we go in public is going to be too loud and not give us the privacy I would choose to have."

She placed a hand on his forearm, and even through the sleeve of his jacket, he felt the warmth of her touch filling him.

Filling his soul...

"I would offer for us to stay here and let me whip up a little something." She smiled wryly. "Unfortunately, the fridge and pantry are empty. It's on my to-do list to stock both tomorrow."

"What if we picked up something and brought it back here?" he asked. "I know a stay-in date is usually something a couple does after they've been out a few times. At least, I think that's the case." He smiled sheepishly. "I can't really tell you the last time I even had a date, Hope. I already feel I've mucked up this one pretty badly."

Her hand fell from his arm, and she said, "I haven't won any awards in the dating department, either, Gideon." She looked at him hopefully. "But I would like to get to know you. I think grabbing takeout and bringing it back here is a great idea."

Relief poured through him, and he said, "Are you a fan of pizza? Romano's makes the best I've ever eaten."

Her face lit up. "You are speaking my language, Chief Ross. You had me at pizza. I'll eat anything as long as it doesn't have anchovies on it."

"Then I'll call in an order for us, and we can run into town and pick it up. Pie, too, if you're still interested in dessert."

He held out a hand. Surprisingly, she took it, and Gideon led her to his SUV. He opened the passenger door and helped her inside the vehicle and then came around and slid behind the wheel.

He started the SUV and turned up the heater to warm the inside of the vehicle more quickly while calling the pizzeria.

Mrs. Romano answered, and he said, "Hi, Mrs. Romano. It's Gideon. I'm going to need a large supreme—no anchovies—and two salads to go."

"*Two* salads?" she asked with interest. "Why, Chief Ross, either you're extremely hungry tonight—or you have a date, young man."

"Guilty as charged, ma'am. I'll swing by in a few minutes to pick it up."

"It'll be waiting for you. And maybe I'll squeeze out of you who your date is," Mrs. Romano said, laughter in her voice. "Give me fifteen minutes."

Gideon hung up and said, "It's going to take about fifteen minutes for the pizza. If you'd like, we can stop by the diner and pick up dessert first."

"That sounds like a plan," Hope said. "One which my sweet tooth appreciates."

He drove to the town square and parked in the center by the gazebo.

"Would you like me to keep the car running so you can stay warm while I run in to Ida Lou's?"

"And let *you* pick out my flavor of pie?" she said teasingly. "Never."

They both laughed, and he came around to her side, helping her from the car. They walked across the street to the diner, which was about half-full. Immediately, he knew they drew attention from every patron present. Sugar Springs residents were interested in everything that went on in their town, and here was their brand-new police chief with a pretty stranger.

Ida Lou came to greet them, two menus in hand. "Nice to see you again, Dr. Keller. And it's always good seeing you, Chief." She paused. "Are you together?

Hope took the lead. "We are—and please, call me Hope, Ida Lou. I'm not much on formality."

"We just stopped by to grab a couple of pieces of pie," Gideon added. "To go, please."

Ida Lou's eyes lit up in interest. "Well, come over and pick out what you'd like," she told them.

Hope waffled back and forth, debating between banana cream and coconut cream pie, while Gideon went with his usual apple. She finally said she'd go banana this time but would try the coconut in the near future.

"Let me get some boxes for you, Chief," Ida Lou said.

Hope turned to him as Ida Lou went to get the containers and said, "Apple pie, Chief? I guess you are the all-American boy."

"Nothing wrong with liking apple pie," he said. "I have been known to step out of my comfort zone and eat cherry or pecan every now and then. Not often, though."

Ida Lou returned and cut generous slices of pie for both of them, and Gideon handed her a ten-dollar bill. "Keep the change."

"It was good seeing you again, Hope," the diner owner said. "I suppose I'll see you tomorrow for lunch. Richard Bisch is a regular."

Hope laughed. "Yes, he told me he eats here several times a week. See you soon, Ida Lou."

They left the diner, and Gideon said, "The pizza should be ready by now. Feel like going into Romano's and having everyone stare at you again? I'm sure you noticed the interest you drew at the diner just now."

"It was a little unnerving," she noted. "I've never lived in a small town before, and I'm not used to such scrutiny. I'm a Houston native. I went to college and vet school in College Station, and I thought it was a small town. I see now that I was wrong about that."

As they walked to Romano's, he said, "The people in Sugar Springs have good hearts—and extremely curious minds. You're a new face in town, and people will be pumping Ida Lou now to find out everything she knows about you. Especially since it was obvious she'd already met you when she greeted you by name."

"I guess I'll have to get used to being gossiped about," she said.

"Turning up with me in tow cranked it from mid-level gossip

to Defcon-5," he joked. "I hope you don't mind being seen with me."

"No, I don't. Despite the previous blip, I am looking forward to talking with you over our dinner."

He held the door open so she might enter first, and he followed behind her. The pizza parlor was about three-quarters full and once again, every patron in the restaurant turned his attention to Gideon and Hope.

Mrs. Romano met them, saying, "The pizza is just coming out of the oven. Eduardo is slicing it for you now." She regarded Hope with interest. "We haven't met. I'm Sophia Romano. My husband and I have owned this place for many years."

"This is Dr. Hope Keller, Mrs. Romano. I was telling her your husband makes the best pizza I've ever eaten. Dr. Keller is in town to work with Dr. Bisch."

"Oh, I heard he's moving to Aggieland to become a professor. Will you be taking over his practice, Dr. Keller?"

"Please, it's Hope. And that remains to be seen. Dr. Bisch has given me the opportunity to work at his clinic for a couple of weeks, in order to see if it's something I might want to consider purchasing."

"Of course, you will," Mrs. Romano said. "Sugar Springs is a wonderful place to live." With a twinkle in her eye, she added, "And raise children. I'm assuming you aren't married since you are the date of our esteemed police chief, and your figure is too good for you to have had children."

Hope looked taken aback for a moment, and then she laughed heartily. "No, I've never been married and don't have any children. Just a beagle named Jake."

"Well, you need to think about having some, young lady. I raised my Dante and Viviana here, and Sugar Springs was a wonderful place for children to grow up."

"Do they still live here?" Hope asked.

"No. Dante has just opened his own restaurant in Dallas two

months ago. You must have Chief Ross drive you over there some day. Let me know when you go, and I'll tell Dante to give you the royal treatment."

Gideon watched Hope's cheeks flood with color, and he added, "Vivi also works at a restaurant in Dallas."

"Not for long if I have anything to say about it," Mr. Romano said, handing over a box of pizza to Gideon. He looked at Hope, and Gideon introduced the pair.

Mr. Romano thanked Hope for trying one of their pizzas.

"We'll get going now," he said. "I'm sure Hope will be back to sample more pizza because she'll be hooked on it after she eats some tonight."

They left the pizza parlor, and Hope said, "You aren't kidding about a small town. Mrs. Romano was quiet...opinionated."

"You mean because she was trying to convince you to stay and raise all our children in Sugar Springs?" he asked jokingly.

She laughed. "Well, do you want two? Three? Four?"

Playing along, Gideon said, "Anything but one. I'm an only child, and I didn't like that much. I made friends with Walker Cox when we were barely out of diapers, and he's been like a brother to me ever since."

As he helped her into the car, she asked, "Does Walker still live in Sugar Springs?"

Gideon handed her the pizza box and bag from the diner and said, "Yes. He recently moved back and took over his dad's law practice."

He shut the door and came around to his side of the vehicle. He started the SUV and continued, saying, "Walker and I went to college together, and we both stayed in Dallas afterward. I was a patrolman and then made detective. Walker went to law school and then joined a prestigious law firm."

They drove back to Lizzy Lou's and hurried inside since the wind had picked up.

"I didn't think to order drinks for us," he apologized.

"That's okay. I'm a water drinker," she reassured him. "I do have dishes and glasses. Hopefully some ice in the freezer."

She took out two plates and as he placed slices of pizza on them, she filled two glasses with ice and water.

Jake, who had met them at the door, followed them back to the couch, where Hope told the beagle he had to stay down while they ate. Jake curled up on the floor next to her feet.

"He's a good little dog, isn't he?" Gideon asked.

"He really is. I've had him for a little over a year now. Adopted him when he was a year old. Jake has been terrific company for me. I was just happy that Lizzy Lou agreed to rent to me since I had an animal. Not many places would have done that. She's even asked that I drop off Jake at the house each day so that he can keep her company."

"Lizzy Lou and Ida Lou are good folks," Gideon agreed, biting into the pizza.

Hope did the same, and then she made an appreciative noise as she chewed.

He grinned. "Told you. Best pizza I've ever had. And as a detective, I pretty much lived on pizza."

She swallowed. "You aren't kidding. Why, I could eat this every day. Then again, I'd have to up the mileage on my run by a few miles to keep the carbs off."

"Oh, are you a runner?"

"I ran track in high school, but volleyball was my one true love. I do enjoy all kinds of sports, though, playing and watching."

Hearing this made him decide something on the spot. "I don't want to be presumptuous, but I'm going to a Super Bowl party this weekend at Walker's house. He got married over Christmas to a teacher at the high school. Rory. They're having a few friends over for the game. I think you might enjoy going. Maybe you could even make a few new friends beyond me."

She looked pleased at the invitation. "That would be really

nice, Gideon. I'm a football fanatic. I've even played in fantasy football leagues for several years." A shadow crossed her face. "Not this past year, though. It's been... an off-year for me."

He held his water glass up in a toast and said, "Then I hope you will find that you belong here in Sugar Springs, Hope Keller. I hope it will bring a happiness which has evaded you this past year."

Her eyes welled with tears as she clinked her glass against his and then drank deeply. Gideon wondered what difficulties Hope had been through and said, "I know we've just met, Hope, but I'm a good listener. It's a skill I picked up during police work. If there's anything you want to share with me, please feel free to do so."

She looked at him thoughtfully. "I may wish to do that when we know each other a little better. But I'm going to put you on the spot now, Gideon. You almost blew this date tonight before it ever started. Why? What did I say that made you curl up inside and push me away?"

He took a deep breath, knowing he owed her an explanation.

And dreading dredging up his past.

"My mom was my whole world from the time I was young. She read to me. Played with me. Told me there wasn't anything I couldn't do if I put my mind to it. Mom encouraged me. Cheered me on." He paused.

"And my dad killed her."

6

---

ope sucked in a quick breath, shocked at what Gideon
had just shared. Instinctively, she reached for his
hand, wanting to bring comfort to this appealing man
she barely knew and yet already found herself liking very much.

"I won't ask you for details, Gideon. You've had to live with
them. It's not my business." Her gaze met his. "But I am very sorry
for what you have been through, especially loving your mom as
much as you did."

He raked a hand through his hair and leaned against the
sofa's back. "No, Hope. I want to talk about it. With you."

Gideon fell silent, and she didn't push. She knew he was on
his own timetable now, and so she sat patiently, waiting for him
to articulate whatever was in his heart.

Staring out into space, he said, "They never should have
gotten married. It was because of me. Mom turned up pregnant
—and for probably the only time in his life, my dad did what
should have been the right thing."

"It must have been difficult for her, finding herself in that
position," she said gently.

"Yeah. She was barely nineteen when she had me. She

worked as a clerk at the drugstore and cleaned houses in her spare time. My dad was five years older and a mechanic at the local body shop. He might have married her—but he sure didn't stay faithful to her. That's one of my earliest memories of him. Him coming home smelling of booze, cigarettes, and another woman's perfume."

"Did your mom ever think about leaving him?" Hope asked.

He shook his head sadly. "No, never. She was pretty religious. Mom never called him out on any of the affairs. Or his drinking. The few times I tried to do so? Let's just say he had a pretty heavy hand and wasn't afraid to use it on me."

Hurt rippled through her, thinking of Gideon as a young boy, trying to defend his mother and stand up to his bully of a father.

He glanced to her. "It really wasn't all bad. Like I told you, Mom and I did a lot of things together. She called out my spelling words to me. She was great in math and helped me understand long division and fractions. She taught me to read and made up all kinds of crazy, funny stories." He sighed. "She was just working a lot of the time, leaving me by myself. That's when sports saved me."

Gideon fell silent again, and Hope continued to hold his hand, wishing she could erase all the terrible memories he held onto.

"I played sports. A lot of them. But I was the best of anyone at football. I had good speed and a nose for the ball. I was offered several scholarships my senior year in high school, and Walker's dad convinced me to take the offer to play at SMU. It was his alma mater, and Walker had been accepted there, following in his dad's footsteps. Mr. Cox told me that even though I had received offers to stronger football programs, a degree from SMU would go a long way after my football days ended."

He smiled wryly. "The Coxes were like surrogate parents to me all my years growing up in Sugar Springs. I told you Walker and I were like brothers, and that really was the case. I spent more time at their house than I did my own. When I went to play for the SMU Mustangs, Mr. and Mrs. Cox came to a bunch of my home games to support me."

"Did your parents ever watch you play in any games?"

"Mom made a point to come to my games in high school. She would leave work at the drugstore and clean one house, then arrive around halftime on Friday nights. Mr. and Mrs. Cox would always save her a seat, and they would catch her up on the passes I'd caught during the first half."

"And your dad?"

"He never came to a single game," Gideon said flatly. "Friday nights were a time for him to booze it up and find someone to fuck."

His tone was so angry, and she knew Gideon had unresolved issues about his father. "What about in college? Was your mom able to come see you play then?" Hope asked.

She read the pain in his eyes, almost wishing she could take back her question.

"Saturdays were busy for her," he said. "Mom usually cleaned houses all day. Clients didn't like to be put off. Once a year, though, she would somehow work out her schedule and ride with the Coxes into Dallas to see me play a home game."

His mouth hardened. "Except for that last time. My senior year."

Once again, Gideon stared into space, lost in thought. Hope sat quietly by his side, continuing to hold his hand, his fingers now entwined with hers. She wanted to will strength from herself into him, knowing the worst part of his story was yet to come.

Finally, he seemed to come back to reality.

"The second game into my senior year, my dad said it was about time he saw me play. By then, I had been named an All-American my junior year and was a preseason pick at wide receiver for my senior year. He wanted to see if I lived up to all the hype. I didn't come home summers between years in college," he told her, his face flushing. "I would find a job in Dallas and stay because I didn't want to be near him. I regret that now. I should've come home and been with my mom."

"Gideon," Hope said softly, "your mom had made her decision to stay in a bad marriage. You were old enough to be making decisions for *your* future."

He blew out a long breath. "I know you're right. Anyway, he told Mom they would go to a game of mine. Knowing her, she was thrilled they would actually be spending an entire day together. But he was drinking the whole time on the way to Dallas. When I took the field for warmups, he made his way to the bottom of the stands and started barking at me. I tried to ignore him at first, but he kept on. I came over and told him not to make a spectacle of himself, or he'd get thrown out of the stadium."

Gideon swallowed. "He told me I better have the game of my life because he'd heard there were NFL scouts in the stadium. He said I owed him. That I needed to sign a fat contract so he wouldn't have to work another day. My coach called me over. I was so embarrassed."

He paused. "That was the last time I ever spoke to my dad." He leaned up and grabbed the glass of ice water, downing the entire contents before sitting back against the couch.

"On their way home from that game, they were in an accident. A bad one. My mom was killed instantly. That's the only thing I'm grateful for. That she didn't have to suffer any. He was thrown from the car, not wearing his seatbelt, as usual. He lied and said that she was the one driving, but he wouldn't have allowed that. I never saw them get in the car with her behind the wheel, no matter how drunk he was. I told the police that later. He protested when they took his blood alcohol level anyway. It was point eighteen."

Hope was shocked at the astonishingly high number, but she figured if Mr. Ross were the heavy drinker Gideon had said he was, he would have built up a tolerance for alcohol in larger and larger quantities as the years passed.

Knowing she had to hear the end of his story, Hope asked, "Was he sent to prison?"

"I wish he would've been. I wished they would've dropped him in a hole and left him there to rot." His gaze met hers. "He was rushed to the nearest hospital and wound up dying from his internal injuries on the operating table. End of the story."

But something told Hope that Gideon had not closed the door on this incident.

"How did you handle your mom's death?" she asked.

"Pretty poorly. I failed a test the next week because I couldn't concentrate when I tried to study. I never should have played in the game the following week. I was distracted. My head somewhere else." He hesitated and then added, "I was injured in that game. Tore up my knee. I never played another down of college ball."

She could hear the bitterness in his voice, even after all these years.

"Your rehab must have gone well because you wouldn't have been able to pass the police department's physical otherwise."

"Oh, I put my heart and soul into rehabbing my knee. I was determined to spit on my father's grave and make a name for myself in the NFL. I was undrafted but signed with the Falcons and went to their summer camp. I wound up getting quite a bit of playing time in preseason and was cut when they trimmed their roster to the final fifty-three men."

"That's fantastic, Gideon. To come back from such a serious injury and experience that much success?"

He looked at her, his eyes misted with tears. "A part of me wanted to play pro ball, but I realized my heart wasn't in it anymore. I had offers to sign to a couple of teams' practice squad, but I turned all those down. If I couldn't set foot on the field as a professional player and compete at that level, I knew I would just be wasting my time chasing a dream which had passed me by. Besides, I'd always wanted to help people. I guess it was the former Eagle Scout in me. Mrs. Cox, who'd been one of my teachers in high school, told me that I had a servant's heart. I decided to apply to the police academy in Dallas. I had no reason to ever come back to Sugar Springs."

"I'm sure you've had a very rewarding career," she said encouragingly. "Else you wouldn't have been named police chief here at such a young age."

"I was a good cop. And detective. I had good instincts and always followed them. When the opportunity arose and Chief Hamilton told me he was retiring, I agreed to come onboard once I finished my current case. A bonus was having Walker back here, as well. Even though we were both busy with our jobs in Dallas, we made time to get together and play racquetball and grab breakfast at least once a week over the years."

"I'm glad you've been able to come back to your hometown," Hope said. "I believe you will make a difference here."

She squeezed his hand, and he looked down, seeming surprised to find their fingers joined.

He released her hand and reached for his plate again, picking up a slice of pizza and biting into it.

"It's gone cold," he said, "while I shared my tale of woe with you."

"I'm glad you did, Gideon. I'm glad you trusted me enough to listen to it."

He set the plate on the coffee table. "Well, this hasn't been much of a date. I apologize for that, Hope. These are things I never really talk about with anyone. Walker knew instinctively how I felt, and he did the guy thing and never really asked. He's just always been there for me, picking me up when I was low."

Gideon rose. "I should go. I've depressed you enough."

She came to her feet and took his hand again, surprised at her boldness. "Don't go, Gideon. Stay. I can reheat the pizza in the microwave."

He searched her face, and she found herself going warm under his intense gaze.

"You really do want me to stay," he said, wonder in his voice. "I've bored you. Depressed you. And yet, you're still hanging in there with me."

Trying to lighten the mood, Hope grinned at him. "Well, we have yet to get to that slice of pie you promised me."

He burst out laughing. "Got a sweet tooth on you, Dr. Keller?"

She sensed his mood shifting. "Guilty as charged, Chief Ross."

"Then let's heat up the pizza and try again. If that's okay with you."

"That's fine with me," she said firmly, not wanting him to leave.

They used the microwave to heat the remaining slices and then sat and talked about the things people on a first date usually discuss. He liked country music, while she was a fan of rock. They both liked action movies and legal dramas, but she added that she was also a sucker for romantic comedies. Neither of them had really traveled much, and she told him her goal was to apply for a passport and fill the pages with stamps from other countries.

"Where would you go first?" he asked.

"I think Greece," she told him. "I've seen a few movies set there, and it seems like heaven on earth. I love the water. Living in Houston my entire life, my folks and I—and later my friends— would drive to Galveston and swim in the warm waters of the Gulf of Mexico. I find water to be very peaceful. In fact, I often-times put on an app of the ocean, falling asleep to the waves coming in and out."

"I've never seen an ocean, much less the Gulf of Mexico. I think I would want to go to England first. See London and all it has to offer and then go out to the countryside and soak it up. I remember a guy in one of my political science classes talking about a trip he and his brother took, just the two of them. They'd gone on a bike tour through France one summer. They biked from town to town, staying in inns along the way."

"That would be a great way to see a country," she agreed.

"Maybe one day," he said wistfully.

Gideon looked at her then with a yearning that felt as if he pierced her soul. It frightened her, and Hope leaped to her feet.

"Let me get those pieces of pie for us," she said, hurrying over to claim the Styrofoam containers and two forks.

She returned with their desserts and handed him his container and a fork. Taking her seat again, they ate their pie while he asked her about herself.

"There's not much to tell," she said guardedly. "I had a happy childhood. Was an only child. Became an Aggie like my dad and graduated from the university and then went to vet school in College Station. Did a few years post-graduate doing some research for a beloved professor. Then I got itchy feet and wanted to put my degree to use. I came back to Houston and found a position in Dr. Wallman's clinic."

"What made you leave that practice? I'm assuming you were happy there."

"Yes, very much so, but Dad got pancreatic cancer. He wasn't diagnosed until late Stage 4, and by then, there wasn't much to do for him. He tried and gave up on the chemo and radiation treatments, which made him miserable. They weren't able to do much for him."

"That must've been tough on you and your mom."

"It was. Dad was always the rock of our family. I lost him and mom around the same time, and it caused me to reevaluate my life and what I wanted. What I was doing. Where I was headed. I knew I needed a change."

"And so you moved from the big city to a small town."

"Maybe," she said. "I'm going to work a couple of weeks at Dr. Bisch's clinic and see whether or not it will be a good fit for me."

Gideon leaned toward her and said, "I think you are meant to stay in Sugar Springs, Hope Keller."

Then his lips touched hers.

7

As Gideon pressed his mouth to Hope's, he wondered exactly what he was doing. It was crazy to even think to kiss her, and so he broke the kiss, pulling away.

But Hope was having none of that. She clutched his shirtfront and jerked him toward her, his lips colliding with hers.

Then greed took over, overwhelming him. It had been so long since he had kissed a woman—and meant it. He'd always thought kissing was an intimate act and rarely did so with the few one-night stands he'd had over the last decade.

Hope Keller's lips, though, were so inviting. He wanted to gobble her up but restrained himself. Instead, Gideon began brushing his lips slowly against hers as he inhaled that wonderful vanilla scent wafting from her skin. He gradually applied more pressure, his arms going around her, needing to draw her closer to him. Her palms came to rest flat against his chest, and he knew she was feeling the drumbeat of his heart, which was beating out of control.

He teased her mouth open with his tongue and pushed inside, gently exploring her. Tasting her.

Wanting her...

Although he wanted to continue the kiss, he broke it, moving his head away from her, her hands falling from his shoulders, her mood unreadable.

"I'm sorry," he began. "I—"

"You really are out of practice as far as dating goes, Gideon," she said lightly, and he clearly saw the disappointment in her sky blue eyes. "You started the date off poorly. There was a lot of good stuff in the middle, however, but now you're blowing it at the end. I'll have to give a lot of consideration as to whether I accept a second date with you or not."

He couldn't help but laugh. "Hope, you're killing me. And yes, I can't remember the last time I had a date. Or even kissed a woman. I know, pretty pathetic."

"A handsome guy like you?"

He shrugged, liking the fact that she thought he was handsome. "I guess you could say I've been married to my job for a long time now. I haven't had much of a social life. The last case I worked on in Dallas went over nine months long. It involved a serial killer."

Her eyes widened at that revelation. "Did you catch him?"

"We did," he said. "That's the only reason I was able to come to Sugar Springs and take over as chief. Roscoe Hamilton wanted to retire, but I told him that I couldn't come home and take the job until the task force had found our killer."

Gideon didn't want to get into the grisly particulars of the case with her and hoped that she wouldn't ask about them. Instead, he asked, "So, the beginning and end of the date was a bust?"

"Pretty much," she agreed, her eyes twinkling at him. "Although I was enjoying the kiss. Even if I'm out of practice myself. I haven't dated much these past few years, Gideon. Like you, I've poured a lot of myself into work."

"I was thinking you were bored tonight," he admitted. "I went on and on about all my woes. Things in the past that I should let go of."

She placed her hand over his, and warmth flooded him. "I was never bored. I feel honored that you opened up to me the way that you did." She smiled. "Besides, we did do a little of the first date stuff. Talking about music and movies. And we were smart enough to avoid any talk of politics."

"Do you lean left or right?" he asked.

"I'm afraid I don't lean any way," she told him. "I think politicians are only out to help themselves and not their constituents. I'm embarrassed to say I really don't vote. I don't even keep up with the news. School shootings. Serial killers. Tornadoes that wipe out an entire town. It's all so depressing to me. I'd rather spend my time helping and treating animals. Or curled up with a good book."

"I guess I'm your polar opposite. I vote in every election. Pour over websites where candidates express their views. But I guess we can agree on not talking about current events."

"Unless it's sports," Hope prompted. "I love all kinds of sports. I'm a huge fan of the Houston franchises. The Astros. The Texans. The Rockets."

He waved his hands in protest. "That is so wrong," he said, laughing. "You're living in East Texas now. This is Dallas Cowboys country. Sugar Springs loves the Cowboys. The Mavericks and Rangers, too."

"Well, I do root for one Dallas team. The Stars. Houston doesn't have an NHL franchise. I've never been to a hockey game, but I love the speed and boldness players show on the ice. The Stars' captain is amazing. He's one of the fastest guys on the ice, and he's led the team in scoring for three consecutive years."

"Maybe we could drive into Dallas and go to a game since they're in season now. We could give Mrs. Romano the heads up and have her contact Dante. We could eat at his restaurant. I know where it is."

Her face lit with enthusiasm. "I would really like that, Gideon."

"Well, I think that should be our third date."

She frowned. "What happened to the second one?"

He smiled. "Since you're having to decide whether or not to go on a second date with me, let me tempt you now with sports—and remind you that I'd mentioned that Walker and Rory are holding a Super Bowl party this coming Sunday. Just a few friends—and a lot of great food. You did agree to go to it with me, Dr. Keller." He paused. "Or do you need to reconsider?"

She pursed her lips, pretending to ponder his offer, and all Gideon could think of was how much he wanted to sink his teeth into her full, bottom lip. He couldn't remember the last time he had felt desire stirring within him.

And it scared the hell out of him.

"Since I look around and see there's no TV here, that means I'll either have to find a sports bar on Sunday or take you up on your invitation. I suppose I could go out with you again, Chief Ross. Maybe let you redeem yourself in the dating department."

"If Sunday goes well, then I'll check the schedule and see when the Stars play at home next," he said. "Date number three."

"How far are we from Dallas?"

"About ninety minutes, depending upon traffic when we hit the Dallas city limits. Maybe it would be better to aim for a weekend game," he suggested. "I assume you have to be at Dr. Bisch's clinic early. A weeknight game would have us getting back to Sugar Springs pretty late."

"Vets always open shop early. We usually start seeing patients by seven. I'll probably get there half an hour or so before seven, just to familiarize myself each day with the appointments coming in."

He glanced at his watch. "Then I suppose we should call it a night."

Gideon rose and Hope did the same, walking him to the door

as he shrugged into his jacket. Although he hadn't planned to, he framed her face with his hands and briefly grazed his lips against hers in a sweet, gentle kiss. He pulled back and smiled at her.

"Thanks for the pizza and pie," she said. "And the conversation. Which was not boring."

"Thanks for giving me a second chance," he replied. "Do you mind if I call you tomorrow and see how your first day at the clinic went?"

She looked pleased. "I'd like that. A lot."

"Goodnight, Hope."

"Goodnight, Gideon."

She opened the door, and he stepped outside, reluctant to leave her, which was a first for him and any woman. Even his ex-wife. As he walked down the stairs to his SUV, he wondered if things might heat up with Hope.

He got into the vehicle, warning himself not to become too invested in her. Until she decided to stay in Sugar Springs, it would be wise to hold his feelings in check. She was a big city girl who might have trouble adjusting to small-town life, or she might not think purchasing Dr. Bisch's practice was a good idea in the long run.

Yet Gideon knew he was fooling himself. He already was invested. Hope Keller intrigued him to no end. For the first time since his divorce, he was picturing himself being with someone. Building a life with her.

He cursed aloud, thinking how ridiculous it all sounded. And yet Walker had told him that there was something instantaneous that occurred when he had met Rory. She had been a little prickly toward Walker in the beginning, but he had known without a doubt that he wanted her and pressed her accordingly.

Was he looking at them—or at Cole and Nova—and simply wishing for the closeness those couples had? How could he not? He was thirty-six years old and back in his hometown. A place where people married and raised families. Gideon had been alone for many years now, not succumbing to the loneliness because he buried himself in work.

His life had changed, though. While he was still dedicated to keeping Sugar Springs safe and willing to put in as many hours a week as it took to do so, his workload was markedly different from his detective days in Dallas. Since his return a month ago, he had been restless, especially when he came home to his empty apartment at night.

Did he think Hope Keller would simply fill a hole? Or did the possibility of more between them exist?

It remained to be seen since she had yet to commit to buying Dr. Bisch's practice.

When he reached home, Gideon poured himself a stiff drink, bringing the whiskey to the breakfast bar and firing up his laptop. First, he checked work emails, answered a few, and then called his dispatcher, inquiring if anything of interest had gone on since he'd left the station several hours ago. When he learned all was quiet, he thanked Grady and hung up.

Then he did something he had never done before. He'd watched fellow cops check out their dates online all the time, using police databases to dive deeply into their research. He'd no intention of doing that, but curiosity drove him to type Hope's name into the search box, wanting to learn what he could about her before their next date this weekend.

Several women with her name popped up, and he scrolled through, trying to locate any article about her. When he couldn't, he refined his search, adding *Doctor* in front of Hope Keller and *Houston* after her name.

This time, one Dr. Hope Keller popped up, an oncologist at M. D. Anderson.

Where the hell was his Hope?

Gideon began drilling down, putting her name in with Houston veterinary clinics and animal hospitals. He tried her name and Texas A&M University and the vet school. Again, nothing.

It was as if Dr. Hope Keller, veterinarian from Houston and graduate of Texas A&M School of Veterinary Medicine, did not exist. Warning bells went off in his head. Why wouldn't Hope have left any kind of digital footprint on the Internet?

It troubled him that she had arrived out of thin air, ready to buy Dr. Bisch's practice. She said her parents had died recently, and so he typed in *Keller, Houston,* and *Obituaries.*

Again, no hits leading to his Hope.

His detective's mind whirled at warp speed now, fantastic thoughts swirling in his head. Maybe she was in witness protection, and that's why she had no history on the Internet because she hadn't done anything under this name. Or what if she had, in addition to experiencing her parents' death, gone through a nasty divorce and taken back her maiden name? If that were the case, then she would be listed on the Internet under a different surname with the dots he was trying to connect.

Being a cop wasn't always good in these situations because his thoughts went dark places it shouldn't. What if she had killed someone and was trying to outrun the law, taking on a new identity and name?

"This is crazy," he said aloud, raking his hands through his hair in frustration.

Gideon closed out of the sites he'd been scouring and stepped away from his computer, his thoughts in a jumble.

Dr. Hope Keller didn't seem to exist—and yet she had turned up in his town, intriguing him, capturing his attention, making him want things he had long ago set aside.

He got ready for bed, promising himself when he got to work tomorrow morning, he would use every resource at his fingertips to discover who the hell Dr. Hope Keller really was.

8

Hope awoke before her alarm went off and prepared for her usual run. After Gideon had left last night, she had pulled up a map of the area where her rental was located and studied the streets, finding several routes she could take with Jake.

As she ran with the dog, she made certain her mind didn't wander since it was her first time running along the streets of Sugar Springs. Part of her run took her through the center of town, and she also passed the fire and police stations off the square, along with the bank, which was two short blocks down from the police station. This time, the police building had far greater significance to her since her date with Gideon last night.

She studied the stores along the square with more interest now, finding herself growing more invested in this town and her possible move to East Texas. Of course, everything depended upon her impressions of the clinic and whether or not she wished to take over Richard Bisch's practice. Her gut was telling her this would be a good move for her professionally.

And personally.

No, she couldn't let thoughts of Gideon Ross distract her. This important decision would need to be made with her head.

Not her heart.

She tamped down the growing feelings she had for a man she'd only spent a few hours with and told herself she was a pragmatist. She would weigh the pros and cons of taking on the responsibilities of not only being a veterinarian in a small community but actually owning her own practice. It would have to make financial sense, as well as be a situation where she could see herself practicing animal medicine in.

Returning to Lizzy Lou's, she raced up the stairs to the garage apartment, Jake following on her heels. Once inside, she took him off his leash and gave him food and water before eating a protein bar she had stashed in her purse. She hoped the clinic had a coffee maker since she could certainly use a cup. After work would have to include a trip to the grocery store. She needed to stock up on food, drinks, and a few household supplies, such as toilet paper and detergent. Lizzy Lou had told Hope that she was welcome to use the washer and dryer in the main house, and she planned to take advantage of that instead of loading her laundry into the car and searching for a laundromat.

She told Jake to come as she slipped into her lab coat and then her regular coat before picking up her purse, thinking to take his leash in case Lizzy Lou might want to go on a walk with the beagle. Using her key, she let herself in the front door and walked straight to the kitchen, finding her landlady sitting at the table, drinking a cup of coffee, pouring over the comics.

"Good morning," Hope said brightly, in good spirits.

"I see you're up bright and early," Lizzy Lou said. "Even after company last night."

Feeling the blush tinge her cheeks, she said, "Yes. I had some pizza and pie with Chief Ross."

"I knew about the pie. Ida Lou said you came in for some. How did you find Romano's pizza?"

Shaking her head at the information Lizzy Lou had on her, Hope said, "It was delicious."

The older woman gave her a mischievous smile. "Hopefully, the company was, too."

The heat rose in her cheeks. "Chief Ross had promised me a piece of pie when I met him yesterday."

"You aren't from a small town, are you, Hope?"

"No. Born and bred in Houston. That's also where I worked."

"I see. Well, if you haven't figured it out, gossip flies fast and furiously in Sugar Springs. It's not malicious, for the most part, but folks are interested in what other folks are doing. Especially a newcomer. I think half the ladies in Sugar Springs have been wanting to fix up Chief Ross, and here you breeze into town and wind up on a date with him your first day here."

Hope could see how she would need to be careful regarding her personal life. She definitely wouldn't overshare with her landlady, who most likely would convey anything said between them to her cousin. With the diner being in the center of town, Hope guessed it to be the heartbeat of all gossip, which would flow from the owner to the patrons. She liked both Ida Lou and Lizzy Lou, but it was hard wrapping her head around the fact that a good many people in Sugar Springs already knew she had been with Gideon Ross last night.

Holding up Jake's leash, she said, "I'm dropping off Jake for the day as you suggested. If you want to walk him, I brought his leash."

"Why, that's a fine idea, Hope. I always like to stroll a few blocks every day. I'm not one for a fancy gym and all those machines and weights. Walking suits me just fine." She leaned over and patted the beagle. "Mr. Jake and I will do just fine together."

"All right. I'm off to work then. I'm not certain how late the clinic is open, so I'm not sure when I'll be back to pick him up."

"Closes at six Monday through Wednesday. Five-thirty Thursday and Friday. And it's open eight until one on Saturdays."

Again, it struck Hope how different a small town was from where she had grown up and lived.

"Thanks for that information, Lizzy Lou. I'll see you tonight. If you get tired of Jake, feel free to take him back to the apartment."

"I usually start dinner at five. I think I'll drop him off before I do that, so you don't have to stop here to pick him up each day." Lizzy Lou paused. "I usually provide breakfast and dinner to guests at the B&B. I really haven't for the garage apartment occupants, but I'm happy to do so if you want to join me."

Thinking she would cherish a little peace and quiet after a long day at the clinic, Hope decided to decline the invitation.

"That won't be necessary," she assured her landlady. "I almost always have a protein shake or bar in the mornings. And I enjoy cooking, so I'll make my own dinner."

"All right then, dear. But if you change your mind, just let me know."

"Thank you. I will."

Hope left and went to her car, driving the short distance to the clinic. When she arrived, a Honda pulled in beside her. Shirley got out and greeted her.

"Still cold today, Dr. Keller," the older woman noted.

"It is," she agreed. "Houston usually is several degrees warmer this time of year."

"Oh, honey, it's Texas. Blink—and the weather will change. I remember Thanksgivings when I've had to run my air conditioner some years and other years, we've had snow on the ground."

They walked in together, and Sally greeted them. "Good morning. No Jake today to keep Sam and me company?"

"I'm staying at Lizzy Lou's. She's looking after him today."

Sally nodded. "That's good. Poor Lizzy Lou lost her pug not

too long ago. Misses him like crazy. Little Jake will be just the thing to perk her up."

"May I see my schedule today?" Hope asked, slipping out of her winter coat and hanging it on the coatrack.

"Come around and look at the computer screen, hon," the receptionist said. "We only have appointments scheduled for Richard. He's going to let you take on all of those today, while he observes. For the next week or ten days—however long you are testing us out—I'll make appointments for the both of you. Surgeries, too, if you're up to it."

"I'm happy to see whoever comes in, and I'm ready to do surgeries when needed," she replied.

Hope studied today's schedule, wondering how the pet owners coming in would take to her seeing their animals when they'd previously booked Dr. Bisch. She had full confidence in her abilities, though, and didn't mind the more experienced vet observing her in action. She knew he wanted to hand his clinic over to someone he had confidence in.

She was ready to prove to him that she was the person who could replace him with ease.

"Is there any coffee?" she asked. "The apartment didn't have a coffee maker." She chuckled. "And I haven't had a chance to hit the store for groceries yet."

"Yes, it's in Richard's office," Sally said. "We're so small that we don't really have a breakroom. I just buy pods. Let me know if you have a particular flavor you enjoy, and I'll pick up a box of it."

"I'm good with anything available, as long as it has caffeine. I stayed away from it until I graduated from college. Vet school had me up super early, though. A hit of caffeine, via coffee, always helps jumpstart my engine."

She went to Dr. Bisch's office and let him know she needed to use the coffee maker. Opening the drawer below it, she saw a nice variety of flavors and chose hazelnut this morning.

"Have you seen the appointments scheduled for today?" he asked.

"Yes, I looked through them when I arrived."

As her coffee brewed, he filled her in on the pet owners who were coming in and then said, "Of course, there are always the emergencies. We see a few of those each week."

Hope doctored her coffee, stirring in some stevia and creamer. "I don't wish that on anyone, but I do hope you can see me work a few of those cases. Sally told me you'd be sitting in on the patients I see today. I want you to observe me not only with routine exams, but also with surgeries or in an emergency that arises."

"I hope to do that," he responded. "I already have confidence in you, based upon Dr. Wallman's recommendation, but I think it's important to watch you with patients. See your knowledge and professionalism at work. Your demeanor. How you operate. I'm sure you know our job doesn't merely consist of tending to animals, but it also involves managing their owners."

"I agree. For vets, bedside manner involves both patients and their owners. I'd like to think I'm good with both." She took a sip of her coffee, feeling the surge of caffeine hit her system.

"Sally always pulls the records of pets coming in before noon when she arrives," he said, taking Hope to where these file folders had been placed in an open box in a hallway connecting to the examination rooms. "She places the afternoon appointments into the box before she takes her lunch."

He pulled out a clipboard for her to use, showing her where the pre-printed well-exam sheets were located so that she could record the information on them and saying this would go to Sally once the visit concluded so she could bill the pet owner appropriately.

"I like a hard copy, so Sally types these up, along with any notes we want to give her. I usually dictate my notes, and she'll transcribe whatever I record onto the office visit report document. We also keep a digital file, and she'll print out a copy, as well, for the paper files."

"Those are behind the reception desk, right?" she confirmed, remembering seeing the long cabinets.

"Yes. Here's where you can place the files of the patients after you've seen them." He pointed to a different tray nearby.

"I know today is more about me seeing patients under your guidance, but I will want to look at the financials of the clinic at some point," she told him. "I'd also like to see your monthly and yearly budgets and learn how supplies are ordered. Meds, too."

"Of course." He hesitated. "Not that I'm testing you..."

"But you are, Dr. Bisch," she said. "I get that. You've built something remarkable here, and you don't want to turn it over to someone who is sloppy or uninformed. Ask away."

He nodded in approval. "All right then." He picked up the file on top. "Our first appointment is a well exam for a three-year-old German shepherd. What are you looking for?"

"What I look for in a routine exam will be the diet and exercise a dog receives. I'll check his breathing as I ask about his behavior and habits, especially his elimination patterns. I'll physically examine him and make recommendations for any preventive medicines and give him any vaccinations which are due. I'll look at his coat and skin. Check his teeth. Suggest any lifestyle changes that might be appropriate, based upon his age, weight, and health status. Listen to his heart and lungs. Give—"

"Enough," he said jovially. "I'm glad I've already taken the professorship at A&M because if they'd heard you speak, they might have offered you the job instead."

She laughed. "I'm happy for you to take that position because I plan to be practicing veterinary medicine for a long time."

"Then let's go see our first patient."

They went to an examination room, where a woman in her mid-thirties stood next to a German shepherd, Shirley petting the dog.

Good morning," the woman greeted them. "Shirley tells me I get to have two vets at Max's appointment today." Offering her hand to Hope, she said, "I'm Margaret Mason. I work as a receptionist for Walker Cox, who's an attorney in town."

"Yes, that name is familiar to me," she said. "I met Chief Ross yesterday, and he mentioned being friends with your boss. So, this is Max." She approached the dog, holding out a hand for him to sniff. "How are you today, Max? I'm Doctor Keller."

Hope then went through a typical, routine checkup for a dog of Max's age, talking through what she was doing the entire time, asking Margaret if there were any behavior issues that needed to be addressed and letting the client know what she was doing to her pet.

"I'm auscultating now. Listening for his heart rhythm. If he has an abnormal heart rate. Moving to his lungs." She paused and listened. "No evidence of increased or decreased breath sounds. That's good."

She moved again, saying, "Palpating now. Checking the pulse in his hind legs. Checking the lymph nodes in his legs, then head and neck. I'm not seeing any signs of swelling or reaction to pain."

The exam continued. "Max's muscle condition is good. His body weight is spot on. His coat has no dryness or oiliness. Skin is also good."

Moving to his face, she looked into the shepherd's eyes. "No redness or discharge or cloudiness. Eyelids close the way they should. No abnormal lumps or bumps on his eyelids." She looked inside the dog's ears. "No signs of discharge or thickening."

She paused, looking to Margaret. "So far, so good. Now, let's see those teeth, Max. "Hmm. A little tartar build-up. It's not significant at this point, though. No broken teeth or ulcers. No excessive salivation. Do you brush his teeth regularly? I would suggest once a day to prevent tartar from occurring."

"Sometimes, that gets put on a back burner," Margaret admitted. "I have a ten-year-old son who feeds and walks Max. He's supposed to also brush his teeth. That doesn't always happen. With the boy or the dog."

Hope laughed. "I'm running my hands along him now. His belly. Legs. Looking for any muscle or nerve problems. Seeing if anything is wrong with his organs. Oh, his toes look terrific!"

She lifted Max from the table. "May I have his leash? I want to walk him a bit. See how he walks and stands. Check how alert he is." As she attached the leash to the collar, Hope added, "Be right back."

Opening the door, she led Max from the exam room and walked him around the reception area, pleased by everything she saw.

Hope returned to where Margaret and Dr. Bisch waited and asked, "Did you bring in the requested stool sample?"

"Yes, I gave that to Shirley when we came in."

"Good. We'll process that sample and evaluate it to see if any parasite eggs are present."

She told the pet owner what vaccines she would be giving Max today, as well as asking if she could do a complete blood count, along with urinalysis and thyroid hormone testing, explaining what these tested for.

After drawing blood for the tests, she gave Max his shots and then petted him, praising how good he'd been during his physical.

"I'll call you about the bloodwork and urinalysis when the results come in, Margaret. Tell your son he's doing a great job of walking Max and keeping the weight off him." She paused. "But they both need to work on that teeth brushing."

"I'll be sure to pass that message along, Dr. Keller. It was so nice meeting you. I hope you'll consider moving to Sugar Springs."

"If all my patients are as healthy and sweet as Max, it'll be a no-brainer," Hope joked, handing Shirley the clipboard and petting Max again. "You're all set to go. Please call me if you have any questions or if Max shows a reaction to his vaccines. Sometimes, dogs will be a little lethargic after their shots. Not as playful as usual for a day or so."

"Thank you, Dr. Keller," Margaret said again. "It was nice meeting you."

"Nice meeting you and Max, too."

After Margaret and Shirley left, Dr. Bisch said, "You are thorough. Friendly. You know how to put an animal and its owner at ease. I don't need to sit in and observe any other appointments today, Hope. You can see all the patients while I catch up on paperwork and a little research. I do have a spaying tomorrow morning at seven for a cat. Another surgery at one-thirty tomorrow afternoon for a dog neutering. I'd like to watch you perform both of those if you don't mind."

"Not at all," she told him, pleased that he didn't feel the need to look over her shoulder the rest of the day. "If you have those animals' files, I'd like to review them after we close today."

"I'll ask Sally to pull them for you. Shall we meet up for lunch? I heard you had pizza last night, so maybe we could do Ida Lou's again."

Did everyone in town know about her and Gideon's evening?

They both left the exam room, she to claim the file for the next patient and Dr. Bisch to have the surgery files pulled.

As she read through the next pet's file, seeing that the appointment was because the cat had suddenly begun peeing outside its litter box, Dr. Bisch returned, files in hand.

"I'll set these surgical files on the shelf here. I'm sorry you don't have any office space, Hope. We can share if you'd like."

"No, I don't want to disrupt your routine. I can either take things home with me to work on, or I can wait until you go home and access your computer to input data. I'm sure Sally will fork over your password."

He laughed. "She's the one who remembers things like that. I'm the kind who would use *password* as my password if it were left up to me."

Just then, Sally appeared and as Hope started into the exam room, she heard the receptionist say, "It's Chief Ross on line two, honey. He sounded like it was urgent."

Gideon hadn't mentioned anything about owning a pet. Hope couldn't help but wonder what Sugar Springs' police chief wanted to talk to Richard Bisch about.

And hoped it wasn't her.

9

Gideon stuck to his usual morning routine, trying his best to block out all thoughts of Hope Keller.

It didn't work.

He saw her in his mind as he jogged the streets of Sugar Springs. When he showered. When he downed two ibuprofen tablets with his coffee because his head ached from lack of sleep.

The woman had gotten under his skin.

He arrived at the police station at six-thirty and immediately went to see dispatcher Gladys Cameron. In her mid-fifties, with bleached blonde hair and eyes and ears that missed nothing, Gladys had been with the department over thirty years. Her son Grady was the night dispatcher, and Gideon thought the son was even more efficient than his mother.

"Morning, Gladys. Anything?"

She took a sip of her coffee. "Nada, Chief. Grady said it was a quiet night. Let's hope it continues that way."

Next, he stopped by the front desk. Sergeant Leland Brown manned it and was also Gideon's patrol commander, issuing the daily assignments. They chatted for a few minutes about today's rotations before Brown gave Gideon a knowing look.

"Heard you had pizza last night with the new vet."

He didn't let his irritation show. He loved his town, but he could see how it might take the gossip a step too far.

"Pizza was good," he said non-committedly.

"I heard Dr. Keller is nice. From Houston," Brown said, obviously fishing.

"She is nice. Whether she stays or heads back to Houston remains to be seen." Gideon hoped his tone would shut down this line of conversation. "Be sure to update me on the rookie by week's end."

"Will do, Chief," the sergeant said.

Next, Gideon went to his office, checking emails and his calendar for the day. He wouldn't meet with his detectives until they came in at eight o'clock. He'd been pleased to find Sam Douglas on staff when he'd arrived at the department. Sam had been a senior and all-state running back when Gideon was a freshman. Sam had been a patrolman in Tyler and later made detective there. He was raising his family in Sugar Springs, though, and when an opening occurred, Roscoe Hamilton had hired the former football player and made him lead detective.

He left his office to go to roll call, part of his daily routine. Gideon thought it important that his patrol officers see him on a regular basis. Besides, he liked being knowledgeable about which cops were riding together and what the morning briefing held.

Once it ended, he went to his office and closed his door, not wanting to be interrupted. To start, he searched for how to find a person who had changed his or her name beyond marriage or divorce, knowing the State of Texas issued name changes through a court order. Usually, any member of the public could access court records unless the file had been sealed for some reason.

He started his search by browsing the official state links on the National Center for State Courts website. It linked case and docket information, but he drew a blank, wondering if Hope had changed her name and the proceedings had been sealed. He knew he was merely following a hunch that she had done so.

He didn't have the time to delve deeper here, so he looked up the Harris County clerk's office phone number. He could request the county clerk to provide information on where Hope had lived —if she did come from Houston—and also ask how to access the court records regarding name changes. The offices wouldn't be open until eight, so he called to leave a voicemail. Surprisingly, someone answered.

"Yes, this is Police Chief Gideon Ross in Sugar Springs, Texas." He provided his official law enforcement identification number so the clerk could ascertain he was who he said he was.

"Yes, Chief Ross. How can I help you?"

"I'm investigating a woman who has turned up in my community who claims to have lived and worked in Houston the past few years. A Dr. Hope Keller. She's wanting to purchase the practice of our local veterinarian, and he can't seem to find anything on the Internet about her. I suggested that she might have changed her name, so I'm trying to track that angle and see if that's the case."

"Give me the name, Chief, and I'll put one of my admins on it. My slate is full today."

"Do you know when I might hear from you?"

"Tomorrow at the earliest. But I will get back to you."

Gideon provided the information and his cell number and thanked the clerk before hanging up.

He didn't want to wait until tomorrow. He wanted to know now.

And then he figured out a way he could learn something about Hope's background. She had to have provided excellent references to Dr. Bisch, or the vet never would have had her come to Sugar Springs in the first place. If Gideon could speak to her former employer, he might be able to clear up the mystery—and set his mind at ease.

Looking up the clinic's website, he located the phone number and dialed it.

"Sugar Springs Veterinary Clinic. This is Sally. How may I help you?"

"Hi, Sally. Chief Gideon Ross here. I have a matter that I need to discuss with Dr. Bisch. Is he available?"

"Yes, Chief. I believe he is. Can I put you on hold?"

"Sure."

As he waited, elevator music played. The song was a saccharine version of Guns N Roses *Sweet Child O' Mine*. If he ever ran and was elected to the Texas state legislature, Gideon planned to sponsor a bill to outlaw elevator music.

"Hello, Chief Ross. How can I help you? Sally said it was urgent."

Damn. He hoped that Hope Keller hadn't been around to hear that.

"No, nothing urgent, Dr. Bisch. I guess it's that deep rumble I have in my voice that always makes me sound serious."

Gideon paused, not having thought of a cover story, knowing he needed to come up with one quickly.

"One of my patrol officers has a middle school-aged cousin interested in veterinary medicine. The boy lives in Houston and is wanting to shadow a vet for some school project. It's just for a day. I recalled you mentioned the other day that Dr. Keller worked at a practice of a friend of yours. Do you mind if I get his name and info? Maybe I could smooth the way for the boy and see if your friend wouldn't mind having him in for the day."

"Sure. Let me get the number for you."

After a brief pause, Dr. Bisch rattled off the name, number, and website of his friend, a Dr. Wallman, and said, "I hope things'll work out for your officer's cousin. It's never too early to start encouraging young people to choose a career path."

"Thanks, Dr. Bisch. I appreciate it."

He hung up and saw it was time to meet with his three detectives. Gideon did so and returned to his office twenty minutes later.

"No calls for now, Cyndi," he told his administrative assistant. "I've got a business call to make."

"Sure thing, Chief."

Closing the door, he felt his heart rate pick up as he called up Dr. Wallman's website, browsing the different tabs for background to learn a little more about the veterinarian. While several staff members were listed, no Dr. Keller was among them. When he felt prepared, Gideon dialed the number and asked to speak to Wallman.

"He's with a patient now," the receptionist said. "May I have your name and number, and I'll have him return your call."

"This is Gideon Ross," he stated, not wanting to mention his title just yet.

He provided his cell number, and the woman said, "Dr. Wallman should be available in about twenty minutes, Mr. Ross."

"Thank you."

Hanging up, he fiddled with some paperwork until his cell rang a short time later.

"Hello?" he said, forgoing his usual response of identifying himself by title and name.

"This is Dr. Wallman, Mr. Ross."

"It's actually Chief Ross, Dr. Wallman, of the Sugar Springs PD. I'm acquainted with a friend of yours, Dr. Richard Bisch."

"Oh, Rich and I go way back," Wallman said breezily. "We roomed together our last two years at A&M and then moved off-campus to an apartment while we attended vet school together. Of course, he and Sally got married just before our last year, so I kept the apartment, while he got the girl."

Gideon chuckled and then said, "The reason I'm calling is as a favor to Dr. Bisch." He then launched into his white lie. "Dr. Hope Keller arrived in town yesterday, and she'll be working at Dr. Bisch's clinic for a week or so. She's interested in buying the clinic since Dr. Bisch will be heading to teach at A&M in a few months."

"Yes, Rich is very excited about that opportunity. And... Hope... is a wonderful vet. Bright. Nurturing. I gave her an excellent reference." Wallman paused. "I'm confused. Is something wrong, Chief Ross? I'm not quite sure what favor Rich has requested from you."

"He told me about your glowing recommendation of Dr. Keller. It looks as if she will purchase the clinic. But Dr. Bisch was curious and googled her. He couldn't seem to find any information about her online, other than the reference he received from you. He's a little reluctant to sell his practice to her because of this. Could you possibly fill me in? I told him I would contact you and try to solve this little mystery."

"Did you call me on your personal cell, Chief?" the vet asked.

"Why, yes, I did."

"I'm going to call you back on one of your office lines. Give me a moment to look up the number. I'll speak with you shortly—if you are who you say you are."

The line went dead. Dr. Wallman had hung up abruptly.

And the mystery surrounding Hope Keller deepened.

Gideon went to his office door. "I have a call coming in shortly from a Dr. Wallman, Cyndi. Would you go ahead and put him through right away? Thanks."

He closed the door again and sat at his desk. Less than a minute later, his phone rang.

"Dr. Wallman is on line three for you, Chief."

"Thanks, Cyndi."

Punching the third button, he said, "This is Chief Ross," trying to sound as official as he could.

"Thank you for humoring me, Chief," Dr. Wallman said. "I simply needed to make certain you were who you said you were and not claiming to be the Sugar Springs police chief."

"Why are you so guarded about a request for information about Dr. Keller?" he asked.

"Because she doesn't want to be found," Wallman said flatly. "This is all in confidence, Chief?"

"Of course," he assured the vet.

"Hope isn't really Hope at all. She's Dr. Deborah Busby. Hope Keller is the name she changed to. It was all legal, you see. I do know the record was sealed in its entirety. She only shared this information with me because she put out her résumé under her new name and knew prospective employers would need to contact me in order to ask about her track record. I was delighted to hear from Rich and sang Deb's—Hope's—praises to him. But she doesn't want anyone knowing her old name."

"Do you know why Dr. Busby took legal action to change her name?" he pressed. "Usually, legal name changes are public record. Sealing the record is unusual. Unless it's a case of domestic violence," he said, fishing for the answer.

"I... I believe that would be something you can take up with Dr. Keller," the vet said stiffly. "I can convey to Rich that he shouldn't have any doubts about her abilities, though."

"No need to call him," Gideon urged, trying to cover his tracks. "I'll let him know we spoke and that Dr. Keller has nothing in her background to alarm him."

At least he hoped that was the case.

"I'd appreciate it if you wouldn't share our conversation with Dr. Keller," he added.

"I won't. I don't speak with her anymore."

That statement sounded odd to Gideon, but he didn't think he'd get anything else out of the Houston vet.

"Thank you for your time, Dr. Wallman."

He hung up, looking at the notepad where he'd scrawled *Dr. Dehorah Busby. Deb.*

He'd been right in thinking she had changed her name. Fortunately, she'd gone through legal channels, so she wasn't some criminal or even in witness protection, as he'd first suspected. Still, he had a name now.

And a burning desire to learn more about Dr. Deborah Busby.

An hour later, Gideon understood why Deb Busby had wanted to hide her identity and become someone entirely different—and why the court had agreed to keep the proceedings sealed.

First, he had searched her name, getting dozens of hits. It had been difficult to read about the murder of her parents by the man who had been stalking her. Apparently, luxury car salesman Cris Calder had become instantly smitten with Deb Busby after bringing in his dog to Dr. Wallman's clinic. His obsession grew, and he had sent her countless presents and emails. When she made it clear she did not want anything to do with him and informed him she had taken out a restraining order against him, Calder had abruptly left and gone to the home of Deb's parents, where he killed both of them.

Dr. Busby had pointed the police to Calder, saying he had followed her for weeks and showered her with unwanted attention. They had even found a tracker on her car which Calder had placed there. While her father had been diagnosed with pancreatic cancer and would have died within a week, his death—along with his wife's—had been extremely brutal. Deb Busby had testified at Calder's trial, and Calder had been given a forty-year sentence.

Gideon leaned back in his chair, hands pillowed behind his head, trying to take it all in. From what he'd poured through, it was likely Dr. Wallman had either fired Deb or let her go because of a few incidents employees at his clinic reported. With her parents dead and Calder behind bars, Gideon supposed Deb merely wanted to start over, hence the name change and seeking to work at a new clinic away from Houston and all the terrible memories.

He couldn't tell her what he had learned. It would be up to Deb—Hope—to share the nightmares from her past with him. It did make him want to wrap her in his arms and keep her safe, though.

It would be important to keep this knowledge to himself. Hopefully, she would reach a point where she trusted him enough to share her past with him.

And when she did, Gideon would be there for her, every step of the way.

10

Four o'clock came, and there were no more scheduled appointments at the animal clinic. Dr. Bisch told Hope he was leaving for the day and that she should use his office and computer for whatever she needed.

Earlier in the day, she had taken a half-hour and spent it with Sally, learning the basics of the vet clinic's computer system. It was an easy one to pick up. If she purchased the clinic—and she was definitely leaning in that direction—she would digitize everything. While Dr. Bisch's system might have worked well ten years ago, she knew people were used to going to a doctor or dentist and seeing their healthcare provider walk in with a tablet. It would be so much more efficient for her to check off and mark her observations as she performed an exam and directly after. Typing was much faster than writing by hand, and then there would be no need to type up notes hours later, when a detail or two might slip her mind. People could receive the report from their pet's visit via email or text, as well as be updated with any lab results. The clinic could provide a hard copy, if requested. Either way, she believed the documentation system needed to be overhauled.

Hope went to Dr. Bisch's office now and logged into his computer using the password Sally had shared, filling in a few extra notes on patients she had seen this afternoon. By the time she did so, it was five o'clock. The clinic's hours stated they were opened until five-thirty on Thursdays, however, and she felt an obligation to be on the premises in case an emergency case was brought in. She decided to look at the budget folders she saw listed on Dr. Bisch's computer since she had extra time to do so and knew the vet wouldn't mind.

After studying them, along with supplies which had been ordered over the last six months, Hope saw the clinic was in good financial standing. Next, she did some quick research on what veterinary practices were going for on the market, both in large cities, smaller towns, and rural areas. It gave her an idea what Dr. Bisch might ask for his practice. While she wanted him to receive a fair price, she had a figure in mind which she wouldn't go over.

She only hoped that their figures would come close to matching.

Hope went to the reception area, carrying this afternoon's updated files, and saw Sally packing up, ready to head home for the day.

"Were you able to find everything you needed, Hope?"

"Yes, thank you." She handed Sally the folders. "And here are the files on patients I saw today for you to input the info and my notes."

Sally gave her a knowing look. "This isn't a system you're used to, is it?"

Answering honestly, Hope said, "No. I'm used to everything being digital."

The receptionist shook her head. "I've tried my best to pull my husband from the dark ages, but he can be set in his ways. He's old school in that he likes the feel and look of a paper trail on a pet he's seen. I know if you decide to buy us out that you'll definitely make some updates to the practice." Sally glanced around. "Including this waiting room, I hope. Talk about the dark ages!"

Both women laughed, and Hope asked, "Have you tried to get him to make changes to this area?"

"Only about a hundred times. Richard didn't want to pour any money into the reception area. It pretty much looks the same as when he took over the practice years ago—and it looked old then."

"I believe since it's the first thing people see when they walk in the door, it definitely needs a facelift," she said.

"I do hope you will consider buying the practice, Hope. We'll sell it because we have to. Richard is dying to get back to College Station and into the classroom. I believe you would continue the legacy of quality care for the pets of Sugar Springs. I know the two of you talked about you working for a couple of weeks before you make your decision, but I can tell you now how pleased Richard is and that you were his first choice."

"I want to make my decision soon, Sally," she revealed. Grinning, she added, "But you might want to start looking at real estate websites for homes in College Station."

The receptionist laughed merrily. "Oh, I've been doing that ever since my husband accepted the vet school's offer. I have two target areas in mind—and my eye on one house, in particular. Maybe he and I can drive down on Saturday and look at it after the clinic closes. We don't have a realtor in the area yet. Maybe it's time to get one."

"If Dr. Bisch trusts me enough to handle things on Saturday, why don't you go down early that morning? That would give you all day in College Station."

"I think I'll hit him up with that idea tonight," Sally said. "Between the two of us, we'll see everything is settled here and our move to Aggieland happens sooner than later. I still have two close friends who live in the area. One teaches at an elementary school in Bryan, and the other works for the university in its financial aid department. It'll be nice to be back with longtime friends."

"And closer to your children," Hope added. "I haven't been given any keys to the clinic, and I understand why. I'll leave with you so the place can be secured."

"I'll have keys cut for you tomorrow in town during my lunch hour," Sally promised.

Shirley and Randy appeared, asking how Hope liked her first day as the four of them left the clinic and walked to their cars. Hope told them it had been a good start and said goodnight.

She was still full from a large lunch at Ida Lou's diner earlier. Today's blue plate special had included a generous portion of meatloaf, macaroni and cheese, and broccoli. If she kept eating a big lunch, she would be able to eat lightly or even snack for dinner, having soup and salad or a sandwich and a piece of fruit.

Not feeling up to a big Walmart stock-up trip, she decided to stop at the small family grocery store she had driven by two blocks off the square. She would run in and pick up a few items, such as cans of soup, bread, milk, and lunchmeat. She still would hit Walmart this weekend after the clinic closed on Saturday in order fill her pantry. While there, she planned to buy a coffee maker. While having one at the clinic was nice, she wanted one at her rental, as well, especially for use on the weekends.

As she pulled into the parking lot of McKinley's, her phone rang. Hope saw Gideon's name on the screen. She still was a bit uneasy about what he had spoken to Dr. Bisch about earlier today and hoped she might lead the conversation around to that in order to ease her mind. Cutting her engine, she answered the phone. "Hello?"

"How was your first day at the clinic?" Gideon asked.

"It was really good," she told him, surprised at the tingles she got just hearing his voice. "My first appointment was with someone I'm sure you know, your friend Walker's receptionist."

"Margaret is a terrific lady," he said. "She's been on her own, a single mom for a long time, but she does a great job with her son. Was Max sick?"

Leave it to the chief of police to know the name of someone's pet.

"No, he was in for his yearly checkup. He passed with flying colors although he could stand to have his teeth brushed a little more often."

"Any crises?"

"Not really. Well, Margie Echols might consider her cat peeing outside the litter box a crisis because she said her entire house is carpeted, but I think we got that straightened out. I saw one dog with gastrointestinal problems. Another couple of well checkups. No emergencies came in. All in all, it was a satisfying day."

"What was it like with Dr. Bisch hovering over you?"

"Actually, he backed off from doing that after he sat in on Max's appointment. He grilled me beforehand. I felt like a student back in vet school with my professor testing me to see if I were prepared or not for a semester exam. Dr. Bisch seemed to like what he heard, however. After Margaret and Max left, he told me he was comfortable enough with me seeing the rest of today's appointments by myself."

"Did all the pet owners take to you? Especially since they were expecting Dr. Bisch?"

"One older lady seemed a little put out, but by the time the exam ended, I think she was more than satisfied. She was very protective of her poodle. I get that."

"Then I'm betting it was Mrs. Dunaway and Precious."

"How did you know?"

He laughed. "She's known for being a little ornery, but she has a good heart. And she loves Precious. A lot."

Hope decided to plunge ahead and see if she could lead Gideon into revealing why he had called Dr. Bisch earlier.

"Do you happen to have a pet yourself? I heard Sally tell Dr. Bisch that you had an urgent question for him."

"Nope. No pets for me. I wasn't home enough when I was in Dallas. It would've been cruel to leave an animal alone so much. My hours are decent now, though. Maybe it's time I think about getting a dog."

He paused, and Hope thought he was going to avoid answering the rest of her question. Then he said, "I was asking Dr. Bisch about your old boss, as a matter of fact."

Fear enveloped her. She tried to keep her voice calm as she asked, "Why so?"

"Long story, but I know about a kid in Houston who wants to be a vet and needs to do a shadow day with one. I asked Dr. Bisch for his friend's number so I could try and facilitate getting that set up."

Relief flooded her, her suspicions evaporating. "Did Dr. Wallman agree to do so? He's an excellent vet. It's also a large practice, with other vets on staff."

"That's good to know. It might allow this kid to see several vets in action and write up a good report about his day. So, what's on your agenda this evening?"

She wondered if he might wish to come over again. "Well, I just pulled up at McKinley's. I thought I would run in and pick up a few things for dinner the next few nights. I'll do a bigger trip this weekend when I have more time to stock up on what I need. That reminds me. I want to bring something to the Super Bowl party on Sunday. Could you send me Rory's number so I can call her?"

"You don't need to do that. I'm sure she'll have enough to feed an army."

She snorted. "Spoken like a typical man. He shows up—and everything is provided for him. I *want* to bring something to the party, Gideon. I don't want to show up empty-handed."

"Okay, I get that. I'll text you Rory's number now and let you go do your shopping. Glad that you had a nice first day at the clinic. Talk to you soon."

"Bye," she said, trying to quell her disappointment, thinking how much she wished he would come over this evening.

That was utterly foolish. They both had full-time jobs. He had already set up a date for them this weekend. It wasn't as if they were exclusive and seeing each other several nights a week. They'd just met.

As she got out of the car, her phone dinged. She saw the text from Gideon. She might as well call Rory Cox now and see if she might be able to pick up the ingredients for something to bring on Sunday as she shopped now.

Hope dialed the number as she walked toward the store's entrance. Another woman was coming out the doors, and her phone began ringing. She said hello into her cell as Hope passed her, and Hope paused, asking, "Is this Rory?"

"Yes, it is." Slowly, the woman turned and faced her, giving her a smile. "It seems like we're having a conversation. How about a face-to-face one?"

Both women ended the connection, and Hope stepped out of the store, offering her hand.

"Hi. I'm Hope Keller, and Gideon has invited me to your Super Bowl party on Sunday, whether you know it or not."

The auburn-haired woman laughed. "Actually, I do know. Gideon told Walker you were coming, and my husband passed that along to me when he got home from work a few minutes ago."

Rory held up a sack and said, "I had to run out to pick up eggs. We're having a teacher luncheon at the high school tomorrow. Something we do the first Friday of every month. A potluck thing. Social Studies is assigned desserts for tomorrow. I got ready to bake brownies—and discovered I didn't have any eggs."

"I won't keep you then. I was just calling to find out what I might bring on Sunday."

"Oh, Hope, you don't have to bring anything. I already have Nova and Brynn bringing stuff. Just come and enjoy."

Hope knew how judgmental women could be. Especially since she didn't know any of these women, she was going to make certain she brought something tasty to this party. She couldn't afford any gossip to get out about the poor impression she had made, all because she didn't think to bring something to eat or drink.

"I'd like to bring something if you don't mind. I enjoy cooking."

"Okay. I'm making chili. Brynn is going to bring a salad, while Nova said she has desserts covered."

"I think I'll bring some queso and chips to munch on if that sounds good," she volunteered.

Rory chuckled. "You will be my new best friend if you do. I could easily make a meal off that."

"I won't keep you then. It was nice meeting you before Sunday. I look forward to meeting Walker, too."

"We're so glad to have you coming," Rory said, sounding sincere. "Gideon is very special to both of us. You'll love Brynn and Nova. Brynn works at school with me as our district's psychologist. Nova is an artist."

Hope thought a moment. "Is she the one who owns Playful Painting? I saw that on the square."

"Yes, Nova mostly creates pottery and jewelry. You can see both of those on display at Playful Painting."

"Does she give lessons there?"

"Actually, it's a place for groups to come and paint together. Maybe you've heard of wine and painting parties? Like that."

Hope hadn't, and Rory quickly explained the concept to her.

"That sounds like a lot of fun."

"Are you artistically inclined, Hope?"

"I liked to sketch as a kid. It came in handy during college biology and vet school classes. Anatomy."

"We'll have to get a group together and do a night at Playful Painting. Nova holds date nights. Maybe I can talk Walker into the four of us going to one."

She felt the blush rise in her cheeks. "We'll see," she said, not wanting to put Gideon on the spot. "I'm looking forward to Sunday. See you then."

Entering McKinley's, she found it had everything she needed though it didn't have much of a variety in products. She took her purchases to the checkout and was soon on her way home.

Jake greeted her enthusiastically, and she set down the grocery bags and knelt, scratching his ears. "I hope you were good for Lizzy Lou today."

She picked up her bags and took them to the kitchen counter. Spying a note, she read it.

JAKE IS A LITTLE LOVE. We did a two-mile walk this afternoon around three. He was my shadow all day. He curled up next to me while I worked on my needlepoint.

Please drop him off every day, and I'll return him. I really enjoyed his company.

Love,

Lizzy Lou

"WELL, since you had a nice long walk this afternoon, I don't think you need another one," she told her pet.

Hope put away her groceries and while she heated soup in the microwave for herself, she fed the beagle and gave him fresh water. She ate her soup as she scrolled through news on her phone, something she never did. But Gideon was interested in the world around him.

And she was interested in Gideon.

She spent a couple of hours studying examples of business

plans on the Internet and researched different types of software used by businesses which included healthcare and veterinary care, liking two quite a bit. She would reach out to sales representatives at both sites tomorrow, sharing that she was thinking of buying an existing practice and seeing how much it would be to purchase the license and install the software and whether or not records could be transferred over. If not, she would need to hire someone to do so because inputting that much information would be a massive project.

She took Jake outside for a final piddle and then changed into her pajamas, thinking she had nothing sexy to sleep in. Her nighttime wardrobe consisted of flannel pajamas in cold weather and t-shirts and pajama pants or shorts in warm weather. It didn't matter. She didn't need anything sexy to wear to bed. Gideon might never ask her out again after Sunday's Super Bowl party, much less want to have sex with her.

Climbing into bed, Jake snuggled beside her. Hope told herself the beagle was all the bed partner she needed. That Gideon Ross was just a passing fancy and nothing would come of their acquaintance, except possibly, a friendship.

As she drifted off to sleep, Hope continued lying to herself.

11

Hope knocked on Dr. Bisch's office door just after five o'clock on Friday. She had seen their last appointment of the day. The older vet had observed both surgeries she performed today, being assisted by Shirley during the first one and Randy during the second.

"I guess you want my computer to update your notes from today."

"Yes, I need to do so while things are fresh in my mind."

"I hear you're the one responsible for us taking off from the clinic tomorrow. I believe you and my wife have formed a conspiracy."

She grinned. "Sally is eager to begin house hunting, Dr. Bisch. You can't blame her. She's ready to figure out where you'll live."

He studied her a moment and then said, "I don't believe after seeing you these past two days with patients and in surgery that we need to prolong this decision, Hope. I'm happy to turn over my practice to you with no reservations."

The vet named a price for the practice, and she asked, "Does that include the clinic itself and all its equipment?"

"Of course." He reached for a folder on his desk and handed

it to her. "I've had my accountant prepare all the financials for you covering the last five years. I own both the clinic and the land it sits on outright. I know you said you've already been looking at my monthly budgets and profits."

She accepted the folder, glad she would have access to a bigger picture than previously. "Yes, I've been familiarizing myself with them. I'll need to get with my own financial adviser and my attorney to see if this is doable, Dr. Bisch."

"I've already spoken to Gene Smith at the bank here in town. He's the VP and head of their loan program. Gene knows how high I am on you and how I want to turn over the practice to you. If you need to go in and see him about a loan, he'll be all ears."

"Thank you. I have a lot to think about this weekend before committing to you."

He looked at her steadily, a look she had seen from her own father many times before. "Tell me you're leaning Sugar Springs way, Hope."

"I am," she confided. "But this is a very large undertaking for me, you see. I had thought merely to join a practice—not take over one."

"I hope the information in that folder will give you enough food for thought. On a different note, Margie Echols—of the peeing outside the litter box cat—will be at the reception desk tomorrow for Sally. She was an English teacher at the high school and still does some subbing there. She and Sally have been in a book club together for years. Anytime Sally's had to be out, Margie pinch hits for us. She's familiar with the way we run things, so you won't have to babysit her in any way."

Hope laughed. "She might know more than I do."

Dr. Bisch rose. "I guess I'll call it a day. I'll check in with you tomorrow afternoon to see if anything came up."

"Enjoy your time in College Station with Sally," she told him. "I hope you're able to find something you like."

After he left the office, she took his seat and logged in, adding the notes regarding this afternoon's dog neutering and the other handful of pets she had seen.

Hope closed out of the program and shut down the computer, leaning back in the leather chair. She couldn't help but be a little disappointed that she hadn't heard from Gideon today. Again, she told herself that they already had plans for Sunday night, and she shouldn't expect too much from him after their one date. She hadn't dated anyone regularly in years, and she really didn't know how people even went about dating these days. She doubted he would want to make their relationship exclusive. That was fine with her. She needed to keep her focus on the clinic.

Taking a chance, she dialed Marc Saunder's number as she opened the file folder Dr. Bisch had given her and began skimming the figures there.

Marc answered and she said, "Hi, it's Hope Keller. The veterinarian I told you about does want to sell me his practice. It includes the clinic and the land it stands on. He owns it all, scot-free, so I wouldn't have any payments to take on regarding either."

"How do you feel about that?" he asked.

"Actually, really good. I like the town. It's a little bit slower pace of life than I'm used to, but I think it's what I need. I would be the only vet on staff, with two vet techs assisting."

"How much is he asking?"

Hope told him and said that she would send him some documents to look over but that her gut was leaning toward making the purchase, no loans involved.

"I'm about to head out now, but it's my Saturday to work tomorrow," Marc told her. "So, whatever you send me, I'll review tomorrow morning first thing and make a recommendation to you."

"Sounds good. Talk to you soon."

She took several pictures of the documents in the file and forwarded those to Marc. She also had downloaded, with Dr.

Bisch's permission, financial statements and the past year's monthly budget for the clinic earlier, and she also included those in her email. Leaving the office, she turned off the lights and went to the reception area.

Shirley was there, putting on her coat, and said, "Randy's finishing up a grooming. The owner's picking up his retriever in a few minutes. He'll lock up for us."

"Great," she said, heading out the door and toward her car.

She'd only made it a few feet outside when she saw Gideon's SUV pull into the parking lot and park beside her car. He got out and made his way toward her. Hope told her heart to quit hammering as if she had just sprinted down a football field.

"Hey," he said. "How was your day?"

"Busy. I performed two surgeries. A cat spaying this morning and a dog neutering this afternoon. Saw a few patients, as well."

"I know we have plans on Sunday, but I was wondering if you might like to go to the high school basketball game tonight. You said you're a sports fan and really like basketball," he added, looking at her hopefully.

Her beating heart raced even faster. "Yes, I'd like to go. Even though I've never lived in a small town before, I think it's important as a community member to support the schools and their sports programs."

"Would you like to grab a bite to eat before we go? You can leave your car. I can drop you off here later."

"Okay. What time is the game?"

"It's starts at seven. It's the next to last of the season. We can clinch the district title tonight if we win, so I'm expecting the gym to be packed." He hesitated a moment and then said, "There's actually a spaghetti dinner at school beforehand. It's a fundraiser for the girls and boys basketball teams. If we eat there, we'll already have a good parking spot and be able to walk down to the gym."

She looked at him steadily. "That means a good portion of

Sugar Springs' residents will see us together, Gideon. Is that what you want?"

His gaze pinned hers. "It's exactly what I want."

His words caused a delicious chill to run through her.

"Spaghetti sounds good to me," she said, her voice shaking a little as she began walking to his vehicle.

Gideon opened the door for her, seeing she was settled, and then he went to the driver's side. Before he started the car, he turned to her.

"I know this is a big step, Hope, and that you might not even be staying in Sugar Springs, but I want to spend as much time as I can with you while you're here."

His words made her throat grow thick with emotion. She swallowed the lump.

"I would like that Gideon. I like *you*."

He beamed boyishly. "I like you, too, Hope Keller."

His hand cupped her nape, pulling her closer for a gentle kiss. He broke the kiss and started the car, beginning to whistle.

As they drove to the high school, he said, "I played basketball for the Sugar Springs Knights back in the day."

"Besides football?"

"In a small town, you do all you can. While football was always my first love, I enjoyed the pace of basketball. Besides, all that running up and down the court kept me in shape for playing wide receiver. Spring training was a breeze because I was in better shape than most when it started."

"You said that you won a scholarship to SMU. I'm sorry I didn't get to see you play then."

"I loved my playing days. The camaraderie with the guys on the team. I found a new team, though, when I went into police work. The blue always has each other's backs."

They arrived at the school, and she saw the parking lot was already three-quarters full.

"Hmm, I see a lot of other people had your same idea."

"I've been to these before. Don't worry. The line will move fast."

They went inside, and Gideon was stopped every few feet, with people wanting to say hello to him. He introduced her as a visiting veterinarian, and Hope knew she drew the curiosity of others.

Finally, they made it to the line and received their spaghetti and salad. They had a choice of a cookie or brownie for dessert, and she looked back and forth, debating on which one to take.

Gideon leaned over and said, "Take the brownie. I'll get the cookie. We'll split. That should end your dilemma."

It surprised her how he already knew her, and she thought his offer of sharing a sweet to be very sweet.

They had their choice of iced tea or water, and Hope chose a bottled water as they walked with their trays to the long tables of the cafeteria. She saw a couple wave at them and turned to Gideon, who was nodding at them.

"That's Cole and Nova," he told her. "Mind if we join them?"

"Not at all."

They sat opposite the couple, and Gideon made the introductions.

"Rory told me you were coming to the Super Bowl party this weekend," the curly-haired, hazel-eyed woman said. "I'm making two of Rain's—my aunt's—desserts. She was known for her cakes and pies."

"I saw your store on the square," Hope said. "Rory told me that you're an artist."

"Yes, but I've become a businesswoman ever since I came to Sugar Springs last summer. I opened Playful Paintings with the money Rain left me in her will."

"It's turned out to be a huge success," Cole added, smiling warmly at his wife. "I'm so proud of everything Nova's accomplished."

She could see the love for his wife shining in Cole's eyes and said, "I hear you're the head football coach."

"I am. Also, the district's athletic director. I try to go to as many other games to support my fellow coaches and their teams as I can. Our son plays football, and he's also going to play baseball this spring."

Hope couldn't help but think how young Nova must have been to already have a child in high school. She knew the couple had recently married and thought it sweet that Cole referred to his stepson as his son. Many people would have made a point to make a distinction between those two relationships.

"Speak of the devil," Cole said. "Leo!" he called out, waving. "Come meet someone."

She saw the lanky teenager did not favor his mother. Cole said, "Dr. Keller, this is Leo Turner. Soon to be Leo Johnson," he said proudly.

The boy beamed at his stepfather and then turned to Hope, holding out his hand. "Nice to meet you, Dr. Keller."

"Hope is a veterinarian," Nova told her son.

"Oh, is Dr. Bisch retiring? Are you taking his spot?"

"Dr. Bisch is moving to College Station," Hope shared. "He'll be on the staff of the vet school there. As for his practice, I'm seriously considering purchasing it."

A pretty teenaged girl came up, holding her tray. She said hello to those at the table and then said, "Come on, Leo. Jake saved us a seat."

"I'll see you later," Leo told them, leaving with her.

"He's a fine-looking boy, Nova," Hope said. "Great manners."

"He's blossomed since we moved to Sugar Springs from Austin," Nova said. "Leo is near the top of his class academically and is enjoying playing sports." She looked to her new husband. "Cole is going to adopt Leo. We've just completed the paperwork."

"He's a great kid," Cole said proudly. "I can't wait to make it official."

They finished their dinner, and Gideon broke his cookie in two, handing her half. She picked up her knife to cut the brownie.

"No, the brownie's all yours."

"I thought we were sharing. You've already forked over half of your cookie."

"I want to keep that sweet tooth fed, Dr. Keller," he said, grinning at her.

They walked to the gym with Nova and Cole, the two women stopping at a restroom.

As Hope came out of a stall, she spied Rory Cox washing her hands and said, "Hi, Rory. How was your staff luncheon today?"

"Hey, Hope. It went well. I ate the most amazing hash brown casserole and got the recipe for it. I know it doesn't sound like it would go with chili, but I'm making it for the party anyway."

Nova emerged from her stall. "You had me at hash browns. If that were the only dish you were serving, I'd be happy."

"Have you decided what luscious dessert of Rain's you'll make for us?" Rory asked.

"I'm going to do two. A cheesecake because Rain was known for those, but I knew we might have a few chocoholics in the group, so I'll also bring a chocolate fudge cake."

Hope said, "What if you serve one dessert first? I'd be happy to eat one, then the chili, and bookend it with another dessert."

Rory and Nova laughed. Rory slipped an arm around Hope and said, "I knew you were my kind of girl. Let's go find the guys and sit together."

They left the restroom and found the three men waiting for them. Rory introduced Walker to Hope, and she found herself immediately liking Gideon's longtime best friend.

"Gid says you're a sports fan, Hope. He said you played volleyball and ran track."

It surprised her that Gideon would share something so trivial with Walker.

"Yes, I enjoyed both and still run in the mornings. I do feel a little like an outcast since I grew up in Houston and have been a fan of all their franchises my entire life. Gideon tells me I'm now in Dallas Cowboys country, though."

They paid for their tickets and entered the gym. As they climbed the steps in the bleachers, Walker said, "But we have a chance to turn you into a Stars fan. I hear you and Gid are taking in a game soon."

Once again, she was astonished that Walker knew this, too, knowing guys seemed to rarely talk about their relationships between themselves.

Gideon led them into a row and they filed in, Hope following him. As they sat, Walker was on her left.

He leaned in, quietly saying, "I was afraid Gideon wouldn't be able to find the right woman for him. I'm placing all bets on you, Hope."

12

F ans packed the gym, and Gideon found himself pressed against Hope's side.

Which wasn't a bad thing at all.

To make it a little easier on both of them, he slipped his arm around her, giving them a little breathing room, and yet still allowing them to remain close. He caught that intoxicating vanilla scent which seemed to cling to her, and desire welled within him. If they weren't sitting in the middle of half the town, he would pull her to her feet and make a quick exit.

Doing so, though, would only fuel the flames of gossip which must be shooting through the gymnasium. While most people present were here to cheer on the Sugar Springs Knights to victory over their perennial basketball and soccer enemy, the Lexington Lions, it didn't mean their eyes were solely directed to the court. Hope was right. He was a public figure with a pretty stranger accompanying him. Any date he might have in public would bring scrutiny, but especially one which concerned a woman who had so recently come to town.

Yet the thought of gossip didn't matter a whit to Gideon. What did matter was he'd put aside any worries about the gossip which would be generated by their joint appearance tonight and decided being with Hope was more important than thinking about gossip.

It was only natural for people to be interested in him outside of police work. He was the former golden boy who'd led Sugar Springs to countless victories on the football field. Many in town had become SMU Mustangs fans simply because he'd won a scholarship to the school. When he'd returned to his hometown at the beginning of the new year, he was welcomed with open arms, the handpicked choice of retiring Police Chief Roscoe Hamilton. While some of the residents in town had attended his wedding to Melinda almost fifteen years ago, the majority of Sugar Springs' citizens knew he'd been divorced the past nine years.

Because of that, everywhere he went, Gideon had found well-meaning people trying to set him up on dates. Sugar Springs was still old-fashioned enough to want its town leaders married, with children. One woman had told him that he was the most eligible bachelor in town, especially since Cole Johnson and Walker Cox had both married over the holidays. He'd turned down every opportunity to be fixed up on dates, blind or otherwise, sticking to his belief that he had come home to protect and serve the citizens of Sugar Springs, not marry one of them. His opinion on marriage had soured, both while he was married and in the years since his divorce.

Hope Keller was a fresh breath of air, though. Gideon couldn't explain exactly why he was so attracted to her, only that he felt the chemistry between them. And it wasn't all physical. Hope was smart as a whip and funny, too. He could see how she would be an excellent vet because of the nurturing spirit surrounding her. She was kind and a good listener.

And all he could think about was kissing her.

And more...

He wouldn't be disrespectful and treat her like one of his one-night stands over the last few years. Even then, those had become few and far between. No, Gideon could see a future with this woman, which was absolutely absurd after one date with her. He kept going back to Walker and Rory though, seeing how they'd connected instantly. From what he gathered, Cole and Nova had been the same way.

Hell, he was in his mid-thirties. He didn't have time to play games. He was feeling something special with Hope.

Gideon only hoped she was feeling the same way.

They announced the starting lineup for the game to thunderous cheers. He had attended two other games since he'd arrived in town, and quickly, Gideon told Hope something about each of the starters.

"The star of the team is its captain, Freddie Otts," he told her after the introductions had concluded. "Cole said that Freddie has drawn the notice of a few of the smaller schools in Texas. Stephen F. Austin. Sam Houston State. Abilene Christian."

The game got off to a quick start, with Freddie hitting two, three-pointers in the first ninety seconds. After that, the teams played neck-in-neck throughout the first half. Gideon was impressed with how much Hope knew about the game and how quickly she got into it.

"Did you see that flop?" she demanded.

"What's a flop?" Rory asked, leaning around Walker.

"He intentionally fell," Hope explained. "Hardly any contact or no physical contact. He's just trying to draw a foul." Turning back to the court, she shouted, "Open your eyes, ref!"

Minutes later, she hollered, "Goaltending! Yes! Finally, that ref is watching the same game I am."

He chuckled. "You do know basketball."

She looked at him, her brows raised. "I told you I'm a sports fan. I wish now that I would have played basketball, but between school and club volleyball commitments, I was tied to that sport almost year-round. I had to walk a fine line, trying to balance it and running track at the same time."

Halftime arrived, and Gideon asked if she wanted anything.

"Maybe some hot chocolate? That lady in front of us has some, and it smells so good."

"One hot chocolate coming up. Anyone else?"

Rory and Nova both opted for hot chocolate, as well. Walker said he would accompany Gideon to the concession stand. Cole had already excused himself just before half to go to the locker room and offer Stan Watson, Sugar Springs coach and Cole's good friend, some support.

As they waited in line, Walker said, "You've got a live wire on your hands, Gid."

He chuckled. "Hope told me she's crazy about sports. Now that I've seen her at an event, I believe it."

"I like her, Gid."

His gaze connected with his friend's. "I do, too, Walker. More than I thought possible. Of course, I don't even know if she's staying in Sugar Springs. She came here to work for Dr. Bisch, not take over his practice."

"Is she opposed to buying him out?"

"No, she's become open to the possibility. They're doing some trial thing, where he's getting a good look at what she knows and how she handles animals and people. But buying a practice is taking a huge bite."

"From what I've seen, Hope can take on whatever she wants," Walker said drily.

"She is pretty special, isn't she?"

"Rory likes her. I do, too, Gid. I hope this can work out for you. I know Melinda's been in your rearview mirror for a long time now, and you haven't been interested in even thinking about marriage since your divorce."

"Melinda is a distant memory," he told his friend. "And I'm warming up to the idea of trying again."

"Have you told Hope you've been married before?"

"No," he said. "It hasn't come up. I mean, come on. We've had one date before tonight. Talked on the phone some."

"But you showed up here with her tonight. That didn't happen by accident."

"No. It didn't." He grinned sheepishly. "I found I couldn't stay away. The thought of not seeing her again until your party on Sunday was eating away at me. I thought coming to something like this would give us a chance to get to know each other a little better."

"Are you going to see her tomorrow?" Walker asked, moving up a step in line.

"I don't know. She's got to work until one. Then she's mentioned buying food and things. I gather Lizzy Lou didn't have much stocked in the garage apartment Hope's renting. Maybe I need to give her a little bit of breathing space."

"Ask her. All she can say is no," his friend advised.

"Ask her what?"

Walker looked at him patiently. "If she wants to see you tomorrow. If she wants a breather, I think Hope is the kind of woman who would say so. And if she doesn't? Then it's simply bonus time for the both of you."

"Good advice," Gideon said, stepping up to the concession worker and ordering three hot chocolates. "You want anything?" he asked Walker.

"Only for my best friend to find happiness. Other than that, I'm good."

He paid for the drinks and handed one to Walker, carrying the other two himself. They returned to the stands, where the three women were deep in conversation. Quickly, he figured out that Hope was explaining different types of offenses, from motion and Princeton to continuity, as he passed out the hot beverages.

"So, the wheel offense is also a continuity offense?" Nova asked, her brow furrowed.

"Yes. It's designed to combat either man-to-man or zone defenses."

"That's the one where the players keep moving in a circular motion, right?" Rory asked.

"Exactly!" Hope cried. "And wheel offenses seem to work best if your team is made up of strong shooters and good ball handlers."

Nova giggled. "I hate to say this, but you explained this way better than Cole or Leo. Football was pretty easy for me to understand. But while I think I actually like watching basketball better, I've been in a daze about what goes on sometimes."

"Same," Rory agreed. "I watch our bench and coach and when they clap, so do I. Then I know to look at the ref. Hey, maybe we should watch some basketball games together. You could be our color commentator, Hope."

"I'd say that would be better than a book club," Nova added. "Maybe we could ask a few other friends and do a potluck and game watching night."

Gideon saw the happy flush cross Hope's cheeks. Knowing what she had been through in her recent past, he couldn't help but be pleased that she was making friends.

Especially if that convinced her to remain in Sugar Springs.

A little guilt ran through him, though. He knew Hope's secrets, thanks to a bit of investigative work. He had never set out to lie to her and wondered if he should give her a heads up about what he had discovered. Still, a part of him knew she was trying to escape her past. He didn't want her to cut and run from Sugar Springs. He still thought it best to wait for her to tell him about her past when she was ready to do so.

It didn't make him feel any less guilty, though.

Cole returned to his seat. "Stan did a nice job of getting the team pumped up again during his halftime pep talk. They know that the district title—and their pride—are on the line. I'm hoping they'll come out strong."

The Knights did just that, running off a dozen unanswered points. The Lions got into foul trouble after that. Their opponent also kept trying to make up points by shooting numerous threes, very few which fell into the basket. The game ended, with the Knights becoming district champions, winning the game 67-54.

"That was fantastic," Hope told Gideon.

"I'm glad you had a good time."

They moved down the bleachers with the crowd and said their goodbyes to their friends before heading to his SUV. Horns were honking in the parking lot, with students shouting, happiness at the victory spilling over.

He eased his vehicle through the traffic, glad he had assigned two patrolmen to traffic duty tonight. It made getting out of the parking lot much easier.

"Shall I drop you at your car?" he asked.

"Or what?" she countered.

Gideon glanced over and saw the smile playing on her lips. "Maybe you'd like to stop by my place for a while? I've got some Bluebell buttered pecan ice cream in the freezer."

"You're on, Chief."

He liked that she didn't protest that she'd already eaten plenty of carbs with the spaghetti and sugar with the two desserts. Most women would have shut him down.

Then again, Hope Keller wasn't most women.

He pulled into his complex's parking lot, gliding into a spot directly in front of his apartment. Getting out of the car, he came around and opened Hope's door. He laced his fingers through hers and led her to the door, unlocking it and stepping inside.

The living room was dark. He'd been gone since six-thirty this morning and didn't like to leave a light burning all day. Gideon pulled Hope into the apartment, closing the door, but left the lights off. Faint light came through the window next to the door as he nudged her against it, his body pressing against hers.

His mouth sought hers as his free hand captured hers,

pushing up her hands beside her shoulders. He kissed her hungrily, need pouring through him. She made little noises that let him know she was onboard. Teasing her lips apart, his tongue plunged inside her mouth. Taking. Giving. Tasting. He could feel his body heating.

Breaking the kiss, he released her hands, tearing off his jacket and dropping it to the floor. He wrestled her coat from her shoulders and down her arms, letting it pool at her feet before he captured her hands again, lifting them high over her head. Using one hand, he pinned her wrists to the door, leaving one hand free to do as it pleased. His mouth fused to hers as his hand skimmed her face, her neck, going lower to her breast. He squeezed it, loving its fullness.

Hope squirmed against him as his lips trailed down her throat, his tongue circling the pulse point in her throat. It beat rapidly, letting him know she was affected by what he did. He kneaded her breast and tweaked the nipple, causing her to gasp.

"I want you," he said hoarsely. "I know it's too soon to say that, but I do."

Gideon lowered her hands, taking them in his, and kissed her long and slow. After several minutes, he broke the kiss. Both of them were breathless, panting. Her face was mostly in shadow, but he sensed the need in her.

"I want you, too," she echoed. "I've never said that to a man before. But you're no ordinary man, Chief Ross."

He kissed her again, hard and swift, wanting to brand her as his, thrilled that she wanted him as much as he did her.

Breaking the kiss, he rested his forehead against hers. "I think we need to wait," he said.

"Are you sure about that?" she asked, her voice low and tempting.

"No. But I don't have any condoms. Unless you have one in your purse?" he asked hopefully.

Hope laughed, a throaty laugh that almost undid him. "No. I

haven't needed one in quite a while. If I had been carrying any, they would already have expired."

Now, he laughed. "I do want to make love with you, Hope. But not yet."

"Should I call you a tease?" she asked playfully.

"No. Just a man who wants to do the right thing by a woman. We barely know one another."

"I think we know each other pretty well, Gideon," she countered.

"I don't want to rush something between us," he explained. "When I do make love to you, I want you to know it's no accident. That it's not just something physical between us. I want it to have deeper meaning."

He kissed her again, this time softly, enjoying the feel of her and the vanilla scent that was driving him insane.

"Do you have a timetable in mind?" she asked, and he could hear the amusement in her voice.

"No. Just not tonight. When I do make love to you, I want to have all the time in the world."

"I can accept that," she said.

He kissed her again simply because he liked doing it so much. The kiss went on until they were both breathless again. This time she broke it.

"I think you promised me ice cream, Chief Ross."

He chuckled. "I believe I did, Dr. Keller."

Gideon released her and turned on a light. He went to the kitchen, Hope following, taking a seat on one of the barstools.

"One scoop is enough for me," she said. "I usually don't eat anything this late, but I'm a sucker for buttered pecan."

"One it is," he said, dishing out her scoop into a cup and placing a spoon in it before handing it over.

He filled a cup for himself and took a seat beside her. They talked as they ate, mostly about sports and Sunday's game. Her knowledge of the two teams playing in the Super Bowl startled him.

"If you hadn't gone into medicine, you would have made a great color analyst," he told her.

She looked pleased at his remark. "I think that's the best compliment anyone's ever given me."

When they finished their ice cream, he rinsed the cups and spoons and placed them in the dishwasher.

"You have an early day," he said. "I need to get you to your car."

"All right."

Gideon drove her back to the animal hospital, getting out of the car so he could pull her into his arms for a final kiss.

"I'll follow you home," he said after breaking it.

"You don't have to do that."

"I know. I want to do that."

He opened Hope's door and returned to his own car, shadowing her as she drove to Lizzy Lou's. When she got out of her car, she came to him. He rolled down the window.

"Thanks for a wonderful night. I enjoyed the game and meeting your friends."

"They certainly like you. Maybe more than they like me."

"You're being silly now."

"Maybe you make me feel silly," he flirted. Then he grew serious. "Do you have plans tomorrow? Other than work?"

"Walmart. I've got to buy a coffee maker, or I won't make it through the weekend. Tom Cruise may feel the need for speed, but this girl always wakes with the need for caffeine."

Gideon laughed. "Want some company at Walmart? I've got a much bigger vehicle than you do. I can carry more groceries."

"Sure. Meet me back here at one-fifteen?"

"I'll be the guy with the goofy grin on his face, waiting to see you again."

Hope bent and leaned inside, giving him a last kiss. "And I'll be the girl eager to see you."

Gideon watched her climb the stairs to the garage apartment. She turned and waved at him before entering. He drove the entire way home, but he believed he might have been able to fly.

Something in him had come alive with Hope Keller's arrival in Sugar Springs, and being the excellent detective he was, he reached a gut conclusion.

He was in love. Head over heels in love.

And he didn't care who knew.

13

Hope left the house with Jake, running the route she was now familiar with after a few days in Sugar Springs. The February cold spell had broken and while this morning was still chilly, it would warm up to the high fifties this afternoon.

Her solo time at the clinic yesterday had gone well, with routine appointments and vaccines being given. Just before closing at one o'clock, Dr. Paulson, the large animal vet in the area, had stopped by to introduce himself, saying that he looked forward to working with her in the future.

It was all but settled now. Hope had spoken with her financial adviser yesterday. After reviewing the documents she had forwarded to him, Marc thought her purchase of Dr. Bisch's practice would be a good investment, both personally and professionally. They had talked about several factors, including whether she could envision any growth and whether she might want to add on to the clinic at a future date. Hope had said she didn't think it would be necessary in the immediately future, but it was always a possibility down the line. The land the animal hospital sat on would allow for expansion if and when that time came.

She didn't know if she would ever have enough business, however, to hire a second vet, unless it was on a part-time basis, one who might even take over the Saturday shift in case she needed the entire day free.

To spend with Gideon.

They had been in one another's company for most of yesterday, and she realized she was experiencing a true relationship for the first time. While she had dated sporadically over the years and had a steady boyfriend after she finished grad school and remained in College Station a few years, she understood that relationship did not have the ease and give and take as in the one she had already established with Gideon in such a short time. Hope didn't know where their relationship was going, but now that she had decided to stay in Sugar Springs, she wanted to see how things played out between them. If he were as serious as she already wanted them to be. So far, Gideon and she had been on the same page, but it remained to be seen if they were both willing to take the relationship to the next level at the same time. She wouldn't press him at this point. Rather, she would let things unfold naturally although she would never hesitate to talk with Gideon. They communicated extremely well.

She had also spoken with Winston, and her attorney was happy that she would be building a life that helped her move past her parents' murders. He told her he would help in any way with the purchase of the clinic. She told him a local attorney would most likely draw up the sale papers but that she would have Walker send them to Winston to peruse before she signed them. They agreed that it would be in her best interest not to take out a loan but buy the clinic and practice outright with the inheritance she had received from her parents' estate.

As she pounded the pavement, Hope thought about today's party, which she and Gideon would be attending. He had gone with her yesterday to Walmart, where once again, they had been stopped several times by members of the community wanting to chat briefly with their police chief. Gideon had helped to bring in the numerous groceries and supplies she had bought, including a coffee maker. She would use her mother's slow cooker later that afternoon to make the queso for the Super Bowl party.

After all her items had been brought in and stored away, Gideon had taken her on a drive around the area. Hope found Sugar Lake to be particularly enticing, hoping she would be able to waterski or swim in it when summer came.

They had gone to Tyler, which was less than half an hour away and was the largest town close to Sugar Springs, with familiar chain restaurants and stores. He took her to dinner, and the time had passed quickly. For once, she was with a man who seemed endlessly curious about her and everything around him. Hope was glad he'd encouraged her to pay more attention to politics and the news. She had liked history when she was in high school and told herself that she needed to look at what was unfolding now as the history of her life.

She finished jogging her loop and raced up the stairs to her apartment, Jake happily accompanying her. The beagle seemed to be taking to Sugar Springs as much as Hope was.

Gideon had told her he would be busy preparing state reports today and would pick her up for the party at four-thirty. He said he wanted to be there in time to start watching the crazy commercials.

Hope found herself taking a nap early that afternoon, a luxury she rarely indulged in. When she awoke, she prepared the queso and hopped into the shower.

Gideon arrived on time, something she appreciated since so few people these days seemed to pay attention to time. Unplugging the slow cooker, she allowed him to carry it to his SUV while she toted the bags of tortilla chips. He placed the slow cooker in the floorboard of the passenger's seat, and Hope held it in place on the short drive to the Coxes' house.

Walker greeted them at the door, accompanied by a beautiful Irish setter.

"This is Comet," he told Hope. "He's two and will be seeing you soon for his annual checkup. He's a bundle of energy, but we love him."

Hope reached down and stroked Comet, scratching between his ears. The dog's blissful look had her laughing.

Rory appeared and said, "Hi. You can bring everything to the kitchen. Nova and Cole just got here."

She said hello to Cole as they passed the large den and entered the kitchen.

"We need to plug in the slow cooker, Rory. Where would you like me to do that?"

"Right over here, Gideon," their hostess instructed as Hope set down the bags of chips.

He did so and left the three women in the kitchen, and she asked for a spoon to stir the dip, as well as a spoon rest. Rory provided both, and they stood in the kitchen talking, hearing the guys' laughter come from the den.

Hope admired the layered chocolate fudge cake resting on the island and admitted that she had a sweet tooth.

"Then you'll love this," Nova said. "But if you're too full to sample both desserts, you can take home a slice or two of the cheesecake. It's in the fridge."

A woman appeared carrying a large bowl and said, "Hello, everyone." She was probably five-ten in height, with blond hair and penetrating green eyes. The man who accompanied her was a couple of inches over six feet and had warm brown eyes and brown hair.

He held up two six-packs of beer. "Can I put these in your fridge, Rory?"

"Sure thing, Ray. I want to introduce you both to Dr. Hope Keller. She's a veterinarian."

The woman offered her hand. "I'm Brynn Mattson. I work with Rory at school. I'm the district's psychologist."

The man closed the refrigerator door, offering his hand. "I'm Ray Barker. I teach biology at the high school, and I'm on Cole's football staff. I also work with the pole vaulters and shot putters on the track and field team in the spring. Nice to meet you, Hope."

Brynn asked, "Is there room for the salad in the fridge?"

"I'll make room," Rory told her. "If we need to take the beer out and put it in an ice chest, we can do that. I had Walker pick up a couple of bags of ice, just in case."

Ray left the kitchen, and the women stood around talking. Hope felt extremely comfortable with the three, never having seemed to fit in so quickly with a group of women. She had spent most of her college and vet school years in the company of men since they outnumbered women usually three-to-one in that area of study.

A burst of laughter came from the den, and Brynn said, "I know they're laughing at those idiotic commercials. Ray was looking forward to seeing them as much as the game." Turning to Hope, she asked, "Are you much of a sports fan?"

"I won a scholarship to A&M and played volleyball there, but I'm crazy about all kinds of sports. I've learned that the teams I root for aren't exactly the ones Sugar Springs supports. I'm from Houston. Die-hard Texans, Rockets, and Astros fan."

Brynn laughed. "That's great to hear. I'm from New Orleans originally, and I'll be a Saints fan until the day I die."

"Well, I'm becoming a sports fan," Nova said. "Thanks to Leo and Cole. I'd never really paid attention to any sport until Leo started playing football last fall. With Cole's line of work, though, it seems as if our house is sports central. I hear about sports. I dream about sports."

The others laughed, and Rory said, "I guess we should join

the guys. What can I get everyone to drink? I've got wine. Iced tea. Sparkling water."

The women grabbed beverages for themselves, and Rory carried in a six-pack for the men. She also suggested they get into the queso and chips and get settled before the game started. Everyone filed into the kitchen and ladled queso into the paper bowls Hope had brought, scooping handfuls of chips, as well, and placing them in their bowls.

After they all settled around the TV, Walker took a bite of the queso and said, "Wow! This is great, Hope. What's so different about it?"

"While I melt the cheese and Rotel tomatoes together, along with a little garlic, I cooked a couple of pounds of sausage and drained it, putting it into the dip. And believe it or not, it also has a can of cream of mushroom soup in it, too, along with a block of cream cheese."

"It's delicious," Brynn complimented. "I may pass on the chili to eat more of this."

The latest flavor of the month sang the national anthem, followed by team introductions, and then the kickoff occurred. The Rams were playing the Chiefs, and Hope wasn't rooting for any specific team, only wanting to see a competitive game. It pleased her that several people went back for a second helping of her queso.

When halftime came, the Rams led 17-14, and everyone traipsed into the kitchen with their empty bowls. They lined up and scooped chili into new bowls, topping it with items Rory had placed out, such as cheese, onions, crackers, and corn chips. Brynn took the salad out of the fridge, and everyone also piled salad high into different bowls.

They had agreed to forgo the halftime entertainment, an act Hope had never heard of, and took their meals to the large dining room table. The conversation was lively, and Hope felt comfortable diving right into the thick of it, not feeling as if she were a stranger to this group. She did notice, however, that Nova seemed to pick at her chili, although she did eat all of her salad.

"It's about time for the game to start again," Walker said. "Let's head back to the den," he suggested. "Honey, when do you want us to eat dessert?"

Rory declared, "I'm always ready for dessert."

The group agreed, and they brought their plates and bowls back to the kitchen, where Rory told everyone to leave their dirty dishes in the sink. She would handle them later. Nova took a poll of who wanted which dessert, and Hope offered to stay behind and help her dish those up.

After the others left the kitchen, Hope retrieved the cheesecake as Nova took off the glass covering from the fudge cake and began slicing pieces.

As Hope brought over the small dessert plates, she asked, "Are you feeling all right?"

Nova looked startled by the question. "Yes," she said nervously. "Why?"

"I just noticed you didn't eat much of your chili. Are you not a fan?"

A blush colored the artist's cheeks. "No," she said slowly. "I actually enjoy chili. Just not today." She took a deep breath and blew it out. "I think... I think I might be pregnant."

"Is that a good thing?" she asked quietly.

Nova grinned. "It would be a wonderful thing. I know Cole and I just got married, but we're both eager for more kids. My period was supposed to come last week. Actually, I hadn't noticed that I missed it until this morning. I was queasy when I got up. At first, I thought I might be coming down with something and was upset I'd have to miss the party. But the feeling passed." She paused. "It was like this the last time. With Leo."

Hope took Nova's hands. "Then I hope you are. When will you tell Cole?"

Her new friend laughed. "I'll buy a pregnancy kit tomorrow

morning after he's left for school. If it's positive, I'll tell him the minute he gets home."

Nova went back to slicing cake, while Hope found a knife and cut pieces of cheesecake.

"I won't say anything until you're ready to tell people," she promised.

"I appreciate that," Nova said. "If I am, I'd like to give it another month. Just to be sure."

"How will Leo take to being a big brother?" Hope asked.

"He'll be over the moon. He's almost as eager as Cole for me to have another baby."

They took the desserts into the den, where the score was now 21-20 in favor of the Chiefs. As they ate and talked and watched the game, she couldn't help but think how much she liked this group of people. No, not people.

Friends.

The game ended with the Chiefs intercepting a pass in the endzone with only two seconds on the clock, guaranteeing their victory. They watched some of the post-game show, and then the party broke up. Only a few spoonfuls of queso remained, and Hope placed it in a small storage container and left it and the bag of chips with Rory. She and Gideon both took home a slice of cheesecake, Gideon threatening to eat his in the car on the way home.

As they got ready to leave, Hope addressed the group, saying, "Thank you for making me feel so welcomed tonight. I appreciate Rory and Walker opening your home to me and for everyone being so friendly and nice."

Brynn gave Hope a hug. "It was great meeting you. I hope you decide to stay in Sugar Springs, Hope. You could join our book club."

"And come and paint at Playful Painting," Nova added.

Hope decided to share her news and said, "I'd like to do both of those—and I'll be able to. You see, I've decided to buy Sugar

Springs Veterinary Clinic."

She heard a collective, enthusiastic "yes," and each of the women embraced her.

"This is wonderful news," Rory said. "We'll need to get together and celebrate, just us girls."

"Let's wait until I confirm with Dr. Bisch," she warned. "I'm thinking he'll ask Walker to draw up the papers to seal the deal."

"I'm ready and eager to do so," the attorney said, beaming at her. "I'm glad you've decided to stay in town, Hope."

She and Gideon said their goodbyes and headed to his SUV. Once inside, she thought he would comment about her announcement. Instead, he began talking about the game, mentioning several plays that had been controversial.

When they arrived at Lizzy Lou's, she didn't know whether or not to ask him in as he walked her up the stairs and to the door.

"Thank you for inviting me to the party tonight," she told him. "I really enjoyed myself."

"Could I come in for a few minutes?" he asked.

"Of course," she said quickly.

Unlocking the door, she pushed it open. Jake greeted them.

"Let me take Jake out for you," Gideon said. "Be right back."

He clipped the dog's leash to his collar, and Hope closed the door behind them. Her heart raced, wondering what Gideon might want to talk about as she placed the cheesecake she'd brought home inside the fridge and hung up her coat.

Two minutes later, man and dog returned, hurrying inside since the night breeze had picked up. Gideon removed Jake's leash, and the dog trotted to the sofa and jumped on it, curling up beside Hope.

Gideon strode toward her, taking her hands and bringing her to her feet. His arms enveloped her, pulling her into his muscled chest. His body heat warmed her as his mouth came down on hers in a hard, possessive kiss which stole her breath.

When he finally broke it, Hope gazed up at him as he said, "I don't think I've ever been happier than when you said you're staying in Sugar Springs." His voice was low and husky, sending a delicious chill through her. "I know you're smart enough to have made the decision based upon what's good for you professionally, but I hope you're also happy personally, Hope. Because I know I am."

He kissed her again, this time an achingly tender kiss.

"And now that you're going to be living here permanently, I want to ask you something."

"Okay," she said, her breathing unsteady.

"I want us to be exclusive," he told her. "I think it would kill me to see you out with another guy. What do you think?"

Without hesitation, she said, "I think it's the best idea I've heard come out of your mouth, Chief Ross."

A slow smile crossed his handsome face. "I like you, Dr. Keller. A lot. More than a lot. I think you're like an onion and have a lot of layers for me to peel away. Starting now."

His gaze was so intense, she trembled in his arms.

"I want to make love to you, Hope. Do you want the same?"

14

Hope hadn't known this man for long—but it seemed as if she knew him better than anyone who had come into her life. Gideon Ross was loyal. Honorable. Respected. Intelligent. Curious.

Most of all, he treated her with consideration. He truly listened to her when she spoke. She had faced gender discrimination during her coursework, with several male students telling her she didn't belong in the veterinarian world. Even the small number of men she had dated over the years had never acted as if they considered her an equal.

But Gideon did. Maybe it was the values his mother had instilled in him from childhood. Or the small-town attitudes and standards which had shaped his beliefs. Probably both had made him into the good man that he was.

The man that she loved.

Hope realized that though they had physical chemistry, she was also attracted to Gideon's mind and character. He was the total package.

And he wanted to make love to her.

"Yes," she said fervently. "Yes. I want to be with you, Gideon."

His sunny smile lit up the room. Lit up her world.

Tenderly, he cradled her face in his large hands. "I didn't know if you would be ready to take such a big step, Hope. I know we haven't known each other that long, but to me? It seems like I've always known you. That my heart knows yours, and they beat together in time. We still have a lot to learn about each other, but the one thing I do know is how I feel about you. How I wake up and you're the first thing in my thoughts. How I look forward to seeing you. Being with you. Talking with you."

He kissed her softly. "I want to know everything about you. Everything. Starting now."

Gideon kissed her again, a long, slow, deep kiss. It stirred a yearning within Hope that she had never felt before. Everything was right with this man. She was thankful she had made the choice to stay in Sugar Springs so she could explore a deeper relationship with him.

Her body flushed with warmth as his kisses became more demanding. His hands roamed her back. Desire rippled through her, and she needed to feel his skin against hers. She peeled his jacket from his shoulders, and he helped her remove it, dropping it onto the sofa.

"Wait," he said, reaching for the jacket and slipping his hand into the pocket. "I brought protection." He pulled out a condom and grinned sheepishly. "I wanted to be prepared. In case you said yes."

"We don't need it," she told him, taking the sealed foil condom from his hand and tossing it onto the coffee table. "I'm on the pill. Ever since my high school days. My periods were too erratic, and the doctor said it was because of the physical activity of playing competitive sports. It was easier to be on it and not have to predict when a period was coming. I've stayed on it out of convenience."

He pulled her into his arms again. "Sounds good to me."

His mouth ravished hers, taking her hungrily, showing her

how much he desired her. Hope reveled as one kiss blended into another, delicious shivers running through her.

But she wanted more of him. Something told her that her greed for this man would know no end as she began unbuttoning his shirt, his masculine scent filling her nostrils, causing her desire to spiral out of control. She managed to get the shirt off him and could only stare at the perfection it had hidden. He had a defined six-pack, and her hands went to it, her palms grazing the muscles.

Gideon groaned at the touch, making her feel powerful and very feminine. She bent, pressing her lips to his chest, moving her mouth over his muscles, feeling them bunch in response.

Boldly, she moved to his nipples, her lips grazing first one, then the other before she then touched each with her tongue. He groaned again, his hold on her tightening. Hope found herself thoroughly enjoying herself, teasing him as his nipples stiffened.

"Enough!" he cried, sweeping her into his arms and carrying her to the bedroom.

Slowly, he undressed her, kissing his way along her body as he did so until she stood bare before him. She saw the heat in his eyes, his desire for her scorching her with each sweep of his eyes.

"Let me help you," she said, her voice low.

Her hands shook a bit as she helped him shed his clothes, nerves flitting through her.

Then he stood before her, the most perfect physical specimen of manhood she'd ever seen. Her palms stroked his chest.

"You still look like the college athlete you were," she said.

His hands captured her waist, holding her in place. "I've put on a few pounds. Not many. I never wanted to be the overweight, stereotypical cop."

She ran her hands up his chest and clasped them behind his nape, pulling his mouth to hers in a searing kiss.

Somehow, they wound up on the bed, touching, stroking,

limbs entangled. Gideon murmured into her ear that he was on a mission to kiss her everywhere.

Mission accomplished.

His lips trailed along every part of her body, causing desire to flare again and again. When they reached her belly, the flutters inside her almost drove her to orgasm then and there. Then his mouth went lower. He guided her legs up so that her feet were flat against the mattress. His hands clasped her knees, pulling them apart. His mouth went to her core, and his tongue plunged inside her over and over. Hope writhed beneath him, her head whipping back and forth, the pressure building inside her until it exploded in a violent orgasm.

"Ride the wave, babe," he said as she moved with the pleasure sweeping through her body.

Then his mouth caught hers, and they kissed, his body now hovering over hers.

She broke the kiss. "I need you inside me," she managed to get out.

He grinned. "Your wish is my command."

His swollen cock thrust into her, and suddenly Hope found herself on the ride of her life, moving, rocking, laughing, crying. When he came, she did, too, the first time that had happened for her during sex. They clung to one another, riding out the storm, both physical and emotional. Then Gideon collapsed atop her, panting heavily. He kissed her neck, licking the pulse which beat wildly.

His arms went about her, scooping her up as he flipped onto his back, bringing her with him. Hope lay half atop him now, her ear pressed to where his heart beat quickly, his hand caressing her back, his lips kissing her hair.

They lay like that for a long time, their bodies cooling. She had never felt so cherished.

"I love you."

She stilled. Had Gideon just told her that he loved her?

"I know it's probably too soon to say those words to you," he said, his hand moving up and down her spine tenderly. "But I don't want to hide my feelings from you. I don't expect—"

Hope's mouth came down on his, silencing him. She kissed him with everything she had, wanting to show him how she felt.

When she broke the kiss, she said, "I love you, Gideon Ross. I'm not ashamed to tell you so. I know it in my heart. In my soul. I don't mind sharing my feelings with you. I feel like I'm on top of the world."

His lopsided grin made her heart skip a beat. "No. Just on top of me."

He pulled her down for a lazy kiss and then wrapped his arms around her. "I could stay like this all night."

"Me, too."

They lay together for almost an hour, no words necessary. Just being together was enough.

Then he loosened his grip and kissed her quickly. "Duty calls. We both have to be up early. As it is, we won't get much sleep. At least I won't. I'll probably go home and lie in bed and think about everything we did in this bed tonight. And when I do fall asleep, I hope I dream about it. And you."

Tears sprang to Hope's eyes. "You are a romantic, Chief Ross. I never would have suspected that."

"I never have been, Dr. Keller. Until I met you."

They kissed lazily for a few minutes, and then he climbed from the bed. "I've got to go so you can get some sleep."

She caught his hand. "I wish you would stay. But I know why you have to leave."

Quickly, she slid from the bed and found her robe, pulling it on as he dressed. Hope walked him to the door, where he kissed her goodbye.

"Can I see you after work?" he asked. "Barring any animal or police emergencies?"

"You better," she said, laughing. "I'll make dinner for us. Think about what you want."

"You. Naked," he responded, making her laugh harder.

Gideon kissed her a final time. "I'll see you tomorrow. I love you, Hope. I really do."

"I love you, too," she said softly as he opened the door and closed it.

She locked it and went to the window, watching him head to his SUV. He paused, looking up, and she waved at him. He waved back and then drove off.

In a daze, she went to the couch, where Jake laid, snoring lightly. She scooped up the beagle and took him back to her bed, setting him near the foot.

As she climbed into bed and rested her head against the pillow, she caught Gideon's scent. Leaning into the pillow, she breathed deeply, satisfaction filling her.

She had never been in love before, and the newness and wonder of it amazed her. She wanted to spend all her time with Gideon, but she understood this was the first flush of love washing over her. The physical need for him was great, but she knew eventually this stage would end. It would be what came after that would test them and see if they were meant to make it in the long run.

Hope hugged her pillow and fell asleep, dreaming of her handsome lover.

15

For once, Hope stayed in bed instead of leaping up and heading out for her usual morning run. Jake didn't seem to mind the break, snuggling close to her side. As they lay there, she reflected on her time with Gideon last night. He had proven to be a generous lover, more interested in pleasing her than himself. That was unique in her limited experience. The few men she had coupled with had been all about themselves, rarely concerned if she had been satisfied by their lovemaking. No, she had sex with those partners.

With Gideon, she had made sweet love.

Knowing it was time to rise and get ready for the day, she tossed back the covers and headed to the shower, hating that she would wash Gideon's scent from her. Once she was dressed for the day, she took Jake out to pee and then brought him back upstairs, feeding him while she used her new coffee maker to make a cup of vanilla-laced coffee, downing a quick protein shake while it brewed. She sipped on it as she picked up her phone, seeing she had missed a text from Gideon while she was in the shower.

> Just wanted to say good morning—and how
> much last night meant to me.

GIDDINESS FILLED her as she read the words. Hope felt like a middle schooler, getting a note from a guy she had a crush on. She texted him back, not wanting to go overboard and scare him away.

> Good morning to you, too. Hope you slept well.
> Can't wait to see you again.

SHE TOOK another sip of her coffee, and her phoned dinged again.

> Same. Pulling into the station. Talk to you later.

WARMTH FILLED HER. Hope had never been one to wear her emotions on her sleeve. She was practical and levelheaded, but thoughts of Gideon Ross made her swoon. She hoped they could see one another sometime today. She was definitely up for a repeat of last night.

She fastened Jake's leash to his collar and sailed out the door, using her key to let herself into Lizzy Lou's, and brought Jake to the kitchen.

Her landlady looked up from the paper she read. Smiling, she said, "I hope you had a good time at your Super Bowl party. It was a close game. And even a few of the commercials were funny this year."

"Yes, it was a lot of fun," Hope replied. "I also got to meet a new couple, Brynn Mattson and Ray Barker. They both work with Rory and Cole Johnson at the high school."

She bent and gave Jake a kiss on his head. "Be good for Lizzy Lou," she told the beagle. Looking to her landlady, Hope added, "Jake didn't get his run in with me this morning. I was lazy and slept in after the party last night."

"Then I'll make certain we take a good long walk this afternoon, won't we, Mr. Jake? Have a good day, Hope."

She drove to the animal clinic, getting out of her car at the same time Randy did.

"Did you watch the game, Dr. Keller?" the vet tech asked.

"Yes, it was an exciting one. Close, just how I like them."

"It was a good game. I only wish my Dallas Cowboys would've been playing instead."

She laughed. "I was thinking the same thing about my Houston Texans."

"If you decide to stay in Sugar Springs, you're going to need to change your allegiance," he teased.

They entered the clinic, and Hope saw Sally was already behind the reception desk.

"Good morning," Sally called brightly.

Randy excused himself, and she went to visit with Sally.

"How was College Station and house hunting?" she asked.

"We saw five different houses. Two in Bryan and the others in College Station. The one I told you that I'd seen online was the best of the bunch," Sally declared. "Richard liked it, too." She smiled. "So much that we put in an offer on it and heard back yesterday afternoon. We got it!"

"Congratulations, Sally. What do you like about it?"

"We downsized a bit from our house here. The new one has three bedrooms and two-and-a-half baths. About twenty-two hundred square feet. It does have a nice-sized pool in the back yard, though. Richard wasn't too sure about another pool, but I told him we'd get a lot of use out of it. We can both swim laps to stay in shape, and it may tempt our kids to visit more often and bring the grandkids along."

"I'm familiar with College Station from my years there. Where is it located?"

Sally shared the closest major intersection, and Hope knew exactly where that area was.

"Come around and look at the listing."

Sally called up the site on her computer, and they went through the pictures together, Shirley joining them. Both women complimented the house, with Sally pointing out features she particularly liked.

Shirley excused herself, and Sally asked Hope, "Have you made a decision about the clinic? I'm not rushing you, but I want to close on this house and get to College Station as soon as we can. Richard's been in touch with the dean of the vet school, and there's the possibility he might even begin teaching during the summer session if we're already there."

"I have come to a decision. I want to buy the clinic."

Sally threw her arms around Hope, saying, "You will be the perfect vet to take over this practice. People are going to love you. I guess we should let my husband know. He's in his office."

They walked to the rear of the clinic, and Hope informed Dr. Bisch of her decision.

He stood and shook her hand. "That's wonderful news, Hope. It will also allow Sally and me to get to College Station sooner than we'd expected. Why don't I call Walker Cox and see if he can meet us for lunch today? We can talk about the sale, and he can draw up the papers this afternoon."

"I will need my lawyer to read over the documents, but I'm happy for Walker to create them."

She returned to the front with Sally to check on today's

appointments. Dr. Bisch followed them, saying if she took the morning appointments, he would take over the afternoon ones.

"That way, you can accompany Walker to his office and see that your attorney gets the information. Hopefully, we can close tomorrow if everything is approved."

"I'd like to give you a going-away party," she told the couple. "I'll also need to see about hiring a new receptionist."

She kept to herself the idea of changing the name of the clinic. She thought it important to rebrand it with new owner-ship. That would also mean buying a new domain name and creating a new website from scratch. She would need to start doing the legwork on that, as well as meeting with a contractor to go over the changes she wanted in modernizing the clinic.

Just before they opened at seven, Hope asked Shirley and Randy to meet with her briefly. She told them that she would be buying the practice and asked that the two of them stay on.

"I'd be happy to, Dr. Keller," Randy said. "I have a couple of ideas I might even want to run by you."

"I'm eager to hear them, Randy. I already think of you and Shirley as family. We're in this practice together." She turned to Shirley. "That is, if you want to stay on, as well."

"Dr. Keller, I've got a lot of living left to do. You can count on me to be here with you."

"I know the salaries you've been making since I've perused all the clinic's financial information. I've seen that neither of you has had a raise in two years. I will be giving you both a bump in pay, but that won't start until I'm officially the owner."

Both vet techs beamed, and Randy said, "Thanks, Dr. Keller. We really appreciate that."

"I want to meet with both of you at a later date. Pick your brain about any changes you might want to see made and why. I'll also go over with you some things I want done around here. For now, let's hit the ground running. We have a busy day."

Hope saw several pets that morning, but the most productive

appointment was her last one when she met with Christine Martinez. Christine had brought in her golden retriever Happy for his annual check-up.

"I heard the buzz when I got here, Dr. Keller," Christine said. "It seems you'll be buying the animal hospital from Dr. Bisch."

"Yes, we're having the paperwork drawn up today, so the transfer will occur soon."

"With Sally leaving, you'll be looking for a new receptionist. I'd like for you to consider me for the position, Dr. Keller. I can get a résumé to you as soon as I get home."

"Oh, really?"

"I taught first grade for a few years. Until my son Marco was born. I took off after that to be a full-time mom and just never went back to the classroom. Frankly, I found myself bored with teaching. I have great people and computer skills, though, and I've always been good with numbers. I've been helping my husband's business on the side, as well as doing the taxes for a lot of my neighbors. Marco started kindergarten this year, and I'm ready to commit to a full-time position again. I don't really want to have a commute from here to Tyler, which is why I've been looking for an opportunity in Sugar Springs. Being your recep-tionist would appeal to me, especially if I could do more than that. Keep your books. Order your supplies. Act more as an office manager."

She liked the fact that Christine was close to her own age, which meant if she were good at the job, she might stay for many years. The fact that she was already pursuing the job before Hope even advertised it also showed her that Christine was a go-getter.

"Would you be able to have dinner with me tonight and talk more about this?" Hope asked.

"That would be great, Dr. Keller. Why don't you come to my house for dinner? I would love for you to meet my family, and I'm a good cook."

"I would like that very much, Christine. What can I bring?"

"Just yourself, Dr. Keller. And an open mind."

She finished up with the retriever's exam and sent Christine out to pay.

Shirley turned to her and said, "Christine Martinez would be a great addition to the clinic, Dr. Keller. I know her and Enrique from church. She's always volunteering for this and that and is smart as a whip. She knows how to get along with people. I hope you'll consider her."

"Getting your stamp of approval is important to me, Shirley. After tonight's dinner, we may have found our new receptionist. It would be great for Sally to be able to train Christine before she and Dr. Bisch leave town."

She made a few more notes on Happy's chart and then set the file in the stack for Sally. With her last appointment finished, she went to Dr. Bisch's office.

He glanced up from his computer. "Ready to go to lunch?"

Hope nodded and asked, "Were you able to have Walker join us?"

"He said he would be at Ida Lou's at one." Dr. Bisch looked at his watch. "It's almost that now. Why don't we take separate cars to the diner since I'll be coming back here, and you might head over to Walker's office with him?"

They left the clinic, and Walker already had a table for them when they reached Ida Lou's. Much to Hope's delight, Gideon sat at the same table.

Both men rose to greet them, and Gideon slipped an arm about her, kissing her cheek, before helping her take a seat. She caught Ida Lou eyeing them, and the diner owner nodded in approval as she headed their way.

"What can I get you?" Ida Lou asked.

They placed their drink orders, and all of them ordered today's blue plate special, which consisted of pot roast and carrots, mashed potatoes, and English peas.

"Rolls, cornbread—or both?" Ida Lou asked the table.

"Let's do a mixture," Walker said.

After Ida Lou left, Walker added, "I hope you don't mind that I asked Gideon to join us. We came in at the same time."

"No, not at all," Dr. Bisch said, grinning at Hope. "I hear Dr. Keller is keeping company with you these days, Chief."

Gideon reached for her hand under the table, entwining their fingers. "Yes, Dr. Bisch. We definitely are seeing one another."

"Well, if you're the reason Hope decided to stay and buy my practice, then I appreciate your help."

"No," Gideon said quickly. "Hope made a business decision without my influence. One which will be good for her. The fact that I'll profit from it personally?" He smiled. "That's only icing on the cake."

Ida Lou returned with their food and drinks, and talk turned to business as they ate. Dr. Bisch told Walker what he wanted stipulated in the documents to be drawn up, and Walker turned to her.

"Does all of that sound good to you, Hope? I may be Richard's attorney, but I want to take care of you, too."

"Dr. Bisch and I have agreed on everything he mentioned. I would like to have my attorney in Houston look over the paper-work before I sign anything, though."

Dr. Bisch said, "I thought Hope could go back to your office with you after lunch, Walker. You can work your magic and send the contracts to her attorney for a look-see."

"If that's okay with you, Hope, I'm happy to have you come back with me and get your attorney's contact information."

"Dr. Bisch has given me the entire afternoon off to accomplish that. I've already spoken with Winston this morning, and he'll clear his calendar once you send him the documents. He'll read through it immediately."

"Everything will be pretty straightforward, so it shouldn't take us long," Walker told them. "If we hear back from your lawyer, we might even be able to sign by the end of the day and file the documents. If not, I can have Margaret take those over to the courthouse tomorrow morning."

Dr. Bisch glanced at his watch. "I better get back to the clinic. Looks like it's a wrap here."

They left their table, Gideon walking beside her.

He asked, "Free for dinner?"

"No, I'm not," she said, trying not to let her disappointment show. "I was invited to eat with Christine Martinez and her family. I'm considering hiring her as my new receptionist when Sally leaves."

"I hope dinner goes well then. You free after?"

"I can text you when I leave Christine's."

"I'll be waiting for you, Hope. See you soon."

This time, he brushed a light kiss across her lips, and she knew the patrons of the diner would be filing gossip reports, sending out news flashes. It wouldn't surprise her if someone might have even snapped a picture of the kiss.

Walker paid for the lunches, telling Hope he could write it off as a business expense. They left the diner, and he pointed out his office. They waved goodbye to Gideon, who was talking with Dr. Bisch, and then strolled along the square and entered his office.

Margaret greeted them. "It's good to see you again, Dr. Keller."

"Hope, please. I'm only Dr. Keller at the office. How is the teeth brushing going for boy and dog?"

"I had a talk with Sam when he got home from school and shared what a great checkup Max had—except for his teeth. We talked about how dogs depend upon their humans to do the things they can't do for themselves. I told Sam he wouldn't want to see Max's teeth begin to rot and fall out because he wouldn't be able to eat then. That seemed to do the trick. Now, they both get their teeth brushed by Sam morning and night."

"That's fantastic, Margaret."

Walker said, "Come back to my office, Hope. I'll get the info I need from you, and then you're free to go while I draw up the papers."

They stepped into his office, Walker closing the door, indicating a seat for her to take. She dug for her wallet and pulled out Winston's card, giving it to Walker.

"I meant what I said in the diner, Hope. I want to be sure you're taken care of as far as this sale goes. I also want to thank you for choosing to stay in Sugar Springs. I see how Gid looks at you, and I know you are the one for him. I'm only hoping you feel the same about him."

"We seem to have a lot in common," she began. "A lot of the same values. Of course, Gideon is well-versed in politics, and I usually avoid that topic like the plague."

Walker chuckled. "Gid has always been a news junkie. I actually think if he hadn't gone into police work that he might have made for a good politician. Hopefully, you can put up with that. Melinda sure didn't like it. I told Gid when he married her that she wasn't smart enough for him or interested in anyone around her. I could see the divorce happening even as she walked down the aisle."

Gideon had been married before?

Hope forced a smile to her lips and rose. "I'll let you get to it then, Walker. Feel free to send Winston whatever you come up with. I'll leave the wording between the two of you. Just text me if you need me back here this afternoon to sign the papers."

"Will do."

He escorted her to the door. "I'll check in with you soon," he promised.

She told Margaret goodbye and hurried to her car. Once she was inside, she let the tears slide down her cheeks. It wasn't that she really cared that Gideon had been married before. It was the fact that he had held this back from her.

Since he had kept his marriage a secret, Hope couldn't help

but wonder what else the handsome police chief might be hiding from her?

16

When Gideon came to Sugar Springs, it had been easy to sublet Cole Johnson's apartment. It wasn't far from the station, and Rory had helped in furnishing it. Pre-Hope, it satisfied his needs.

Post-Hope was a different matter.

He would keep from rushing things with her. Knowing what he did about her past, he knew Hope was fragile emotionally, thanks to her stalker murdering her parents and the sensational trial which followed. Also, she was moving to a new town. Taking on not simply a new job but becoming the proprietor of a business, her first foray into ownership, not to mention embarking in a relationship with him. Because of all these factors, Gideon would exercise patience.

But he knew Hope Keller was his future.

At some point down the line, he would ask her to marry him. Because she would have so much of her capital tied up in the veterinary practice, he wanted to be the one responsible for finding them a house. He'd spent very little money in the years after his divorce, having paid only a couple of months of alimony because Melinda quickly remarried, so he'd accumulated a nice chunk of savings which could be used as a down payment on a home in Sugar Springs. Besides, it would look good to the community if he purchased a house and showed he was investing in the place he worked and calling it home.

Gideon had scoured house listings in the Sugar Springs area when he got to work this morning. Not too many had popped up, much less any that he liked. He wanted a large, rambling house because he wanted plenty of space for rambunctious kids to play. A large back yard would be a must.

Then it hit him. Richard and Sally Bisch would need to sell their house when they moved to College Station for his new position.

And their house would be perfect.

So far, it hadn't been listed on any real estate sites, including Tamara Heath's, a local real estate agent, unless it was a pocket listing, one which wasn't placed in any database. Some sellers did that to test the market and see what a house could bring in. Gideon believed the Bisches simply hadn't gotten around to it, wanting to wait to see whether or not Hope would decide to buy their practice. Now that she was in the process of doing so, he figured the Bisch house would go on the market fairly soon.

He planned to make an offer to Richard Bisch right now before it did.

The two men exited the diner and as they walked to the vet's vehicle, Gideon said, "I suppose with Hope deciding to stay that you'll be putting your house on the market soon."

"Yes, we need to get around to doing that. Sally says before we have Tamara Heath come and take a look and put a price tag on it, I've got some cleaning up to do. I'll admit that the garage is a mess. I also need to spruce up things with a bit of paint, both inside and outside."

"Why not just sell it as is?" he asked.

Dr. B chuckled. "Sally doesn't want anyone coming to look

until the place is in better shape. The bones are good. It's just a few cosmetic issues, that's all."

"What if I told you that I'd like to buy it before you even list it?"

Surprise filled the vet's face. "Are you serious, Chief?"

"I am. Roscoe wanted me to start quickly, so I knew I didn't have time to look for a house. That's why I subleased Cole Johnson's apartment when I got here. I've settled into my job now, and I know it's important to a community for its leaders to be invested in their community. That means buying a home. I've looked at a few online and haven't seen anything I liked so far."

"Well, you'd like our house if you like big. It's got five bedrooms. A huge kitchen and a large family room. A study, which I never use. It's a two-story. On a cul-de-sac with only three other houses. Our two kids were able to play in the street. Ride their bikes around. Play basketball." The older man paused, studying Gideon. "If you're looking to raise a family, Chief, our house would be ideal. Yes, it could stand a few updates. And those coats of paint I mentioned."

"But if you sold it to me before doing that, I could paint it in the colors I wanted."

The vet grinned slyly. "Or the colors someone else might want."

"I do want to have a family, Dr. B. I'm not rushing anything. Having the right house would be a good first step toward that goal, though."

"Let me talk it over with Sally. She's the one good with numbers. I'm sure she'll be the one who sets the price."

"Do that. I'd be happy to meet with you once you've spoken with her and have an idea what you're asking for the property."

Dr. Bisch offered his hand. "Will do, Chief Ross. You'll be hearing from me soon."

"Thanks."

Gideon returned to his SUV and checked in with Gladys

Cameron. His dispatcher told him all was quiet, and he said he would be out on patrol. Though he knew he had plenty on the force patrolling the area, he liked to drive the streets himself at least once a day, looking for anything out of place, waving to citizens, stopping to chat with a mom pushing a stroller or someone walking a dog.

He couldn't help himself and drove past the Bisches' place again, hoping no one on the cul-de-sac was counting the number of times he did so. The house had immaculate landscaping, with a large maple tree in the front yard. He wondered about the layout of the house and the fact that he was offering to buy it without having even entered the place. Still, the outside spoke to him, and hearing how many bedrooms it had and the fact it had a large kitchen gave him a good feeling. He would change the paint and trim on the outside, though, getting Hope's input on that.

It would be a fine line he walked now, wanting to hear her opinions and make changes without pressuring her. He would simply tell her he didn't have much taste in design or color and that he knew things needed sprucing up and could use her advice. Fingers crossed, she would choose things she would like in her own home—since he planned for it to be *their* home one day.

As he left the cul-de-sac, Gideon wondered if Hope had seen a therapist after her parents' deaths. She hadn't mentioned it or if she was seeing anyone now that she had moved to Sugar Springs. He figured she would probably need to drive into Tyler to do so. Again, he told himself to be patient. To take baby steps with her. That quote about '*a journey of a thousand miles begins with a single step*' rattled around his head.

He would take more steps with Hope each day.

～

HOPE HAD ALREADY SEARCHED for a local contractor and had found a few online. After reading reviews, she had decided to use Steve Pillar if he were available. She drove to his office now, which was located in a house several blocks off the town square.

Entering, she went to the desk where a woman sat.

"Hi, I'm Hope Keller. I'm hoping to hire Steve for some work updating an animal clinic."

"Hi, Hope. I'm Becky, Steve's wife. He'll be back from a job in about ten minutes. Can I get you something to drink?"

"No, thanks. Do you mind if I wait?"

"Let's go into the conference room. I do a little bit of every-thing around here, including coordinating the schedule of what the crew needs to do. I can also show you some of the places we've worked on, including businesses that we've remodeled."

Becky rose and led Hope to what had been the home's family room. It had a large conference table in the center and skylights, which gave the room extra natural light.

"Our next-door neighbor is Margaret Mason. She told me about meeting you the other day. She's thrilled that Sam is brushing his teeth and their dog's more now. Have a seat, and let's look at a few previous jobs."

Becky handed her a large notebook, and Hope perused it as Becky explained the before and after pictures.

"Hey, hon," a balding, muscular man said, coming into the room.

"This is Dr. Hope Keller, Steve. She's the one buying Dr. Bisch's animal hospital."

Steve shook hands with her. "Great to meet you. I see Becky has you looking at jobs we've completed in the past." He took a seat. "Let's talk about what you want done. I'm assuming to the clinic and not a house."

"No, I've only been in Sugar Springs a short while. I'm renting a garage apartment now. The work I want to commission is for the clinic."

"I haven't been there in probably five years or so," Steve said. "We had to put our cat to sleep. We just never got another one."

Hope made a sympathetic sound. "I'm sorry. It's always hard to lose a beloved pet. Even though that happened years ago, the clinic still looks the same since this last time you were there. According to Sally Bisch, nothing's been done to it in many years."

She explained what she wanted to do to refresh the examination rooms and how she wanted to rearrange the reception area, adding a second entrance and moving the desk.

"I also want to start carrying pet food, so I'll need an area designated for that with shelving."

Steve grabbed a sketchpad and began drawing. She had him change a few things as they talked through her vision of the reception area.

"There. That's what I'm talking about," she said. "You've nailed it. How long would it take to do a project like this?"

He thought a moment. "I'd say five to seven workdays. You'd have to shut down while we were there. It would be too much noise for the pets. I know a lot of times they can be skittish, especially when going to the vet. I'd like to see the clinic in person, though. That way, I can do some measuring. Draw up more precise plans and give you a solid estimate. Get you on the schedule. This is actually a good time of year for a project such as this. Warmer weather is a busier time of year for us."

"Do you have time now to see it?" she asked.

"Sure. I'm supposed to head over to check on a tile job in about two hours, so I'm free until then."

"Let's do it," she said.

Steve suggested they ride over together so they could talk about ideas he might have after he saw the clinic. Hope readily agreed, and they drove to the clinic together in his truck. On the way, she asked for recommendations for people who might do landscaping and signs.

"If you want a sign low to the ground like they have now, one which meets city code, we could handle that. Are you going to change the name after you buy it?"

"I'd like to. I'll know more once I hire a graphic designer. I'll also need someone to design a new webpage."

"I have just the person for you. Enrique Martinez. He's done ours and several others for friends of mine. Even designed my logo and business cards."

"Do you know his wife's name?"

"Sure. It's Christine. She handles his books."

"I'm going to take this as a sign," Hope said. "I'm interviewing Christine to be my new receptionist. We're having dinner at her house this evening."

"Then tell Enrique hi for me."

Steve pulled into the parking lot. They entered the building and said hello to Sally. Hope explained why Steve was here.

"It's about time," Sally said. "I told Hope we needed to update this place years ago. Richard is just too set in his ways."

"Then let me look around and take some measurements," the contractor said.

Her cell rang, and she saw it was Winston. "I've got to take this. It's my lawyer."

"Use Richard's office," Sally suggested. "He's with a patient."

She nodded and headed to the back. "Hi, Winston. Have you had a chance to look over what Walker sent?"

"I have," her attorney said. "I haven't spoken to him yet. I wanted to touch base with you first. Everything is in wonderful order, Hope. This attorney knows his stuff. The language is concise and clear. Everything is spelled out. I have no problem in recommending that you sign the papers. It's a very good price, by the way."

"I think Dr. Bisch made it attractive so I would be eager to buy," she told him. "He's accepted a position to teach at A&M's vet school, and he and his wife are champing at the bit to leave Sugar Springs."

Winston laughed. "With this good an offer, you should see if he's willing to sell you his house."

"I'm not ready to take on home ownership yet, much less a mortgage. I'm sinking quite a bit into this practice. I want to get it running smoothly and be comfortable owning my own business before I extend myself any further."

"Just a thought, Hope. I'll call Walker Cox now and tell him it's a go."

"Thanks, Winston. Send me your bill."

She hung up and rejoined Steve. He had completed his measurements and started walking her through where he would place things. She agreed with everything he suggested.

"Let me take you to an exam room. Those just need fresh coats of paint and a little tweaking."

They visited an empty one, and Steve recommended a few shades of paint to try, ones he thought would be calming to animals and their owners. Hope explained the colors dogs and cats could see, and they decided to look at a color palette when they returned to his office.

They said goodbye to Sally and walked around the outside of the building. Hope shared what plants and bushes she wanted to put in. They both agreed the grass was in good condition although she wanted to add a few trees. She also wanted the walkway up to the clinic refinished.

"Actually, if that's all you want done, my crew can take care of that. You don't need to hire a landscaper. I can go to the nursery and pick out what you want. Or you can even come with me."

"You can do that? Oh, that would be terrific, Steve. I trust you. Just get what you can."

"Okay. Let's go back to the office and talk costs."

On the way to his office, her cell rang. Hope saw it was Walker.

"Excuse me a minute. Hi, Walker. Did you talk with Winston?"

"Yes, and he sang your praises. Said Sugar Springs better take good care of you, or he'd come up and take care of us."

She laughed. "That sounds just like Winston. When do I need to come to your office?"

"Any time between now and five-thirty. You and Dr. Bisch don't have to be here at the same time in order to sign the papers. Margaret's also a notary, so she'll take care of that end of things. She'll file the papers tomorrow morning once we have both your signatures."

"Okay. I'm with Steve Pillar now. We have a few more things to discuss, then I can head your way."

"No rush, Hope. See you later."

At Steve's, she took up Becky's offer and sipped a sparkling water while looking at paint samples, deciding on the ones she wanted for the outside of the clinic, as well as the indoor rooms.

Steve returned, approving of her choices, and presented her with a cost estimate. He went over it, saying she would receive a more detailed one before work began, as well as allowing her to view the plans.

"I had to ballpark the landscaping costs. And I didn't add anything in for the signage just yet."

"That's not a problem. This gives me a good idea what I'm committing to. I'll own the clinic by this time tomorrow, so let's see when you can get me on your schedule."

They looked at his calendar. Becky said she could move two different, smaller jobs so that they had a full seven days in a row, minus a Sunday, to work on the clinic.

"So, you can start two weeks from this coming Monday," she confirmed. "I'll work with Sally to reschedule appointments already on the books for that week."

She gave him her credit card for a down payment on the work, and Steve said, "I'd suggest you get a business credit card,

Hope. You'll need to separate your professional and personal expenses. That's the first thing your accountant will tell you. Why don't you arrange a new account first at the bank, and then you can pay me the funds due? It'll help keep your records straight."

"I appreciate that advice, Steve." She stood and offered her hand. "I really look forward to working with you."

Hope drove to the square and parked in front of Walker's office. Margaret greeted her and took her to the conference room, where she pulled out her notary public book and stamp to record the transaction.

Walker appeared. "This is a big step for you, Hope."

"It is. I came to Sugar Springs, not knowing I would be staying, much less that I would buy a veterinary practice."

"Let me show you where we need your autographs."

He pointed out where she should sign, and Hope did so. Margaret made everything official.

"We'll get copies of everything to you tomorrow," Walker promised. "And I'll send them to Winston's office, as well, for his records."

"Thanks for everything," she told the pair. "I may be back soon, though. I'm probably going to want to do a name change for the business. Put my own mark on it."

"That's not complicated to do," he told her. "When you're ready, give me a holler."

Hope left the office and returned to her car. Once inside, she gave a squeal, happy that her life was turning around for the better. The dark days of Cris Calder seemed far behind her.

17

Hope followed her phone's directions to Christine Martinez's place. The outside of the house was neat as a pin, with a huge oak tree in the yard and a swing hanging from it.

She knocked at the door, and a handsome man in his mid-thirties opened it.

"You must be Dr. Keller," he said. "I'm Enrique, Christine's husband. Won't you please come in?"

"Thank you," she said, entering the house.

"May I take your coat?"

She slipped from it and handed it to him. He hung it on a coat rack standing near the door. Just then, a bright-eyed boy who was a mini-me of his father ran into the foyer.

"Who's this, Papa?"

"This is Dr. Keller. Marco, our son."

"Hi, Dr. Keller. I went to the doctor when my throat was really sore. I missed school. It was..." His face crinkled in thought. "It was..."

"Did you have strep throat?" Hope asked.

The little boy brightened. "That's it! It hurt to swallow. Do you help little boys with strep throat?"

By now, Happy had joined them. The golden retriever came toward her. She offered her fingers to him, and he licked them.

"No, I'm not a doctor for people. I'm a doctor who helps animals. Like Happy. He came to see me the other day."

Marco frowned. "But Happy wasn't sick."

"Sometimes, you go to the doctor even when you are well," she explained. "The doctor can look over you and make sure you stay well. Have you ever gotten a shot before?"

The little boy nodded solemnly. "They hurt. But I get a red sucker, so it's not that bad."

"Those shots are called vaccines. They help you stay well. They keep you from getting things such as chicken pox. It was the same when Happy came to see me. I looked him over. Listened to his heart. Checked his ears and eyes. And I gave him his shots." She smiled. "But he didn't get a sucker."

"Did you give him a treat instead?"

"No, I didn't, Marco, but that's actually a very good idea. Maybe when I give dogs and cats their shots, I should give them a treat."

The boy looked up at his father. "Can I give Happy a treat now, Papa? For the shot he got?"

Enrique ruffled his son's hair. "Of course, Marco."

Marco shot out of the foyer, Happy on his heels, and Enrique said, "He is a good boy. He and Happy are inseparable."

"Do you give him any responsibilities regarding Happy's care? Maybe asking Marco to feed the retriever his breakfast and dinner?"

"We do, Dr. Keller. He also has to make his bed each day."

"Please, call me Hope."

"Come to the kitchen. Christine almost has dinner ready." He paused and smiled at her. "You are in for a treat. Tonight, she has done her special lasagna for you. It's a Mexican lasagna."

They went to the kitchen, and Hope greeted Christine. "I hear that you're making us lasagna tonight. It's one of my favorites."

"Ours, too, but I put a little spin on it. Come, sit at the table and visit while I toss the salad. Enrique, you and Marco need to wash up."

Christine took a large pan of lasagna from one oven and a loaf of bread from the other.

"Oh, you had me at that bread," Hope joked. "Give me a tub of butter and that loaf, and I'd be more than satisfied."

Christine laughed. "You and Marco. He could eat his weight in bread—as long as it's slathered in butter."

Once everything was on the kitchen table, the others took their seats, and Enrique asked if she wouldn't mind if they said grace.

"Of course not," Hope replied.

Marco was the one entrusted with saying the mealtime prayer. It was brief but given from the little boy's heart.

They talked about Sugar Springs over the meal, and Hope explained the duties which Sally carried out at the clinic.

"I printed my résumé for you, but I would be very comfortable taking on all those responsibilities," Christine said.

"I plan to add some additional tasks to the position," she shared. "For one, I want to start carrying pet food for both dogs and cats. I think it would be convenient for people to buy bags and cans of food for their pets when they come into the clinic for routine checkups. Or even when they're running low. The stuff the grocery stores sell is terrible for pets, but I know it's easy when you're shopping for your family to simply place a bag of dog food in your cart. So, another undertaking would be to establish a relationship with the pet food companies and place the food orders for the clinic. Check the shelves to see when we're running low and order so that we can restock things and not run out."

"My wife helps me in my business. She keeps the books and

handles making appointments for me. She's also very good with numbers."

"That is something that is very important with this job. As we talked about the job during Happy's checkup, this is more of an office manager position than a mere receptionist."

Hope explained what the salary would be and the hours Christine would need to work, which went above forty, so she mentioned anything over that number would pay time-and-a-half. She also explained the health benefits package, which Shirley and Randy were covered by.

"Would I be able to have Enrique and Marco placed on my policy?" Christine asked.

"I would have to look into that since both Shirley and Randy are single, but I think that would be an option. I'm trying to get answers to all my questions this week because I have a feeling once Dr. Bisch and his wife close on their new house in College Station, they'll be gone."

Enrique excused himself, saying that he needed to read to Marco and get the boy ready for bed since it was a school night.

Hope helped Christine clean up the kitchen. Christine insisted that Hope take home some of the leftover lasagna and placed it in a container.

"When you leave, I will remind you it's in the fridge."

The two women went to the family room, and Christine asked, "I hope you will consider hiring me, Hope. Even if you don't, I think you should hire Enrique."

"What does he do?" she asked, already knowing some of it from what Steve had shared.

"He is in graphic design and also works with computers."

"I will be looking for someone skilled in those areas. I want to come up with a new name for the clinic, and that will mean having a new website designed, as well."

"Enrique does website design. I can send you some examples of others he's created. Let me get my phone."

After Hope had received the websites via text, she browsed through them. "I like the look he creates. It's very clean and modern. Just what I'm interested in."

They tossed ideas back and forth for new names until Enrique joined them and said, "Marco is ready for his kiss good-night from his mama."

"I'll be back in just a few minutes," Christine said.

Hope caught Enrique up on what they had talked about during his absence, explaining how she wanted to rebrand the clinic to show her new ownership. She shared some of the names she was considering. They discussed the potential for each of them and decided on Keller Critter Care.

"Let me get my sketchpad," he said, leaving the room briefly.

When he returned, Enrique opened it and began drawing furiously, showing Hope each design as he went.

"That's the one," she said excitedly after seeing a few tries. "I like the lines."

"We could use a similar font on the website," he explained. "That is, if you wish to hire me to create it for you."

She felt comfortable with this couple. They were responsible and creative.

"Yes, I would like you to design a new website for me."

"We'll have to apply for the domain name," he said. "I can also host it for you."

"Let's trade cell numbers, and you can text me your proposal. I'd like at least a rough estimate of what the costs will be, both to create the site from scratch and whatever monthly fees would be incurred."

After they had done so, she also sent him her email address, and said, "I'll send you three or four veterinary websites that I like. It should give you an idea of the tabs I will need."

Christine joined them again, and Enrique showed her the logo they would be using for the clinic.

"I can write the copy for the website with Enrique," Christine said. "If you'll just give me the particulars."

"You can either read over it before it's placed on the site," Enrique added. "Or you can let us place it on the page so you can see how it will look. Any corrections to text or pictures are easy to add or delete. Christine is an excellent photographer, and she would be the one to take the pictures for the website instead of using stock photos."

"I like that idea," Hope said. "I might even call up a few pet owners I worked with this week and see if they could bring in their animals for a photo shoot that shows what happens when you come to the clinic." She smiled. "Of course, we would want to feature Happy on the website."

"Ah," Enrique said. "We will have a superstar in our family."

"Are you comfortable with us moving ahead then, Hope?" Christine asked.

"More than comfortable. I want Enrique to start his design work as soon as he has an opening in his schedule, and I would love for you to start work at the clinic tomorrow, if possible. Sally has a lot in her head, and it would be great for you to train under her before she leaves town. I will need to check with Walker Cox, who serves as my attorney here in Sugar Springs. The sale of the clinic goes through tomorrow morning, and the papers will be filed at the county courthouse. I don't know what all would be involved in a name change, but let's push ahead."

Hope rose. "I won't take up any more of your evening, but I want to thank you for a lovely dinner. I'm so happy to be working with both of you."

"Let me get your lasagna," Christine said. "And I'm ready to start tomorrow morning."

After his wife left the room, Enrique said, "This is exactly what my wife has needed. She felt undervalued in the classroom. While she loved being a full-time mom to Marco, she has always itched to do more. That's why she's helped me in my business and also done the taxes of several people in our neighborhood."

She offered her hand, and Enrique took it. "I look forward to working with you, Dr. Keller."

Christine returned with a container and another something wrapped in foil. "A couple of slices of the bread." Her eyes twinkled.

"Oh, the carbs!" she declared. "I guess I'll be running extra hard tomorrow morning."

They walked her to the door, and Hope asked Christine if she could be there at six forty-five tomorrow morning.

"That's fine," her new office manager said. "Enrique can get Marco ready and take him to school."

"Then I will see you tomorrow," she said. "Some animal clinics have their entire staff dress in scrubs, including the receptionist. I'll leave that up to you as to what you'd like to wear."

"Do you mind leggings or jeans? My jeans are in good taste. No holes. A very dark denim."

"That sounds fine. Whatever you're comfortable wearing."

She went to her car and started it so the heat would come on. Then she texted Gideon.

Leaving now. Home in ten.

HE REPLIED with a thumbs up emoji, and anticipation filled her. She wasn't happy that he hadn't mentioned his previous marriage to her, but she was still eager to see him.

Gideon was sitting on the steps leading up to her apartment when she arrived and came to meet her. Hope was barely out of the car when he pulled her into his arms for a searing kiss.

"Come inside, and we can warm up," she told him, already heated by his kiss.

They climbed the stairs, and Jake greeted them when she unlocked the door.

"Let me take him out for you," Gideon said. "Come on, boy."

Jake trotted down the stairs, Gideon following the beagle. Hope hung up her coat and placed her lasagna in the fridge. She put on her new tea kettle and got out two large mugs for them.

Gideon returned and shrugged out of his jacket, coming to her and slipping his arms around her.

"I missed you, Dr. Keller," he said huskily.

He kissed her again, slowly and thoroughly. She lost track of time until the tea kettle whistled that it was ready.

Hope broke the kiss. "Would you like some tea?"

"That's sounds great."

She had already placed teabags in two mugs and squirted a bit of stevia in both before pouring in the hot water. She offered him his mug, and they dunked their teabags as they carried them to the sofa and sat.

He bent and sniffed. "Orange spice. Yum."

"I'm glad you enjoy drinking tea," she said. "Some men turn up their noses at tea."

"Not this one," he said. "True, I prefer coffee in the morning, but I'm happy to sit with you and sip tea anytime."

Placing her mug on the coffee table, she decided she needed to confront him. No, confront was too strong. She merely needed information from him.

"I have something to ask you about," she began. "Something you haven't mentioned to me before."

"I'm an open book, Hope. I thought you knew that."

"Why didn't you tell me that you'd been married before?"

His eyes widened in surprise. "I guess Walker mentioned something about it to you."

She nodded. "I'm not mad. I'm not even upset. Just... curious."

"I guess I didn't mention it because it was so long ago. A mistake that I've put on a far back burner. Frankly, I never think of Melinda. I haven't even seen or talked to her in years." His gaze met hers. "But I'm happy to tell you everything now. You deserve to know."

Gideon explained how he and his ex-wife had met and dated a couple of years in college.

"With twenty/twenty hindsight, I understand that she was never in love with me. Just the idea of her and me. And a me which I could never be."

Confused Hope asked, "What do you mean?"

He told her how he had received numerous accolades during his playing days and had been projected to go in the first or second round of the NFL draft.

"A knee injury early during my senior season ended those dreams. I went through a long, brutal rehab. I wasn't drafted, but I did receive an invitation to go to the Falcons' training camp."

He explained how he'd done well and despite being a tad slower than before his injury, he still impressed the coaching staff enough with his moves and nose for the ball.

"I made some good catches in preseason games for them. In the end, though, it wasn't quite enough to make their 53-man roster. They did ask me to play on their practice squad, with the idea if one of their wide receivers was injured during the season, I might have the opportunity to move up. Not start, but possibly play."

Hope studied him. "You didn't want that, did you?"

"See, you didn't even know me then—and you already understand me better than Melinda ever did. If I couldn't play and perform at the level I expected from myself, I didn't want to bounce around the league from team to team on various practice squads from year to year, holding out hope that one day I might get a chance to play. I wanted more for myself.

"That's when I decided to apply to the police academy. By

then, Melinda and I were already married. She was horrified that I'd decided to become a cop."

"Was she afraid for your safety? Police work can be dangerous."

He snorted. "No. She was upset that she would have to tell her friends what I did for a living. She was from a very wealthy family, and what I made in a month was mere pocket change to her. She was constantly going to her daddy, begging for money. Melinda didn't want to work. Didn't want to build our relationship or a family. She merely wanted to go to spa appointments and lunch with her rich friends and volunteer for work through the Junior League."

Gideon shook his head, his disgust apparent. "We never should have gotten married. We never should have stayed married. I hung in there, not wanting to be a failure at marriage after I had failed with my NFL dreams. Melinda begged me to go to work for her dad instead of being a cop, but being a banker and wearing a suit each day wasn't my cup of tea. I liked what I did. Patrolling the streets. Helping people. Making a difference in the community."

"So, you parted ways," she observed.

"Yeah. Melinda started seeing an old boyfriend. To be honest, I think she had been seeing him long before our divorce was final because they became engaged two weeks after we signed the papers and were married a couple of months after that."

Gideon sighed. "That was almost ten years ago, Hope. I've never seen Melinda since then. I never think about her. I've been married to my job."

He took her hands in his. "I wasn't trying to hide anything from you, babe. I suppose at one point it would have occurred to me to mention being married previously. I hope you'll forgive me."

She looked him in the eye. "There's nothing to forgive. I understand. I understand *you* better now. And I'm touched with how open you've been with me. Honesty is very important to me, Gideon."

"It is to me, too." He framed her face in his hands. "That's why I knew this time was different, Hope. I realize now that I didn't truly love Melinda. She had become more a habit. Like an old pair of shoes you've worn forever and just can't seem to let go of. With you, I feel like myself. I never truly let my guard down around her or her family and friends."

"I love you," she told him. "And I want you to know you can always be yourself with me."

"That's what I love about you," he said, kissing her deeply.

Hope lost herself in the kiss, satisfied that Gideon would never hide anything from her ever again.

18

Hope awoke, enveloped in the warmth of Gideon's arms. She could also feel Jake nestled against her feet. She was in Gideon's bed, where she had spent numerous nights during the past month. Even though they were adults, he was still concerned about gossip and didn't want his car parked in front of Lizzy Lou's all night. When his schedule allowed, they would usually eat dinner together in town or at her place, and then he would take her—and Jake—to his apartment, so that her car remained at her rental. She had teased him that she felt like a teenager, sneaking around, not wanting her parents —or in this case, Lizzy Lou and the neighbors—to know what she was up to.

He was thoughtful in so many different ways. Considerate of her time and feelings. The love she had for him had grown exponentially as they had gotten to know one another better and better. She could see a future with Gideon Ross in it.

They had done a big send-off for Richard and Sally Bisch, holding it at Ida Lou's diner so that there was plenty of room and good food. Sally had done an excellent job of training Christine Martinez. Already, Hope and Christine had grown close, and she knew without a doubt that hiring Christine was one of the best decisions she had made.

Working with Enrique, too, had been a dream. The graphic designer was bold and clever, always open to ideas she pitched, while fielding many unique ones of his own. They had gone with Keller's Critter Care for the name of the new clinic, and Enrique's logo design was perfect, bearing the clinic's name with an adorable cartoon dog and cat. Along with the Martinizes, Hope had worked on the new website until it was perfected. It would go live today, the day of the grand reopening of the practice.

Steve Pillar had also been terrific to work with. The contractor and his crew were friendly and efficient. They had placed the final touches on the veterinary practice yesterday afternoon. Hope and Christine, along with Shirley and Randy, had gone over every square inch of the inside and outside of the building, loving all the updates and improvements, and eager to show them off today to the public. Hope had arranged for free food in the parking lot provided by the local sports bar owned by star basketball player Freddie Otts' parents, finger foods that would be easy to manage.

Freddie himself had gotten involved with the party. Hope learned that the senior in high school was wise beyond his years and had worked on the Hollywood production when they had filmed in Sugar Springs last summer, serving as Tanner Haddock's personal assistant. Freddie had not only helped in organizing the food for today, but he also had plenty of games and volunteers working booths which had been set up. Freddie had even given Christine some props to use at her photo booth, where she would be taking pictures of pets and their owners. Freddie had found or made all kinds of bow ties, visors, and bandanas for the dogs and cats to wear. She would have to make sure several of these pictures appeared on the website, as well as framing some to hang on the walls of the clinic.

Good to her word, Christine had written outstanding copy,

mimicking the websites Hope had forwarded as good examples, and yet putting a small-town, original spin on each of the pages. The new office manager had photographed several pets and their owners going through various stages at the clinic, from washing and grooming to routine exams and shots to surgical recovery and boarding facilities.

Christine had also shot the refreshed reception area from various angles, and by the time Hope had gotten home last night, those pictures were already up on the website waiting for her approval. Her clinic workers now felt like true family to her, and she was grateful she had come across Dr. Bisch's listing for a new veterinarian. She couldn't imagine her life anywhere else. Professionally and personally, she was the happiest she had ever been.

Gideon began nibbling on her neck, one of her weak spots, his hand splayed against her bare belly. By now, he knew all the right places to touch her, and shattering orgasms were the norm and not the exception.

For her part, Hope was sexually confident for the first time in her life. Gideon had helped guide her as she had explored his body, and she knew a good number of ways how to please him, as well as ways of making love she'd never even thought about. She knew this wasn't infatuation. Yes, the sexual sparks between them continued, but the depth of their conversations and how well they had come to know one another told Hope this was the real deal.

He turned her in his arms, kissing her eyelids, nose, cheeks, and finally her mouth. She couldn't believe the number of hours they had spent merely kissing. Kissing—along with being with Gideon—was her new favorite pastime.

"Good morning, Dr. Keller," he said huskily, causing a delightful chill to ripple through her. "Happy Reopening Day."

"Thank you, Chief Ross."

"You've worked hard for this, Hope," he told her. "In the short run, you lost a little income having to shut down for a week, but the results are spectacular. I know you're going to bring in new business. Who knows? Maybe you'll eventually have to hire another vet to work along beside you." Gideon paused. "As long as it's not some guy that will try and sweep you off your feet."

She laughed. "That will never happen. I've already been swept up once. I don't plan on it happening again." Hope sighed. "Everyone has worked so hard on my behalf."

He kissed the tip of her nose. "No one works as hard as you do, babe. Why don't you let me do a little of the heavy lifting right now?"

She put herself in his very capable hands, and Gideon did more than satisfy her.

When they finished making love, she dressed quickly and said, "I want to go home and shower. Do my hair and makeup there. "

"Then let me throw on some clothes, and I'll drop off you and Jake. I can meet you at the clinic later. I do have a breakfast meeting at the diner with Mayor Tommy Milton. I have no idea what he might want. But don't forget—we have our Stars game in Dallas tomorrow afternoon."

"I had almost forgotten about that. I've been caught up in the reopening of the clinic. Thanks for reminding me."

Once Gideon dropped her off, Hope got ready. She took Jake to Lizzy Lou's, and her landlady said she would take the beagle on a nice, long walk and then return him to Hope's apartment because Lizzy Lou wanted to attend the opening of the clinic.

"It's time for me to look for another pet," she told Hope. "I don't know exactly what breed I want, and I think that's a good thing. I want to go into the process with an open mind."

"You'll know the dog you'll want when you see him," she promised. "Some little furry creature will speak to you. Maybe even today. I've invited the humane society to be there in the parking lot. They'll be bringing along several pets who are looking for their forever homes."

Excitement filled Lizzy Lou's face. "Oh, my goodness! I might actually get a dog today." She leaned down and petted Jake. "You won't be getting all the attention anymore," Lizzy Lou teased. "But whatever I do decide, Hope, I still want you to drop off Jake each day. If I do get another pet, Jake could help socialize him. He's such a well-behaved little dog. He would be a good influence on another animal."

"Then I'll see you at the clinic," Hope said.

She drove to her practice and parked in back. She had had Steve and his crew pave over some of the grass in the rear of the building, and they had also cut a door so that she and the entire staff could park in back and enter there, saving room in front for pet owners to park. She decided to lock her purse in the car so she wouldn't have to wag it around because her office would be open to the public. She wanted everyone to see the entire building, including the improved surgical suite.

Once again, as she entered, she marveled at how much Steve and his work crew had gotten done. She'd had to close the clinic on a Friday, and they had worked that Saturday and all this past week to complete the job, but the results were exactly what she'd envisioned.

When she made her way to the reception area, she was surprised at the vast number of balloons she saw.

"My, it looks festive in here," she declared.

"Randy is the one responsible for bringing them," Shirley said. "He just attached some outside to draw more attention. And the food truck is already here. The gaming booths for kids are being set up now."

Hope addressed everyone and said, "Thank you for all you've had to put up with. I know it's been a bit chaotic around here, and it was a lot having to reschedule appointments during the remodeling, but I believe we're all happy with the results."

"Thrilled is more like it," Shirley piped up. "We really appreciate all your efforts, Dr. Keller. Especially on the small break room."

The surgical suite at the clinic had been oversized, as large as two surgeries at her former place of business. Hope had Steve take some of the extra space without sacrificing anything the surgery suite required, and he'd partitioned off a small break room for the employees. She had purchased a microwave, full-sized refrigerator, and had a small dishwasher and sink put in. It even had room for a café table with two chairs. Randy had declared he would probably bring his lunch everyday now, saving on money and gas. The staff had pooled their money and bought a large coffee maker since Dr. Bisch had taken the one in his office with him when he left. She was glad the coffee maker was gone because it would give her more room in her office, with less interruptions from the staff.

Enrique had also convinced her to buy new computers for herself and Christine and new tablets for the vet techs and herself. She had gone with Enrique's suggestions for both. She had had a good idea of the type of system she wanted to implement for pet appointments, which would mirror the same one used at Dr. Wallman's practice. She and Christine had sat with Enrique, telling him of the needs for how they recorded information, showing him different records required.

In response, the tech specialist had written a new program which fulfilled all their needs, as well as having a few bells and whistles no one had thought of. It would make all their jobs easier. She had given Christine free rein on how she would keep the books and order supplies. Once more, Enrique tailored a recordkeeping and accounting program which would be perfect, all for a very reasonable price.

The entire staff had gone to the Martinez house since the clinic was closed, due to the renovations, and Enrique went through everything with them until they were comfortable and had all their questions answered regarding both their hardware and software.

Shirley had thanked Hope profusely for leaving paper behind and going digital. Once all information was input into electronic files, Christine would run a hard copy only if a customer asked for one to be provided in that format. The office manager and Steve had worked together on the reception desk area, and Hope was delighted at how streamlined and efficient things would operate now.

Hope went out the front door and checked in with the humane society members. They had set up a pen with several cats and dogs inside and also had more animals to be adopted in cages. She thanked them for coming out today.

"Fingers crossed more than a few of these pets find homes today," she said.

Hope then spoke briefly with Marvin and Leah Otts at the food truck. Leah gave her a slider to sample, and Hope gave it the thumbs up.

"I'm going to go check in with Freddie," she told the couple.

Marvin laughed. "Oh, he'll be running the show, Dr. Keller. You know our Freddie."

She located Freddie and saw he was managing everything regarding the booths. He'd taken the initiative to talk to the priest at the church across the street. For a small donation, Father Greg had agreed people could park in the parish's parking lot today. She saw several cars already there and assumed they belonged to the volunteers currently setting up the booths in the clinic's parking lot.

"Hi, Dr. Keller," Freddie greeted. "Everything's running smoothly."

"I can't believe you do all you do, Freddie. Your résumé must be jam-packed."

He smiled modestly. "I'm just interested in so many different things, Dr. Keller. And I have great news about college."

Though Freddie had received all-district honors, two other key starters on the Sugar Springs basketball team had gone down with injuries the last game of the season, and the Knights did not advance beyond the first round in the playoffs, which apparently had hurt Freddie in the recruiting process. Gideon had shared with Hope that there was still a possibility Freddie might sign with a school which had previously shown interest in him, and she hoped that's what he would share with her now.

"What's your news, Freddie?"

The teenager beamed. "I have a full ride to USC. I'm going to be a Trojan!"

She knew this university was a private school and how expensive its tuition could be. "Congratulations, Freddie. Was it an academic scholarship? I know your grades are outstanding."

"Even better, Dr. Keller. I became interested in filmmaking when Tanner Haddock came to Sugar Springs last summer and shot a movie here."

Hope knew the film had been the famous action star's directorial debut. "Yes, I saw it. It was fantastic."

"I got my name in the credits. I served as Tanner's assistant during the shoot. I still am leaning toward majoring in business, but the world of filmmaking is really interesting to me. Not that I want to be an actor and director. But I think I've got the organizational skills to be a producer. Anyway, Tanner and Paige are going to pay for my college. They want me to come work for them and their new production company when I graduate."

"That's incredible Freddie, and so generous."

He beamed. "I know. Mom and Dad do pretty well at the sports bar, but anyone in the restaurant business knows you live month to month. The profit margin is extremely slim, even when you look like you're successful. I always knew to go to college, I would need to win a scholarship. This is a dream come true—and no loans to pay back."

"Well, my congratulations, Freddie. I think you'll do an

amazing job no matter what you choose as your major or wherever your career path takes you. I know you didn't want me to pay you for organizing today."

"No, Dr. Keller. Let me stop you right there. I think it's important to give back to a community. Sugar Springs has been the best place in the world to grow up. I always want to do whatever I can to help this town, no matter where I wind up. I can't let you pay me a dime for what I've done." He grinned. "Else I couldn't claim this as volunteer hours for National Honor Society." He winked at her. "Gotta go."

The teenager took off, and Hope was amazed at the maturity of this young man. She thought of how people like Gideon and Walker had been raised here in Sugar Springs, and she couldn't help but think of having children herself.

With Gideon.

They had declared their love for one another, and it just seemed understood that they would remain together. She didn't expect a formal declaration anytime soon since their relationship was still so new, but she hoped that one day it would lead to marriage and children. Like Gideon, she wanted to put roots down in this community and be here forever.

The turnout for the grand reopening was tremendous. Hope saw many of the pets and their owners which she had worked with since she had arrived in Sugar Springs, as well as many other residents of the town. People had been encouraged to bring their pets, and the place had an energy about it due to the animals present. Christine was so busy taking pictures that Hope and Freddie took out their own phones and went around snapping pictures to supplement. The local newspaper was in attendance, as well as a reporter from Tyler, who promised her a nice spread in tomorrow's Sunday edition.

When they closed down the booths and signaled to the food truck that it was a wrap, Hope knew everything had been a success. Her staff, along with Gideon, met in the reception area as she went and thanked Freddie and his cadre of volunteers and his parents in the food truck.

Lizzy Lou was over at the humane society's pen, and Hope went toward her landlady.

"Did you find a pet, Lizzy Lou?"

The old woman beamed at her. "I sure did, Hope. They're going to be checking my references, but since I know everyone who works there, I think I'm a shoo-in."

"Which one will be yours?" she asked.

Lizzy Lou pointed out a black lab and said, "He's three years old, so he's already housebroken and has a little bit of training. His previous owner passed away suddenly, and there was no one to take him. I think Midnight and I will get along just fine."

Hope entered the clinic to talk with her team and was surprised when they popped the cork to a bottle of champagne and handed her a bouquet of roses. Shirley poured glasses for all of them and handed Marco a bottled water. Christine distributed the plastic cups, and then said, "Raise your glass to Dr. Keller and Keller Critter Care."

"Here-here," Gideon said, and they all drank their champagne.

Christine said, "I've already gotten several compliments on our new website, and I checked the voicemail. Seven people have already called for appointments next week."

"That's fantastic news," she said. "I couldn't have done this without you and Enrique."

Christine told Hope to go on and leave. "I'll lock up, Dr. Keller."

"Then I guess I'll see everyone Monday morning," she said.

Gideon went out the back door with her, his SUV parked next to her vehicle. "I have somewhere I want to take you," he said. "Some place I need to show you."

"Where?" she said, curious.

"Nope. No previews. You'll see when we get there."

She reclaimed her purse from her car, and he opened the passenger door for her. They drove up to the square and then turned off it, traveling a few blocks before he turned into a cul-de-sac. He parked in the driveway of one of the four houses there and cut his engine.

Turning to her, he asked, "What do you think of it?"

Hope looked at the house, confusion filling her. "It's really nice. Very large. Why are we here?"

"Because it's Dr. Bisch's house." Gideon paused. "Actually, it's my house now."

19

Gideon tried to gauge Hope's reaction. Her brow furrowed in thought.

"So, you bought a house—and didn't think to mention this to me?" she asked.

Her tone did not bode well. He heard both disappointment and doubt.

"It's not actually mine yet," he told her. "I just have first dibs on it before it goes on the market."

Understanding dawned on her face. "That's what you talked to Dr. Bisch about that day. At the diner. You walked out with him, while I went to Walker's office."

"Yes," he admitted. "I knew the Bisches would have to put their house on the market and wanted to see if I could purchase it before they even listed it. In the long run, Dr. Bisch did me a favor and agreed to sit on it for a while."

"Why?" she asked, clearly confused by his response.

"I wanted to run things by you first. You had so much going on at the time, Hope. Buying the practice. Hiring new staff. Meeting with Steve about all the remodeling. I didn't think it was fair to distract you with this."

"With *this*?" she asked, her voice now rising in anger. "I thought we had this conversation before, Gideon. When you hid your marriage and divorce from me."

His own temper flared. "Come on, Hope. Play fair. I told you I wasn't hiding anything. You said you understood. My marriage to Melinda is buried so far in my past, I never even think about it. I *have* been honest with you."

He cleared his throat and stared straight ahead at the house, which he had hoped would be not his.

Theirs...

"Dr. Bisch told me he was making enough from the sale of the clinic that he and Sally could use those funds to buy their new house in College Station, especially since you paid cash for the practice. He agreed to keep the house off the market for a month and give me a chance to show it to you. If you don't like it, I'll tell him that. He can get Tamara Heath to list it tomorrow."

Gideon turned back to Hope, seeing tears misting her eyes. "I told you I'm in this for the long run with you. And as police chief of Sugar Springs, I do need to buy a house and become more settled. I want to do that. With *you*."

"So, is this... a marriage proposal?" she asked quietly.

"In all honesty, Hope, I wanted to ask you to marry me weeks ago because that's how sure I am about you and me. But I thought you would think it was way too soon for me to bring up something like that. I didn't want to rush you. I know your focus now is—has to be—on your professional life. Establishing yourself and Keller Critter Care. I just want you to know that I'm not going anywhere. I'm thinking about a future with you. Buying this house would be a huge step in our relationship."

She was quiet a moment and then said, "Let's go see the inside then."

He took her willingness to look at the house as a small victory as he came to help her out of the SUV. He hadn't meant to hide this from her. Hadn't even looked at it that way. As he offered his hand and she took it, guilt ran through him, though.

Should he also tell her that he knew about her past? Was this the time to mention his digging—or would that drive another wedge between them? He had hoped she would have shared her story with him by now. Maybe, like his divorce, she was done with the past and didn't want to talk about it with him. Ever.

He linked his fingers with hers and led her to the front door. Unlocking it, they stepped into a decent-sized foyer. Gideon watched as Hope looked around with a discerning eye, gazing up at the light fixture, her eyes moving toward the staircase and then back down, studying the floors.

"The floors look to be in good condition," she commented. "They would need to be re-sanded, but if they look this good throughout the rest of the house, that would be a huge savings."

"I'm glad you know about things like this. I told you how Rory had to help me pick out the furniture for my apartment. I have no taste—or knowledge—when it comes to interior design, and I don't know anything about houses since I grew up in a trailer. Dr. Bisch said that the house had good bones, but that I might need to do some updates."

"It definitely needs painting," she said. "I would change the colors outside to a light beige with a dark brown trim because it would go well with the brick." She glanced at the walls. "The inside also could stand to have a new coat of paint."

"Let's walk through and see what you think of the rest of the place. Be honest. I want your frank impression. I've been through it a few times, but other than the layout, I really didn't know what to look for."

They stopped at the office which had French doors and then went to the large family room, which was completely paneled.

"This room is a terrific size, but it's way too dark with all this paneling," Hope told him. "The paneling really dates it. I would tell you to paint the paneling and maybe put in a couple of skylights for more natural light. In fact, I would take out the windows on that wall and put in French doors leading out to the back yard."

"I can see that. It's a great idea."

They moved to the kitchen, and she winced.

"What's wrong?" he asked, not having a clue what bothered her about it.

She opened a cabinet and then closed it again. "These cabinets definitely need to be repainted and new hardware installed on them. The countertops and backsplash are ancient, Gideon."

He had no idea what backsplash might be and supposed it was the tile on the wall beneath the cabinets. Again, his trailer park upbringing did him no favors now.

"What would you do instead?" he asked her, curious.

Hope told him in detail what should be done, even pulling out her cell and calling up a website, showing him a few pictures to illustrate what she meant.

"I can see it better now. I really like those ideas. What else?"

"I would enlarge the island. Make sure it had seating for four instead of two, as it does now. That would add much more storage space. Let's see the rest of the house."

They walked through the entire downstairs, finding a dining room, laundry room, powder room, and the primary suite. Hope made a few suggestions for both bathrooms. Moving upstairs, they saw a loft which could serve as a TV room.

"I see this as a hangout spot for kids," he told her. "A playroom when they're younger and then maybe adding a TV and sofa and loveseat when they're older. That way, they have a place to bring their friends and have a little privacy."

She didn't comment and instead turned, going to see the four bedrooms on that level.

"The Bisches had two kids. A boy and a girl," he said. "Sally told me that one bedroom upstairs served as a guestroom, and the fourth bedroom was for her use. It had her sewing machine and bookshelves. She said it was her retreat from everything, and she read a lot a books and sewed a lot of clothes in it."

"The upstairs looks really good," Hope said. "Again, besides painting, I would update both bathrooms, as well as those two downstairs which I already mentioned. Overall, though, it is a great house with a terrific floorplan. Especially if you want a family."

She went down the stairs, Gideon following her, still unsure about Hope's feelings toward the house—and him.

"We should look at the back yard," she said, finding the door in the kitchen which led outside. "Oh, I wasn't expecting this. A pool and outdoor kitchen? This is a great entertaining space."

"Sally said they spent a lot of time outdoors. Grilling. There's even a pizza oven. I think I would want to put in a firepit in that far corner."

"Yes, that would be the perfect place for it."

She headed back inside, and he locked the door behind him.

"What do you think? Could you see us living here?" He hesitated and then added, "With kids? I know we haven't begun to talk about anything like that, but I do want children, Hope."

He moved to her and slipped his arms around her waist. "Talk to me, babe. I want to hear your thoughts."

Her gaze didn't meet his. Instead, she stared at his chest. "I always wanted to have kids," she said softly. "You know I was an only child. My mom had difficulty getting pregnant and staying that way. She miscarried twice before she had me. Her doctor told her she didn't need to try again after I was born. I always longed for brothers and sisters."

Gideon tilted her chin up until her eyes met his. "Same. I wanted siblings. Always. Do you see a future here with me, Hope Keller? Do you want to build a family—build a life —together?"

"Yes," she said, the word a whisper.

Relief swept through him, and he bent and kissed her softly.

He broke the kiss, but she yanked him down for a more heated one.

The kiss took on a life of its own, and his hunger for her knew no limits. Desire rose within him, filling him. Hope, too, seemed to be swept up by it, her kiss growing more urgent.

He spun her, backing her into the door they had come through minutes ago, his hands bringing hers high over her head, his body pressed against hers.

"I want you," he murmured against her mouth, his lips going to her neck.

"I want you, too," she managed to say, her breath coming in quick spurts.

Releasing her hands, he unfastened his belt. He managed to push his jeans down his thighs, along with his boxer-briefs. His cock stood at full attention as he lifted her tunic top and jerked down her leggings and panties. His fingers slipped inside her, stroking her, finding her already wet for him. Gideon lifted her, and she wrapped her long legs around his waist as he plunged inside her.

Hope moaned in pleasure as he steadied her back against the door and began thrusting in and out of her. Her whimpers grew louder, and as he climaxed, he felt her own orgasm rippling through her. They clung to one another, riding out the pleasure storm, and then his mouth merged with hers once more.

He was never going to let Hope Keller go.

She finally unlocked her legs from him, and he eased her to her feet.

She smiled shyly at him. "Well, that was... unexpected."

They both replaced their clothing. With a wry smile, Gideon said, "I suppose we'll have to buy the place now after christening it like that."

Hope burst into laughter—and Gideon felt everything was right between them again.

He took her hands and said, "I don't expect you to pay for any of this house. You need to focus your funds on the clinic and making it a success. I'm paid a decent salary by the city, and I know it will look better to the citizens of Sugar Springs and show them I'm committed to life here if I'm a homeowner. I would like it, though, if you moved in with me once the work is completed here. No rush. As far as marriage is concerned, we can take our time. I want you to be certain that I'm the one for you before I ever slip a ring on your finger."

Gideon lifted her hand and kissed her knuckles, praying that day would come sooner, rather than later.

She pulled her hands from his and cupped his cheeks. "I thought you were worried about what gossips would say regarding us. If I move in with you, that could cause quite a stir."

"We're adults. If people have a problem with it, it's their problem. Not ours."

Hope tilted her head, studying him a moment. "What if I don't want to move in unless we *are* married?"

It pained him to hear that, but he said, "Then we'll wait until that happens. I still want your advice on how to make this house a home for the two of us. I can wait as long as you want us to, Hope."

A slow smile played about her lips. "What if I said I don't want to wait, Gideon? What if I told you I'm ready to make that commitment to you? To us?"

Joy rippled through him. "Then I suppose I would need to make it official."

He dropped to one knee, again taking her hands in his.

"Hope Keller, my life hasn't been the same since you arrived in Sugar Springs. I never thought I could find someone who understood me so well and who loved me so much. For me, you are simply my everything. I want more than anything to wake up each morning with you in my arms and know that we will always be together.

"Will you marry me?"

She smiled gently. "That question will be my favorite thing that you will ever say to me. That—and all the *I love yous* which will come throughout the years. It's a yes, Gideon. A thousand times yes."

He sprang to his feet and threw his arms around her, kissing the life out of her.

Many minutes later, he broke the kiss, the adrenaline still racing through him.

"Then I guess we getter call Richard and Sally Bisch and tell them we want the house."

Gideon kissed Hope again, grateful he'd returned to Sugar Springs and would embark upon a life with the remarkable woman he would always love.

20

Hope got ready for their trip into Dallas. Knowing they were going to Dante's restaurant after the hockey game and having Googled it and seeing how upscale it was, she now donned dressy black pants and heels, which she rarely wore in her line of work. She paired them with a blouse she had borrowed from Rory, one in Victory green, one of the Dallas Stars' colors. She layered a black blazer over it, one she had found at a boutique store on the square run by a woman named Dahlia. Actually, Hope had purchased several pieces there, knowing her wardrobe outside work was sorely lacking. When she had mentioned that fact to Rory when she borrowed the blouse, her friend had said that they needed to make a shopping trip into Dallas soon. Brynn and Nova were also onboard, and Hope looked forward to a girls' day outing with them.

She had already taken Jake over to Lizzy Lou's. Her landlady had said she would keep the pup for the day and even overnight, winking at Hope. She supposed they would need to announce their engagement soon. Perhaps they might keep it under wraps until she was wearing an engagement ring.

Hearing a knock at the door, Hope went to answer it, finding

Gideon standing there, his raven-black hair windblown and his gray eyes shining with love, making her breath hitch.

He had a brown paper sack with handles in his hand and said, "Can I come in for a minute?"

"Of course," she said, stepping back to allow him entrance to the apartment.

He kissed her and said, "You look beautiful."

"I don't dress up very often. The pets and their owners see me in my white lab coat and flats six days a week, but it is nice to have somewhere to go and spruce up a little bit."

He opened the sack and pulled out two items of clothing, lifting one and holding it up. She saw it was a Dallas Stars jersey and beamed at him.

"That looks to be just my size. Fork it over, Chief."

Shrugging out of her blazer, Hope pulled the jersey over what she wore. It fit perfectly. Gideon also slipped out of the jacket he had on and replaced it with a matching jersey.

"I thought going to your first Stars game that you needed to dress like a true fan. We can take them off before we go into Dante's place."

She wrapped her arms around his waist and kissed him enthusiastically. "Thank you for the gift. And yes, I noticed it had my favorite player's name and number on the back."

"Don't ever accuse me of not listening to you," he teased.

They headed downstairs and were soon on the road to Dallas.

"Hopefully we shouldn't hit much traffic, other than the usual construction along I-20," he said. "Sometimes, I don't think they'll ever be done with it."

On the way, they talked about the house. They had called Dr. Bisch yesterday and told him they were interested in purchasing it. Hope told the veterinarian that they would commit once they had an inspector give them his report. Dr. Bisch had agreed to their request and congratulated them on their future home.

Gideon had called Walker to get a recommendation for a

home inspector, and the attorney passed along the name of the one he and Rory had used when they purchased their home. Gideon had called the inspector immediately, and he had an opening in his schedule on Monday afternoon at four. Gideon would let him in and stay during the inspection, while Hope would leave work and join them in time for the last of it, as well as hearing the inspector's impressions of the house. If things looked good, they would take the next step with Walker, who had been retained by Dr. Bisch to handle the sale.

They reached Dallas, and Hope studied the city, telling Gideon it was the first time she had ever visited it.

"I know these streets well after my years on patrol in several different areas. Besides Dante's, I know a few other great places to eat. We'll have to come back sometime, and I'll take you on a tour down Memory Lane. Show you SMU's campus. The stations where I worked. That kind of thing."

She looked forward to learning more about her fiancé.

They went to a small parking lot, and Gideon gave his name to the attendant. He waved them in, and they parked a stone's throw from the arena before heading inside. Once their tickets had been scanned, Gideon had them walk the entire circle so she could see the arena, and then he led them down to the ice and their seats.

She was amazed when he kept walking to the very bottom of the stairs, seeing they had first-row seats next to the glass.

"How did you manage to pull this off?" she asked, thrilled at the location.

"I've got a connection. The guy who is head of the arena's security team now used to be a Dallas detective. We worked a few cases together, and I called him to see if he could get us some decent tickets and parking. He was happy to do so."

They took their seats, which were halfway between mid-ice and one of the goals. Excitement rippled through her as the players took the ice for their warmups. Gideon's friend stopped by their seats, and Hope thanked him for the tickets and parking.

"Glad to help out an old friend who's gone on to different— and hopefully better—things. How are you liking heading up the force at Sugar Springs, Gideon?"

"It's a lot quieter than working in Dallas, I'll tell you that."

His friend laughed. "I know. I can't believe I fell into this job. The people are incredibly friendly, and I don't have near the headaches when I worked for DPD."

He frowned and touched his hand to his ear, listening. "Excuse me. I've got a little crisis to manage. Nothing serious. Enjoy the game."

The players' introductions sent a chill down Hope's spine, with the music and lights and booming voice of the announcer ramping up her excitement. Dallas claimed ownership of the puck after the first faceoff, and the Stars dominated the Red Wings from the start. She wondered if she might be lucky enough to witness a hat trick in person.

The Stars led 2-1 at the end of the first period, and Hope and Gideon went to stretch their legs, walking the concourse again. They didn't want to get anything to eat or drink since they wanted to save room for their upcoming meal. Gideon did buy her a Stars pennant, though, and they returned to their seats for the second period. Hope was amazed by the velocity when players hit the Plexiglas in front of them. The Dallas captain, her favorite player, scored a goal during that period, thrilling her.

Near the end of the second period, a huge fight broke out in front of them. She saw it grow from a pair of players to more of a two-team brawl in an instant.

Gideon nudged her, and she looked to him. He pointed to the left of them, and she saw the Stars captain standing apart from the fight, his lips twitching in amusement as he knocked the puck around with his stick, flipping it into the air several times.

Then the hockey player's gaze met hers, and she swallowed

nervously. He grinned at her and used his stick to flip the puck again. This time, however, it sailed high into the air and over the glass. Instinctively, she leaped to her feet and caught it.

Smiling, she waved it at him and shouted, "Thank you," seeing he mouthed, "You're welcome."

By then, the referees had broken up the skirmish. Four players were sent to the penalty box. The period ended with Dallas leading 4-2.

She watched the Zamboni driver glide along, resurfacing the ice, and Gideon teased her about the captain awarding the puck to her, saying, "I should hang a sign around your neck saying you're taken."

Hope laughed. "That's what a ring will do, Chief Ross."

"What kind of engagement ring would you like?" he asked. "That's something we need to talk about."

"Nothing flashy," she told him. "In fact, I'm almost leaning toward not having one. I don't wear any rings now because it's easier to pull surgical gloves on and off, which I do numerous times a day, changing with each examination I perform."

"So, no engagement ring? What about a wedding band? Would you wear that?"

"I think I'd like a thin, white-gold band," she told him. "Maybe a few diamonds in it?"

He leaned over and kissed her. "Babe, if you wanted it, I'd lasso the moon and slip it on your finger. Maybe we can go ring shopping in Tyler next weekend."

"What about you?" she countered. "Will you wear a wedding ring?"

He grinned. "Sure. I want all those women who come on to me because of the uniform to know I'm taken."

Hope punched him playfully in the arm. "Should we make any kind of announcement regarding our engagement? Put something in the local newspaper?"

He slipped an arm around her shoulder. "Let's just keep it

between you and me for now. Maybe once we get the house ready and you move in, we can let people know then."

Play started again, and Dallas went on a shooting spree, knocking in three goals within a five-minute period, all made by their premier forward who'd just been signed to a lengthy contract extension. The Stars won the game 7-2, and Hope couldn't stop talking about having seen a live hat trick.

They left the arena and headed back to Gideon's SUV, where they both removed their team jerseys and slipped into their jackets. She fluffed her hair when she got into the car and asked where Dante's restaurant was located.

"It's in an area called Uptown. Not too far from here."

"Mrs. Romano was tickled that we were coming. She seems very proud of her son."

"Dante was the kid who always wanted to get out of a small town," Gideon said. "He trained at some big culinary school and then worked at a few restaurants in Dallas before opening his own place a few months back. His sister also cooks in Dallas. She's a sous chef at a pretty impressive steakhouse."

They arrived at the restaurant at a quarter till six, entering and giving their name to the hostess.

Her eyes lit up. "You'll be at the chef's table this evening," she said. "Please follow me."

Hope admired the sleek, elegant décor and black and white modern furnishings as they moved through the restaurant.

They had barely been seated when a good-looking man in his early thirties appeared at their table. He had jet-black hair and lively amber eyes and one of the best smiles she had ever seen. She thought immediately that he was probably a player as he turned on his charm.

"Good evening, Gideon. Or should I say Chief Ross?" He turned his gaze upon Hope. "And this must be the enchanting Dr. Keller. My mom has sung your praises."

"Thank you for having us this evening. My friend Rory tells

me your restaurant is quite popular, and it's hard to book a table here. I'm glad you could accommodate us."

"Mom would have had my head if I hadn't given you the best seat in house," Dante said, laughing. "Would you allow me to let you dine from the chef's menu tonight?"

"We're in your hands," Gideon told the chef. "I know you have to do more than basic spaghetti and lasagna. I'm looking forward to seeing what you'll cook for us."

"Thank you for trusting me regarding your choices. My sister's, as well. She will be assisting me."

Dante turned. "Ah, here she is now. Dr. Keller, this is my little sister, who is almost as much a genius in the kitchen as I am. Viviana Romano, Dr. Hope Keller."

The vivacious woman smiled at her. She had the same dark hair and amber eyes as her older brother and was extremely attractive.

"It's so nice to meet you, Dr. Keller."

"Please, I'm Hope outside the clinic."

"Mom said you've made quite a stir. Buying Dr. Bisch's practice—and snagging the most eligible bachelor in town." Viviana turned to Gideon. "It's good to see you, Gideon. We haven't talked since homecoming last October. Congratulations on solving that nasty serial killer case."

She turned back to Hope. "Gideon was quite the rock star at the Dallas Police Department. His name was in the newspaper all the time. I guess you've already realized that you've got a good one in him."

Gideon's hand took hers beneath the table as Hope said, "I know just how lucky I am."

"Enough chitchat," Dante declared. "Vivi will be doing appetizers for you under my direction."

"Give me a few minutes, and I'll be back—and hopefully, I'll knock off your socks."

Vivi left them, and Dante said, "I'm trying to sweet talk my sister into coming to work for me. She works at her steakhouse Tuesdays through Saturdays and has been graciously giving me her time on Sunday evenings for a couple of months. I think I'll have to fight my parents over her, though."

Intrigued, Hope asked, "Why so?"

"First, I doubt I could ever land Vivi. We love each other very much, but like true siblings, we can fight like cats and dogs sometimes. I think it would be hard for her to work in my kitchen on a full-time basis because she has a fiery spirit and too many ideas of her own she wishes to implement."

"Has she ever thought about opening her own restaurant as you have?" Gideon asked.

"No, her finances are in abysmal shape." He shrugged. "But my parents are trying to convince Vivi to return to Sugar Springs and take over Romano's for them."

"They're retiring?" Hope asked, surprised by that news.

"They've worked six days a week for decades now. Long, long days. While they've enjoyed serving their food to the residents of Sugar Springs, they're ready to kick back and enjoy life. Mama wants Pops to take her to the old country for an extended trip. They want to seek out their Italian relatives and bask in the Tuscan sun."

"Do you think they would move there permanently?" Gideon asked.

Dante laughed. "That's Mama's plan. I say, not a chance. The moment Vivi or I get married, they'll have visions of grandchildren dancing in their heads. They might go live in Italy for a year or two, but East Texas has been home to them for too long."

"Do you or your sister have any marriage plans?" Hope asked.

The chef laughed heartily. "Vivi was living with someone, and I thought they would eventually marry, even though I didn't think he treated her right. He died—and she hasn't dated since his death. Frankly, I think it would be good for her if she did return to our hometown and take over Romano's, even if just for a change of scenery. She's told me some of the ideas she would implement if that occurred. But Viv's reluctant to do so, thinking it might be a step back after having cooked at such a prestigious restaurant in a large city."

"She would do more than pizza?" Gideon probed. "I hope she wouldn't take pizza off the menu. I live for Romano's pizza."

"No," Dante assured them. "Vivi would never do that. The name Romano and pizza go hand-in-hand in Sugar Springs. We'll see if she decides to take up my parents' offer or not. As for me? I'm a single man in a city which attracts beautiful women. I have zero plans of settling down anytime soon. And on that note, I have customers to cook for. I will leave you in the hands of my excellent sommelier. He knows what you will be served tonight on the chef's menu and can make recommendations for you."

Dante took his leave, and the sommelier stepped forward from where he had hovered in the background. He described a few different wines for them. Gideon passed, saying he was driving, but told Hope to indulge in whatever she wanted.

She chose a half-bottle of a recommended red blend, saying she would limit herself to two glasses. Once the wine arrived and she sipped it, she told Gideon he had to at least sample it. He did so.

"That *is* good." He paused, smiling at her. "But I'm sure I'll be tasting it on you later tonight."

A hot blush heated her cheeks at his suggestive words. "We'll see about that, Chief."

Hope sipped her wine as they spoke, and a quarter-hour later, Vivi appeared with a server carrying a tray.

"I have your *antipasti*—your appetizers," Vivi said. As the server placed the starters on the table, she pointed to each. "This is mozzarella *caprese*, a staple in any Italian restaurant. It's a house-made mozzarella, along with tomato and basil."

"I'd be happy with this alone," Gideon said, "but what else am I seeing?"

"Here is *polipo alla Griglia,* grilled octopus with freshly-sliced tomato, capers, cannellini beans, and olive oil." Pointing at the final plate, she added, "The last appetizer is *Parmigiana di Melanzane e Zucchine,* which is eggplant and zucchini parmigiana with mozzarella, topped with tomato sauce."

"I see a theme with all that mozzarella," Gideon teased.

"We Italians do love our mozzarella," Vivi declared. "Enjoy!"

They ate the appetizers, Hope sighing and murmuring with each bite. Gideon declared them the best he'd ever eaten in an Italian restaurant. Vivi checked on them and was pleased they had enjoyed their *antipasti.*

"Dante is about to bring you your *primi piatti*—first course," she told the couple.

The same server accompanied Dante, who walked them through that course. It consisted of one dish of pasta cooked in tinfoil with porcini mushrooms, cherry tomatoes, breadcrumbs and shaved *Parmigiano Reggiano.* The second was composed of grilled octopus, fava beans, and clams mixed with ear-shaped pasta. The final dish was an unusual tubular spaghetti in a creamy zucchini sauce, and *parmigiana,* with a touch of herbs and tomato sauce.

"This is all so fantastic," she told Dante after they had finished the course.

"Your *secondi piatti* will arrive shortly," he told them, retreating to the kitchen again.

"I'm glad we have a little bit of a break between courses," Gideon said. "I'm already getting full."

The next time Dante returned, he brought two veal dishes, one a veal chop *parmigiana,* breaded and pan fried, and the other a veal *scaloppini,* served with thinly sliced potatoes and porcini mushrooms. Her favorite, though, was a surprise—a grilled half-rabbit sauteed with rosemary, spinach, potatoes, and carrots.

Hope told Dante, "I've never eaten rabbit before. I was a little leery when you described the dish because I have rabbits as patients, but it was simply delicious. In fact, everything was."

Vivi appeared. "Are you ready for some dessert?"

Gideon groaned. "I know we were served smaller portions because of the variety of foods we sampled, but I am stuffed, Vivi." He looked to Dante. "This was absolutely the best meal I have ever eaten. No wonder your restaurant is doing so well."

"Everything was fabulous, Dante," she added. "And your *antipasti*, too, Vivi. As much as I love a good dessert, I think I'm going to have to pass, too."

"Then you must come back for dessert and coffee another time," Dante declared. "May I take your picture? I told Mama I would send it to her."

He did so, and then the server took his camera, having Dante and Vivi get in the picture as well, the four packed tightly into the tiny booth.

"Thank you," Dante said to the server. "Mama will be happy that you enjoyed yourself. Dinner is on her tonight."

"What? No, Dante, we need to pay for our meal," protested Gideon.

"And offend my mother?" he asked. "Never. She has taken to Hope, and she's always liked you, Gideon."

"Then I will be certain to tip handsomely," Gideon said. "Thanks for a fabulous meal, both of you. It was good seeing you again."

They left the restaurant, Vivi hugging them goodbye and Dante shaking their hands. In the car, Hope slipped off her jacket and shook her head.

"I'm glad you're the one driving home. I don't think I could even press my foot to the gas pedal. I can't remember the last time I ate so much, much less food so tasty. That was nice of Mrs. Romano to pay for our meal. We'll need to stop by and see her soon."

"How about pizza after the inspection tomorrow? It's supposed to last about two-and-a-half to three hours."

Hope groaned. "I don't know if I'll have room for pizza by then. I'm definitely not jumping out of bed tomorrow morning to go run."

Gideon took her hand, threading his fingers through hers. "Skip breakfast and lunch. You'll be plenty hungry by dinner, come tomorrow. That meal will have stretched our bellies to the limit. We'll be starved for pizza."

They drove home in comfortable silence, happy to be in one another's company. Gideon walked Hope to her door and kissed her sweetly.

"I'm going home now," he told her. "I've got a meeting tomorrow which I need to prepare for. I'll see you at the house after work tomorrow. If all goes well, I'll let Dr. Bisch know and give Walker the go-ahead. I'll need to meet with Gene Smith at the bank. He's a VP and chief loan officer. After that, what do you think about Steve Pillar taking on the remodeling job? You seemed pleased by his work at the clinic."

"Steve would be the perfect choice," she agreed, running her hands along his arms. "Are you sure you don't want to stay over?"

"Your offer is tempting, Dr. Keller, but duty calls." He kissed her again. "I'll see you tomorrow."

Hope unlocked her door and stepped inside. Turning, she watched him descend the stairs and get into his SUV. She raised a hand, waving goodbye to him, thinking she was the luckiest woman in the world to have found such a good, decent man.

And bonus points for him also being the hottest guy she'd ever met.

She got ready for bed and was about to turn off the light when her phone received a text. She picked it up.

I had a wonderful time today, Dr. Keller. All I need to do now is get you in a Dallas Cowboys jersey. Or maybe out of one. Let me work on that. ILY.

HOPE TEXTED BACK A FLIRTY REPLY, ending with ILY2. She set her cell on its wireless charger and turned off the light on the nightstand.

It had been a perfect day with the perfect guy. She didn't know if life could get any better than it was right now and then decided each day with Gideon Ross would be better than the day before.

21

G ideon left his office and headed down to roll call. He had learned of a couple of burglaries which had occurred over the weekend and wanted to address his patrol officers regarding them.

He slipped into the back row, nodding at Sergeant Brown, who began the daily briefing. After the usual housekeeping tasks, the patrol commander made his daily assignments and told the patrolmen present about the dual break-ins, citing that it happened to two houses which sat back-to-back.

"The residents in these two houses are good friends, and the families had gone away together for the weekend. They returned last night to find their houses had been burgled."

Brown gave the officers the details they knew, including the fact that only electronics and prescription drugs from the medicine cabinets had been taken.

"Detective Douglas will have his team at both houses this morning," the sergeant continued. "Crime Scene will be dusting for prints and seeing what they might turn up. The families stayed in the homes of friends last night, so the scenes are pristine."

Gideon rose then and went to the front of the room, standing next to the podium instead of behind it. He didn't like any barrier between him and his trained officers.

"Both of these families had members who admitted they had put their plans to be gone on social media. We're never going to be able to get around this, folks. No matter how many times we warn the public not to broadcast their plans to be away, someone invariably does so in advance. Or even posts pictures of wherever they are, giving the criminal element a heads up as to which houses are open season.

"I'll be meeting with Detective Douglas and his team after they've gone over the scenes themselves and interviewed potential witnesses later today. But I want you to keep your eyes open. Be alert to anything different you see or hear in the community. Sometimes, it's those small things that cause us to pause a moment and reflect, which helps solve a case of this nature in the long run. Dismissed."

He spotted the force's only rookie, Scott Winkindale, and called out, "Officer Winkindale. A word."

The patrolman looked startled but tried to compose himself as he made his way toward his boss. Gideon moved to the side of the room as officers were filing out, Winkindale following him. The room cleared quickly.

He looked at the young rookie, who was a Sugar Springs native and former army recruit who had served his country and now, at twenty-four, was ready to serve in his hometown.

He led with, "You're not in trouble, Officer Winkindale."

Relief filled the rookie's face. "I was hoping I wasn't, Chief. I know I have my six-month review coming up next week."

Chief Hamilton had left notes on Winkindale, all of them praising his early performance on the job. Sergeant Brown and Deputy Chief Pete Blest seconded the former chief's opinion. Gideon, who had met with each of the thirty sworn officers, three detectives, and those in civilian positions during his first month in charge already would put Officer Winkindale in his top ten percent as far as eagerness, loyalty, and duty were concerned.

"I think you'll be pleased at your eval meeting with me next week," Gideon told the young patrolman, "but I want to address something a little more personal with you now."

"Sir?

"You're from Sugar Springs, Officer. You know how everyone in town knows your business practically before you do. Like the fact that you have been seeing a pretty, third grade teacher at the elementary school for a couple of months now."

The tips of Winkindale's ears pinkened. "I have, Chief."

"And I know, too, that you're still living with your folks."

"Yes, since I got out of the army. Trying to save money. As a matter of fact, I told my mom just last night that I thought it was time to move out. Nelda and I need some privacy. We're getting pretty serious."

"Maybe I can help you out then. You might have heard that I recently purchased the Bisches' place."

The rookie grinned. "Yes, Chief. Gossip works both ways, including that you are serious about Dr. Keller."

Gideon ignored that observation. "I will need to give up the apartment I've been subleasing from Cole Johnson, the football coach at the high school. I was wondering if you might want to step in and take on the apartment as yours. The lease runs through the end of July. Since Coach Johnson is already married, he won't be renewing it."

He named the monthly rent and then to sweeten the pot, Gideon added, "I would be willing to throw in the little furniture I have there. It would come with a bed and dresser. A couple of barstools. A sofa and coffee table. But the TV would be coming with me."

Officer Winkindale now beamed. "That would be terrific, Chief, but I don't want to take advantage of you."

"You wouldn't be. I am going to have help picking out the

furnishings for my new house. This would give you a chance to get a start of your own. Are you interested?"

"You bet I am," the patrolman said enthusiastically.

Gideon pulled out his phone. "I'm texting you the address and apartment number so you can swing by on your lunch break and check it out."

He removed his keys from his pocket and slid the one to the apartment off his key ring. Handing it to Officer Winkindale, he said, "No pressure. Make your decision and let me know. If you don't take it, I'll need to look for someone else to step in and finish out the lease."

"Let me stop you there, Chief," the rookie said. "I know I'm going to like it, and I'm going to love having some furniture to start out with. I'll still go by and look at it today but count on me to finish out the lease."

The rookie left to join his partner for their shift, and Gideon headed to his office. Cyndi was already at her desk and greeted him.

His phone sounded, and he saw a text from Walker had come in.

Have time to meet at the diner for breakfast?

He texted a thumbs up and added he would head there now. That was one thing he liked about being his own boss. He could take time for something like this, and it never hurt to be seen out and about in the community. It was guaranteed he would speak to the majority of the patrons at Ida Lou's this morning, be it a simple hello or listening to a problem or concern they might want to share with him.

"I'm heading out to the diner, Cyndi," he told his admin.

When Gideon arrived at the diner, he saw that Walker hadn't arrived yet.

Ida Lou greeted him, and he said, "Table for two. Walker will be joining me."

She seated him only after he'd stopped to visit with three different tables. He waved away the menus, saying, "Coffee and water for both of us. We'll order when Walker gets here."

His friend appeared at the door and spotted Gideon, joining him in the booth.

"Glad you had time to meet for breakfast," Walker said. "We've both been busy the last few weeks. I'm glad we can catch up."

Ida Lou returned with their drinks, and the two men ordered.

"How is the house coming along?"

Gideon said, "We're actually doing a walk-through during our lunch hour today with Steve. He's finished up on all the construction projects and cosmetic changes. We're there to check the final work and sign a very large check over to him."

"I know the inspector's report didn't have any red flags. At least you didn't mention anything more than the renovation Steve's been doing."

"The only thing the inspector recommended we see about was a new water heater. The current one is seven years old, and when he asked how many people would be living in the house, I told him I was hoping to fill a couple of those bedrooms in the near future. He recommended anything between fifty and eighty gallons." He grinned. "I went with the eighty. Always pays to be prepared. That's already gone in. We'll wait on the HVAC system. It's nine years old, but the inspector said it was in good working condition."

"Sounds like things are serious between you and Hope," Walker observed.

They had yet to tell anyone they'd become engaged since they had purchased the house and had the updates worked on the past few weeks.

He now said, "We're getting married. We haven't told anyone yet. Don't have any wedding plans or even a date. Our focus has been getting the house ready for us to move in together."

Walker's smile told Gideon how pleased his friend was at the news. "Congratulations, my friend. I'll keep this under my hat—even from Rory. And you know that'll kill me."

"I'll let Hope know that I told you today. I'm sure she'll want to share the good news with Rory. For now, though, keep it quiet if you would."

Ida Lou set their plates in front of them. "Enjoy breakfast, fellas."

Once she left, Walker said, "There actually is a point to this breakfast meeting."

Gideon stopped buttering his toast, instinctively knowing what his best friend would say next.

"It's something we're not letting the general public know just yet. We have told my parents and Granny Bea, however." Walker beamed. "We're going to be parents come the very end of October."

He smiled broadly. Quietly, he said, "Congratulations to both of you. You're going to be amazing parents. And a Halloween baby. That'll be fun."

Walker's smile turned wicked. "Actually, it looks like two Halloween babies. The sonogram showed it'll be twins."

He held his reaction in check, not wanting to draw the attention of those around them. "That is wonderful news, Walker," he said with a straight face. "I can't think of anything better. How is Rory feeling? I haven't seen her in a couple of weeks."

"Oh, pretty miserable. Mornings are a challenge, to say the least. But once she's thrown up a few times, she feels pretty decent. She is extremely tired when she gets home from school every day, though. She's even been taking a nap then. I'm on

dinner duty while she grades papers and does her lesson planning. We eat. Talk a little. She curls up next to me, and we watch a
show on TV—and then she is out for the count. I've had to carry
her to bed several times over the last two weeks."

"It will be a good thing she's resigning at the end of the year. It
would be hard to teach full-time with newborn twins. When will
she hand in her resignation to Joe Bob?"

"Actually, she's doing that this morning. She won't mention
the babies. She'll simply tell him about wanting to pursue her
clothing line. I don't think he'll be surprised."

They finished their meal, and Walker said, "Maybe the two of
you could come over this weekend for dinner." He chuckled. "An
early dinner. The weather is getting nicer. We could cook out
some steaks or burgers."

"That sounds good. Just let us know if Rory is up to it."

"Let's plan for Saturday at five," his friend said. "If Rory hasn't
seen Hope by then, that will give them a chance to swap their
good news with one another."

Gideon returned to the station and met with his detective
team mid-morning, getting an update on the burglaries. He also
worked on the evaluation for Scott Winkindale next week,
wanting to get it out of the way.

A little before noon, the rookie texted him, telling Gideon
that the apartment was ideal and to count him in. He was
relieved, having one more item checked off his to-do list.

He left the station at noon to meet their contractor at the
house. Hope texted that a small emergency had come up at the
clinic and that he should go ahead and begin the walk-through
without her.

Pulling up at the same time as Steve, they walked up the front
sidewalk together. Gideon couldn't but feel a sense of pride,
knowing this place now belonged to Hope and him and that they
would be starting their family soon. She had already gone off her
birth control pills in preparation for that.

"Hope's running a little behind at the clinic," he told Steve. "She said for us to go ahead, and she'll catch up."

Steve led him through the house, pointing out what his crew had done in each of the rooms. Nothing was much of a surprise since he and Hope had visited the house several times during the last three weeks of renovations. Gideon was pleased with the paint job on both the inside and outside, as well as the updates to all the bathrooms. Most of the money had been poured into the kitchen, which now gleamed. He didn't care what it had cost. He wanted to make his fiancée happy.

"Hope is going to be very pleased with your work," he told Steve.

The contractor chuckled. "She's turned into my best customer this year."

"I'm afraid this is going to be it for now, Steve," Hope said, joining them in the kitchen. She glanced around as Steve asked, "What do you think?"

"I think that this will be my favorite room in the entire house," she replied, smiling.

Gideon moved to greet her, brushing his lips against her cheek, whispering, "And here I thought the bedroom would be your favorite."

She blushed profusely as Steve led them from the kitchen. They went through what remained of the house with the contractor. After they had seen all the completed work, Gideon offered Steve his hand.

"You do nice work, Steve. Tell your crew thank you from us."

"Will do. Glad that you're happy with what we've done. You were right about those skylights, Hope. They really brighten up this room. I'll be sending along my final bill since you aren't asking for any adjustments."

"And I'll add another review to your website," Hope promised.

"Let me do that," Gideon volunteered. "That way, people visiting the site won't think you're Steve's only customer."

They all laughed, and Steve took his leave.

Gideon's arms encircled Hope. "Well, we've done it, Dr. Keller. We've got a dream house to move into. We just need to schedule a wedding now. I know it takes women a long time to pull things together. All the dresses and flowers. That kind of stuff. I hope you'll consider moving in with me while all that planning is going on."

She looped her arms around his neck. "I was never one of those little girls who always dreamed about her wedding. I don't need weeks or months of planning, Gideon. All I ever need is you by my side."

Excitement shot through him, thinking Hope would soon be his. He gave her a long, slow, very thorough kiss.

When he broke it, he said, "Then I think we need to apply for our marriage license as soon as possible."

"You're the lawman. I'm sure you know the specifics. Do you think we could manage to get married this weekend? Grab Walker and Rory as witnesses?"

"If that's what you want, babe, I'm happy to have a courthouse wedding. Of course, we need to check on our furniture deliveries. Here in town and in Tyler."

"I don't need a bed to move in, Gideon. A sleeping bag will do. One that I'm happy to share with you," she said flirtatiously, skimming a finger down his chest.

"Why don't we grab a pizza and go to my place? At least I still have a bed there for a while. Not for long, though. I arranged for that rookie cop to take over my sublease. Which reminds me, I need to let Cole know that. Winkindale will be good for the rent. After all, he knows I'd come looking for him if he didn't pay on time. No one wants to get on the chief's bad side, least of all the lowest man on the totem pole."

"Call in the pizza then," she urged. "And more mushrooms

this time, please."

He kissed her, hard and swift. "I think you just might turn into a mushroom with as many as you eat, Dr. Keller."

"There are worse things in life than mushrooms," she said airily, pulling away from him and claiming her purse. "I'll see you at your place."

Gideon called in their pizza order, Mrs. Romano laughing when he requested extra mushrooms.

"I know who rules the roost these days," she teased.

Half an hour later, he and Hope were seated on his sofa, indulging in a large sausage and mushroom pizza.

And hopefully, they would indulge in a passionate round of lovemaking afterward.

Her cell rang. "Sorry, I better get it." She rose and went to her purse.

"No need to explain. We've both got jobs which don't end at the end of the day. I just hope everything is all right."

Hope removed her phone from her purse. Her eyes widened as she looked at it. Gideon wondered who was calling her because of her reaction.

"Do you mind if I step inside your bedroom?" she asked, the color draining from her face.

"Whatever you need, babe. And I'm here."

She moved into his bedroom and closed the door. He worried about her reaction as she saw the Caller ID. He tried to eat another bite of pizza, but he'd lost interest and set down the slice, anxiously awaiting for her to emerge.

When she did, her face was flushed with color, and he felt the anger vibrating from her.

"What's wr—"

Hope slapped him so hard, Gideon saw stars.

Without having to ask, he knew exactly who had been on the other line.

And what she had heard.

22

Hope was horrified by what she had just done—and yet felt justified after discovering Gideon's hideous betrayal. She took a step back from him, needing to put distance between them.

"Hope, I can explain— "

"You wanting to explain lets me know you guessed who was on the other end of the line. You've deceived me. Betrayed my trust in you."

He flushed guiltily. "Yes, I figure that had to be Dr. Waldman on the other end of the line."

"It was. My old boss. But then you knew that already, didn't you?"

Nausea roiled through her as her world fell apart. "He wanted to check with me because he was confused. The Bisches came to Houston this weekend to visit their grandchildren. Naturally, they got together with Dr. Waldman and his wife since the two men are such good friends. Somehow, it came up about you contacting Dr. Waldman."

Hope crossed her arms defensively in front of her. "*You* lied, Gideon. You made up some crazy story so that Dr. Bisch would give you Dr. Waldman's name. And then you pursued it after that, calling him under false pretenses."

"I'm not blameless, Hope. I understand that. I get why you're so angry."

"Do you?" she asked, her voice rising in hysteria. "Oh, I suppose you do," she said sarcastically. "Because you know exactly who I am. And you have known pretty much ever since I arrived in Sugar Springs."

He raked his fingers through his hair in frustration. "Blame it on my cop instincts. I was attracted to you—intrigued by you— from the moment we met. I hadn't seen a woman, much less been interested in one, in a long time. So, I did what most single people do in these circumstances. I Googled you. And nothing came up. Absolutely nothing. These days, no digital footprint waves a pretty big red flag. I wondered who you were. Why you had come here. I wanted to learn about you. I even thought maybe you were in witness protection. And once I did discover the truth, I kept it to myself. No one else in town knows, Hope. I promise. Not even Walker."

"You lied to find out what you wanted to learn, Gideon. You used your status as a cop to do so."

He looked at her, tears swimming in his gray eyes. "I have never lied to you, Hope. I wanted you to trust me enough to share with me about your past. I didn't want to bring it up. I wanted *you* to bring it up to me. Frankly, I pretty much had forgotten about it. Because I fell in love with you. With *you*—not the you of your past—but the you that you are now. Hope Keller. Sugar Springs veterinarian.

"And the love of my life."

His words stabbed her in the heart. She refused to let her anger dissipate and listen to romantic gibberish from him. For once, Gideon Ross wouldn't be able to charm himself out of a mess.

"I changed my name for a reason. A very good reason. To

escape the horrors in my past. But you already know about those. I'm sure once you wormed the name Deb Busby out of Dr. Wallman, you used all the resources at your fingertips to learn about my history. My past."

"I did search your name," he admitted. "I discovered what you had gone through with Cris Calder. How he cost you your job. How he murdered your parents."

She winced, still sensitive to the topic.

"I barely knew you, but I did know you were someone I wanted to pursue a relationship with. A name is just a name, Hope. I don't care if you're Deb or Hope. I love you. *You*."

"You went behind my back, Gideon. You learned my parents had been murdered. I didn't want anyone here to know about that. I wanted to make a fresh start in Sugar Springs." She laughed bitterly. "I even took the name Hope because I hoped that I would have a better life in the future. Keller came from Helen Keller because she's such an inspiring person. A woman who accomplished the impossible, rising above her multiple disabilities to become one of the leading figures of her time."

Hope squeezed her eyes shut, wishing she could vanish. But she was a mature adult. She would face this crisis head on.

Even though beneath her anger, her heart was breaking.

Opening her eyes, she said, "I should have realized it would all come out. I was a fool to believe I could begin again. That I could make a life with you."

He stepped toward her, clasping her elbows. "We can still do that, Hope. I love you. You love me. It doesn't matter what happened in our pasts. It's our present and future which concerns me."

She jerked away, again taking a few steps back. "How can I love you when I don't even trust you, Gideon? Get it through your thick skull. You *lied* to me."

"I never lied to you, Hope," he reiterated.

She snorted. "That's just semantics. It was a lie of omission." Her gaze bore into him. "And it's a lie I can't forgive. Or forget."

Hope spun around and went to her purse, tossing her phone inside and slipping the strap over her shoulder. When she turned, he was there. His fingers dug into her shoulders, and his mouth went down on hers, desperation in his kiss.

But Hope was through with kissing this man. With being with him.

She turned her head and pushed against his chest at the same time, saying, "Let go of me," not bothering to disguise her bitterness and disappointment.

She counted on the fact that above all else, Gideon Ross was a gentleman.

He released her, stepping back, misery on his face.

"Hope, I will do whatever it takes to make this right between us again."

Her eyes narrowed. "There is no more us, Gideon. You saw to that. This engagement is off. It's a good thing we didn't announce it after all. I don't want to ever speak to you again."

Hope turned and rushed out the door, running to her car, hoping, praying, that Gideon wouldn't follow.

And yet hoping he might.

She reached her car and unlocked it, climbing quickly inside and locking the doors. Looking out her windshield, she saw he stood at his apartment's door, anguish on his face. Filled with resolve, she turned away, starting her car and driving home. Her entire body trembled so badly that at one point, she had to pull over and try and calm herself, afraid she would lose control of the steering wheel if she didn't.

Once she did, she managed to drive the rest of the way home, tears pouring down her cheeks. She climbed the stairs to her apartment and entered, where Jake greeted her, his tail wagging happily.

Scooping up the beagle, she went to the sofa and collapsed,

sobbing heavily now as she buried her face in the dog's fur. Hope cried as she never had before, even more tears than when she had learned of her parents' murders. This was similar. The death of her relationship with Gideon. She had pinned all her hopes on him, looking forward to the life they would live together. With kids. In this community.

How could she stay in Sugar Springs after this breakup?

She would have to. She had no choice. She had invested in a business, and she now had people who depended upon her. Sugar Springs was a small town. She wouldn't be able to avoid seeing or hearing about Gideon, but she would have to remain here. Too much money and time had been invested in her veterinary practice to up and sell so quickly.

Besides, Hope was tired of running. She had run from Houston and all the terrible memories created by Cris Calder. She had run from being Deb Busby and the life she had known.

Well, she liked Sugar Springs, Gideon Ross or no Gideon Ross. And she would stay. She worried, though, that the friends she had made would abandon her. Take his side. That would hurt the most. She already felt as if she had found a sister in Rory, and she was growing close to both Nova and Brynn. She would have to leave that social circle and look for friends elsewhere. For now, though, she would need to look after herself. The dreams which had almost become a reality would now be locked away, pushed to the far recesses of her mind. She was an adult. She owned her own business. She would get through this without turning into a hot mess.

But just for tonight, while she was alone with Jake, Hope would mourn the loss of Gideon. As she cried, she somehow knew she would never love another man again.

~

GIDEON CLOSED the door to his apartment. It took all his willpower not to slam his fist through the wall. His life had gone to hell in a handbasket in a single moment.

It was true what he had told Hope. After initially learning her true identity and why she might want to make a clean break with her past, he had put it out of his mind. Instead, he had gotten to know Hope Keller, not Deb Busby, and he had fallen in love with Hope. He realized now the mistake he had made. He should have told Hope what he had learned. It could have led to her ending their relationship early on, but she might have given him a second chance after some thought.

Now, Gideon knew there would be no second chances for him. For them.

Despair filled him, haunting him and the choices he had made. He didn't want to be in Sugar Springs anymore. Coming home and taking over as chief of police in his hometown had been his ideal career move. Now, however, living in a town with Hope—and without her in his life—soured the dream.

He went to his phone and called Walker, needing his old friend more than he ever had.

"Hey, buddy, what's up?"

"I fucked up royally. With Hope."

Immediately, Walker said, "Come over, Gid. Now."

He was silent a moment and then finally murmured, "Okay."

Somehow, he drove to Walker's house, wondering how he had even gotten there when he arrived. As he turned into the driveway, he saw Walker standing on the porch.

His friend came toward the car. Gideon rolled down the window.

"Would you like to come in?" Walker asked quietly. "Or we can just sit in the car and talk. Whatever you want."

Gideon motioned for Walker to come around, and he did so, climbing into the SUV. Neither man said anything for a good five minutes.

Finally, Walker asked, "What happened, Gid? If you talk it out, we can find a solution."

"There is no solution," he hissed angrily. "I screwed up, Walker. I did the one thing Hope could never forgive me for."

Walker placed a hand on Gideon's shoulder and squeezed. "Things may look dark now, but don't give up hope."

He laughed harshly. "I've already given up Hope. Or rather, she's given up on me."

"Then talk about it," Walker urged. "Tell me what happened."

"I'll say all of this to you in confidence. You as my attorney. I don't want you sharing this with Rory or anyone else."

"Agreed. Go on, Gid."

He began at the beginning, explaining how he had been drawn to Hope and couldn't find anything about her, which puzzled him.

"She seemed to have appeared out of nowhere, with a glowing reference from the previous vet she had worked for. I was taken with her. Dr. Bisch was obviously taken with her, professionally. So, in cop mode, I started digging."

Gideon explained the channels he had gone through, trying to find information about Dr. Hope Keller and how she hadn't existed anywhere.

"Then I told this crazy lie to Dr. Bisch, in order for him to give me the name of the vet Hope had worked for previously. I called this Dr. Waldman, who was in Houston, and identified myself as a police chief. That must have scared him into betraying any promise he made to Hope about keeping her identity secret. Waldman explained that Hope had worked for him under a different name and that she had legally changed hers after she left his practice. The only reason she shared this with her former boss was because she'd put out résumés and knew she would need Waldman's recommendation to land another position at a veterinary clinic or animal hospital."

"So, this Dr. Waldman had agreed not to reveal who she was to prospective employers?" Walker asked.

"Apparently so, but here I was, the law. Waldman gave me Hope's original name, and I thanked him. Naturally, I began scouring the Internet for any information about her that I could find." He blew out a long breath. "I found a wealth of it."

Gideon explained who Hope had been previously and how a man had stalked her. How her refusal of Cris Calder's advances had led him to murder her parents. How after a lengthy trial a year after the murders occurred, Calder was found guilty and sentenced to prison.

Walker whistled. "No wonder Hope wanted to change her name and escape her past. Did you tell her this tonight, Gid? Did you want to come clean about knowing who she was since you were going to be married?"

"No," he said miserably, feeling the loss of Hope all over again. "I really had forgotten Hope was Deb Busby before she arrived in Sugar Springs. I fell in love with who she is, Walker, and not her name. Apparently, the Bisches got together with the Waldmans this weekend. The two vets, who are longtime friends, going back to vet school, must have got to talking about Hope. I'm not sure what the conversation was, but something triggered Waldman, and he called Hope tonight to discuss it."

"And she is angry at you," his friend observed.

"Angry doesn't even begin to describe her reaction. She went ballistic. I've never seen someone so angry, Walker. She's hurt. Feeling betrayed. She ended things with me because she feels I lied to her by sneaking around and finding out about her past, as well as not telling her what I had learned. Hope thought she had found someone she could trust. I broke that trust—and I can tell there's no way of getting it back."

Walker thought for a moment and then spoke. "This is all new to her now, Gid. It blindsided Hope. It hurts even more because of how close the two of you have grown. The house. The engagement. All of her hopes and dreams for the future seemed to crumble in an instant in her mind. But I know Hope loves you, Gid. This wave of rage will pass. She'll come to her senses."

"I doubt it," he said flatly. "When she left, she told me she would never forget—and never forgive me."

"That was the hurt talking. Not Hope. Give her a few days. She'll cool down and have time to think things through. She'll realize she flew off the handle. She's not going to throw away the love of a lifetime over something like this."

Gideon shook his head. "You're thinking and processing this as the pragmatic, coolheaded attorney that you are, my friend. I know Hope. I don't ever see her forgiving me, much less trusting me again. And without trust? There's nothing."

"She loves you, Gid. That's what you have going for you. And you love her."

"You think this is just a bump in the road for us, Walker, but it's not. This is an impasse that Hope will never get around. I've got to face facts. It's over between us. I don't even want to be here anymore."

His friend frowned. "Here? As in Sugar Springs?"

Gideon nodded.

"Don't be rash, Gid. Don't go resigning and leave. Don't walk away—from Sugar Springs—or Hope. Promise me."

He shook his head. "I'm not making any kind of promises. I will tell you that I won't act on this now. I'll give it some time. See if I can coexist in this same place as Hope. I won't make any guarantees, however. Something tells me that if I can't live in Sugar Springs without Hope, I may have to leave altogether."

23

Hope somehow managed to get through the next few days without breaking down in front of anyone. If she had been playing the part of herself in a movie, she would have easily walked away with an Oscar. No one suspected anything was wrong with her.

Even though she had shattered into a thousand pieces inside.

She couldn't sleep and was up until the wee hours, dozing fitfully for a couple of hours before rising for punishing runs. She wound up leaving Jake behind, worried that the length and pace of her runs would be detrimental to the beagle.

She avoided going into town during lunch, afraid she would run into Gideon. Sooner or later, it would have to come out that they were no longer seeing one another. Thank goodness they had kept their engagement between them and not announced it to their friends or the public. That was the one saving grace in all this. She couldn't help but wonder if she was keeping quiet about the news of ending her relationship with Gideon because once it got out, it wouldn't only seem real.

It would *be* real.

As she completed notes on her last appointment, a Great

Dane with an ear infection, her cell rang. She froze a moment. Part of her was afraid to look at the Caller ID because it might show Gideon's name. He had yet to call her. She understood why. She had ended things. No matter how he felt, he was a man who would respect her wishes.

But the other part of her desperately wanted to see his name lighting up her phone. Hope had truly been miserable since their breakup. She didn't know how much longer she could go on in her current state. Yet she couldn't take him back. She had lost all trust in him.

Even though the love remained...

Reaching for her cell on the desk, she saw Rory's name. She blinked back tears as she answered.

"Hi, Rory, what's up?" she asked, hoping her voice didn't betray how she truly felt.

"This is spur of the moment, but would you like to have lunch today? It seems like forever since I've seen you, and we only had a half-day at school today. I don't have to stay this afternoon because I've already accumulated enough professional development hours."

Hope looked at her watch. "It's almost one. I'll be honest. I just don't feel like going into town right now."

"What if I picked something up and brought it over?" Rory countered. "We could eat in your office and catch up."

"I'd like that," she said quietly, blinking rapidly because of the tears filling her eyes.

"I just pulled out of the school parking lot. What do you want?"

"Surprise me."

Her friend laughed. "I can do that. Be there in a few."

She hung up and finished her notes. The rest of the staff would be leaving for lunch. She was glad to have the place to herself. Hope decided she would tell Rory about ending things with Gideon. She wouldn't go into specifics, but it would be a start.

Hope tried reading an article in a veterinary journal as she waited for Rory to appear with lunch. She failed miserably. It was one thing to focus on a patient in front of her. Quite another to try and concentrate when no one else was around. She had dutifully played the role of concerned, caring town vet, but she had no motivation when she wasn't in her white coat role.

Aimlessly, she stared into space until she heard, "Earth to Hope. Come in."

Glancing up, she saw Rory had already arrived and looked concerned.

"Hey. Just thinking. Come on in."

Hope moved some things to the side of her desk as Rory set a large sack on it.

"Barbeque sandwiches and fries. It just sounded like it would hit the spot. I didn't think about drinks, though."

"I've got us covered." She spun her chair around and opened the small fridge sitting on the floor. "Bottled or sparkling?"

"Bottled is good," Rory replied, removing items from the sack and placing them on the desk. "I'm glad you had the time for lunch. And we still haven't scheduled a trip into Dallas to shop. I desperately need to do that. For a good reason." She bit into her sandwich. "Mmm. Just what I wanted."

She put a water in front of Rory and opened her own bottle before unwrapping the sandwich and fries.

"Okay, what's your good reason?" she asked and took a bite of tender brisket.

Rory swallowed and grabbed a few fries. "I'm going to need several new things to wear." She popped the fries into her mouth and chewed a moment. "Because I'm pregnant."

"What?" Hope was stunned for a moment but quickly recovered. "That's terrific news!"

She stood and leaned down, hugging Rory fiercely. Wanting what her friend had. A loving husband. A home. A child.

Hope burst out in tears and turned away.

"Hey, it's okay," Rory said, standing and wrapping her arms around Hope. "I'm pretty emotional these days, too. Are you also pregnant, Hope?"

"No," she wailed, her tears falling faster, sobs racking her body.

Rory simply held her, letting Hope cry until her tears subsided. She pulled away, sitting in her chair again.

"What's going on? Does this have anything to do with you canceling dinner tomorrow?"

She looked blankly at her friend.

"Walker had said you and Gideon were coming over this weekend, and we'd cook out. Then he said it was off. He didn't explain why, and I didn't ask him about it." Rory paused, frowning slightly. "Have you and Gideon had a fight?"

Shaking her head, she said, "Not a fight. We've... I've... ended things."

"Oh, honey. I'm so sorry."

Hope wiped her eyes with the sleeve of her lab coat. "I don't really want to talk about it. The reasons are... private."

Rory took her seat. "They can stay that way, but if you do want to talk about it—any of it—I'm here."

Her mouth trembled. "I know. I should've known that. I wanted to call you. But I thought..."

Her friend gave her a knowing look. "You thought I would take Gideon's side. Because of Walker."

"Yes," she admitted.

"I adore Gideon," Rory said. "I always will. But you're also my friend, Hope. I won't—can't—choose sides. I'll just have to stay friends with you both." She paused. "I know this has to be difficult. And I've made it worse by telling you I'm pregnant."

"No," Hope quickly reassured her. "I'm thrilled for you and Walker. You'll be the best parents on the planet. I'm just sad about... well, that it's not me. We had talked about children.

We both wanted them. I'd even gone off my birth control pills."

She froze, trying to recall when her last period had occurred, and came up blank.

"We were engaged," she blurted out. "We weren't going to make a fuss. Just go to the courthouse with you and Walker as our witnesses and get married. This weekend. Oh, what if I'm pregnant?" she wailed. "Maybe that's why I'm crying so much over Gideon. It's hormones. What am I going to do?"

"Take a drink of water," Rory said calmly.

Hope reached for the water and sipped it. "That's better," she said shakily. "I don't know if I can be a single mother. And I've ruined your good news."

"I know you're happy for us. Don't borrow trouble. First thing is to find out if you are pregnant. That's easy. Just pick up a home kit at Walmart."

"What if someone I know sees me doing that? Then they'll know it's Gideon's. And we're not together anymore. You know gossip. It'll take on a life of its own."

"*I'll* buy the pregnancy test," her friend said. "And when I let people know I'm pregnant, no one will suspect a thing."

"I'm sorry I've turned this into all about me," Hope apologized. "Tell me everything."

Rory laughed. "Well, I barf every morning—and then feel pretty good the rest of the day. I get food cravings. Like the barbeque today. The babies are due on Halloween."

"Wait. You said *babies*?"

"Yes. It's twins. We're having a sonogram soon. I definitely want to find out the genders, so we can be more prepared. Our lives are going to change radically."

"Then I guess it's a good thing you're going to be working from home on your skating designs and not standing in front of a class of teenagers, looking like a beached whale," Hope teased.

"It is a good time for me to make this career change."

"I'm happy to go to Dallas and shop with you for maternity clothes whenever you're ready." She thought of having kept Nova's secret and how she, too, would be needing maternity clothes.

They finished their lunch and as they threw away their trash, Rory said, "I'll go pick up the kit now. You want me to drop it by here on my way home?"

"That would be fine. I'll be worried until I take it. I'm not sick in the mornings."

"That doesn't happen for a few weeks. You might be pregnant now, and those symptoms will appear soon. Or you might not be at all. Either way, I'm here to support you. Walker, too. I know his first allegiance is to Gideon, but Walker adores you, Hope."

"He's a good guy," she said softly.

"I'll go to Walmart now. I'll put it in your top right drawer if that's okay. I'll just tell Christine I'm dropping off something for you."

They stood and Hope hugged Rory tightly. "Thank you. I've been so worried to tell you about the breakup."

"Friends forever," Rory assured her.

Hope saw three patients after lunch and then had a break in her schedule. She went to her office and closed the door, finding the pregnancy kit in a paper sack in her drawer. She opened it, skimming the instructions. She thought back and counted, realizing she had missed the start of her period a few days ago. Stress could often halt a period from coming, however, and her life had been full of it the last several days. Still, if she were pregnant, this test could confirm it. If it came up positive, she had a lot of planning to do.

And that would mean including Gideon.

He was the kind of man who would want to be in his child's life, even if they weren't together. She wouldn't keep the baby from him. That is, *if* there were a baby.

Slipping the kit into her lab coat pocket, she went to the

restroom and peed on the stick, waiting for the results. While the kit had said testing in the morning would provide a more concentrated urine sample, she couldn't wait. She would use the second test it came with tomorrow morning to follow up on today's results. She knew false positives were rare, so if she received a positive this late in the day, she believed she would be pregnant.

The lines appeared. Two of them.

She was definitely pregnant.

A feeling of euphoria filled her. This was something she hadn't expected but suddenly realized she wanted very badly. Although she would be a single parent for the most part, Hope didn't care.

She was going to be a mother.

A wave of sadness swept through her, knowing her parents would never get to see their grandchild. They would have been the ultimate grandparents—fun, giving, and incredibly loving. Still, Hope would do everything in her power to give her child a wonderful upbringing, and with Gideon as the baby's father, she knew that he or she would be loved by both parents.

She made a decision not to tell Gideon yet. The chance of miscarriage was higher than most people thought. If she could get through eight weeks of pregnancy, she would make arrangements to see him and inform him they were going to be parents.

Taking out her phone, she texted Rory.

> Test was positive. Please don't tell Walker yet. I want to give it eight weeks before I share this w/Gideon. I don't want to get his hopes up in case I miscarry.

HOPE TOOK A DEEP BREATH, seeing Rory was responding.

Will honor your wishes but my 2 cents? Tell
Gideon now. He deserves to know.

HOPE WOULDN'T LET the idea of having a baby be the reason they got back together. She still hurt from Gideon knowing all along who she was and never revealing that fact to her. Maybe she should tell him this news, though. She would think on it tonight. Her thoughts were already racing with all the things she needed to consider.

Somehow, she managed to keep her emotions intact and finished out her day, making her way to the front to check in with Christine before she left.

Her office manager was a bit frazzled. "I'm sorry, Hope. I forgot Marco has a make-up T-ball game. I was going to do the usual Friday bank deposit, but I can't now. Would you be okay with me locking it up and going tomorrow instead?"

"Give it to me. The bank closes at six. I can do it on my way home."

"The drive-through is crowded sometimes. You might want to go inside," warned Christine.

"Not a problem."

Christine handed over the bag with the cash deposits and checks inside. A majority of their clients used a credit card, but a handful—mostly older people—liked to write a check or pay their bill in cash, thus the weekly deposit.

Grabbing her purse, Christine said, "Thanks again, Hope. You're a lifesaver."

"Enjoy the game. I hope Marco hits a homerun."

She went to her car and headed toward the bank. As Christine had predicted, the line was longer than Hope would want to wait in, so she parked and headed inside. Only one person was being helped by a clerk and as Hope approached, the free clerk waved her over.

"Hi, Dr. Keller. Christine couldn't make the drop today?"

She set her purse on the counter and handed over the zipped bag. "Marco had a T-ball game. I told her I could do it."

As the clerk unzipped the bag and removed the checks and cash from inside, Hope pulled out her phone, thinking she would treat herself and call in a pizza order to Romano's for dinner. Nothing had tasted good to her this week, but she had the baby to think about now. She needed to get something in her. Resting her elbow on the counter, Hope glanced up and saw a man dressed in black from head to toe enter the bank's lobby. He rolled a ski mask down, hiding his features, and turned the lock so the front doors were bolted.

Fear cascaded through her, but she had the presence of mind to hit favorites and tap Gideon's name, thankful that she had resisted the desire to remove it from that list.

Hope heard him say hello and rested the phone on the counter, touching speakerphone as she did, praying he would listen.

"Everyone stay where you are," the man shouted, "and no one gets hurt." He aimed a gun in the direction of the two bank tellers. "Tellers, take five steps backward. Now. Don't trip an alarm, or it's a bullet in your brain. Step from behind the cages and move to the center of the room. We're on the clock."

The robber waved his gun at the two men sitting at desks to his right. "Over here," he barked, gesturing with the gun, and they hurried to the center of the bank.

The bank president came out of his office, his jaw dropping, and the robber said, "You, too. In the middle. Fast."

He glanced to Hope and the other customer, a woman in her late forties, and waved his weapon at them. They joined the others in the center.

She only hoped Gideon heard what was going on.

24

G ideon sat at his desk. "Get a grip, buddy," he warned
himself.

He had been in a terrible mood ever since Hope
ended things several days ago. Normally the calmest of men, his
fuse these days was short and explosive. He knew he had to rein
in his temper but had no idea how to put a lid on his frustration.
And not just frustration.

Call it pure misery.

He wasn't suicidal, but if things didn't change soon, he would
show signs of depression. Already, he was self-medicating, his
fancy term for drinking too much when he got home each night.
The thing was, while he enjoyed an occasional beer, Gideon
wasn't much of a drinker. That hearkened back to his athletic
days. As a scholarship athlete, he hadn't wanted to do anything to
put his career in jeopardy and had almost been a teetotaler in
college. After graduation, when his pro hopes dwindled and then
dried up, he still wanted his body—including his reflexes—in tip-
top shape. He never came into duty hungover.

Last night, however, he had gotten sloshed. He woke up this
morning cotton-mouthed, his eyes bloodshot. He had done what

he'd seen in an old Paul Newman movie, *The Sting*, and dunked his entire head in a sink full of ice and water. That had roused him like nothing ever had before. The dunking—and a quick stop at the pharmacy for some eyedrops to get the red out—and he actually appeared normal-looking this morning. Inside, though, his gut was churning. He told himself no more booze, no matter how miserable he was.

His cell rang, and he winced at the sharp noise. When Gideon saw Hope's name light up on his phone, his mouth went dry. He hadn't called her, not wanting to reach out since she had made it perfectly clear she wanted nothing to do with him.

But this was Hope calling *him*.

Could she have had a change of heart?

He answered. "Hello?"

She didn't say anything. But what he heard chilled him to the bone. Gideon listened, quickly figuring out that Hope was in the bank—and it was being robbed. Someone barked out quick, precise directions. Whoever was in charge sounded like he knew what he was doing.

Gideon jumped to his feet and tore out of his office, his cell glued to his ear as he raced to the dispatch room. He grabbed Gladys by the arm and hustled her outside.

"Listen," he instructed quietly. "Stay quiet. Open line," he warned.

Then he hurried into the room, closing the door. He didn't want the robber—or robbers—to hear him as he took control of the system.

Using the APCO ten codes, Gideon flipped a switch and broadcast to every officer on duty, be it in a squad car or on foot, "This is Chief Ross. 10-18." He paused a moment, letting the urgent alert message kick in.

Though no bank alarm had been sounded, he said, "We have a likely 10-45. A 10-64 now. 10-65. First National Bank." At least he prayed Hope was in the bank in town.

In cop speak, he'd just alerted all personnel on duty that a crime was in progress, an armed robbery.

"10-40. Repeat. 10-40. Hostage situation. I'll be in front. Get the drive-through lines vacated and alert tellers silently."

The 10-40 was a warning not to use sirens or flashers. He didn't want to warn any getaway driver waiting outside, much less alert the people involved inside the bank itself.

"Ross out."

Gideon hurried to the door, where Gladys held the phone to her ear, her face grim. She lowered it, pressing it to her chest.

"He knows what he's doing, Chief." She paused. "And he has Hope helping him."

Fear shot through him. He grabbed the phone and ran out the station's side door. The bank was only two blocks away. He could reach it faster on foot and possibly detain any driver outside.

He held the cell to his ear, running the short distance, dodging a car as he crossed the street. As expected, the Friday drive-through line was long. He would let arriving patrolmen deal with that. Cutting across the parking lot, he saw Hope's car, which was like a knife twisting in his gut. Few cars were parked in front, which meant other than bank personnel, a limited number of hostages inside the building. He did hear a car running and saw it was empty.

Gideon hurried to the entrance and ducked, pulling his gun with one hand and testing the door with the other as he glimpsed several hostages face down on the floor in the center of the lobby.

Locked.

The double glass doors would allow him to see in, but that meant the criminals inside would also be able to see him outside. Quickly, he moved to the side, out of view. If the man or men inside were so conscious about time, he or they would be coming out in less than a minute.

And Gideon would be waiting.

HOPE FOLLOWED the gunman's instructions, going flat on the floor, facedown, spreadeagle. Everything was happening so fast. More than anything, she hoped Gideon had been able to hear what was happening and figure out where she was. She hadn't had time to give him any kind of clue. But he was smart. He hadn't advanced to the position he held without honing his instincts.

Suddenly, she was lifted off the floor, the gunman latching onto her elbow and dragging her to her feet. He marched her to where she had been standing moments ago.

She didn't want him to see the phone open on the counter, and so she said, "My name is Hope," trying to distract him and have him look at her.

"I don't give a rat's ass." He pulled something white from his pocket and thrust it at her.

She looked down, seeing it was a Target bag, with other Target bags stuffed inside it.

"Behind the counter." He shoved her. "Open the drawers. Fill a bag two-thirds full. Start another one after that. Take everything in the drawers."

She was already behind the counter and had pulled out the extra bags by the time he finished speaking. Hope opened the drawer and began placing cash into the bag. She had always remarked on how strong Target bags were and had used them to carry all kinds of things. It was almost comical that this robber also knew just how great Target bags were.

"Twenty seconds!" he shouted at her.

Not bothering to look up, she moved to the second drawer and grabbed as much cash as she could in the time allotted.

"That's it. Come here. Now!"

Hope could hear the agitation in his voice. She had looped the first Target bag over her wrist, and it now hung from her forearm. She carried the other one and tried to give it to him.

"You carry them," he ordered, grasping her arm again, his fingers digging into her flesh.

He pulled her across the lobby. As they got to the door, he paused. "Don't get up for three fucking minutes. Don't call anyone until then," he warned those lying on the floor.

Then out of nowhere, the robber fired his gun without provocation. The bank president yelped, clutching his thigh.

"Take care of him before he bleeds out."

The gunman threw the lock and pushed open the right-side of the double glass doors. As he pushed Hope through the opening, she trusted that Gideon was on the outside. Waiting for the gunman.

Waiting for her.

Two steps out the door, she dropped to the ground. The gunman started to jerk her arm and then released it. A shot sounded, a noise so loud that Hope shrieked.

Then he fell to the ground beside her. For a moment she saw the stunned look on his face. Then his eyes went wide. He was dead.

Strong arms lifted her, rushing her away from the body. She dropped the Target bag she carried, but the other one remained looped on her arm as they halted. She looked up.

And saw Gideon.

He jerked her to him, his mouth coming down on hers. Hope clung to him, kissing him back, thinking how foolish she had been to let this man go.

He broke the kiss, his hands on her shoulders. "Are you all right? Did he hurt you? Did he hurt you? Hope? Hope?"

Her voice wouldn't work. It was as if her vocal cords had been frozen.

Gideon cupped her face. "Nod if you're okay, babe."

She did, her head moving in quick jerks.

Gideon enfolded her in his arms again. "You're going to be fine, Hope. I'm going to turn you over to one of my officers."

"No!" she said, clinging to him.

He looked at her steadily. "I have things that need to be done," he said gently. He glanced up. "Officer Winkindale is going to take good care of you. He'll escort you to the station. You're going to need to give a statement."

"When will I see you again?" she asked frantically.

"As soon as I can finish up here."

"He shot someone. You need an ambulance."

"We'll take care of it."

Gideon motioned, and a patrolman hurried over. "This is Officer Winkindale, Hope. He's going to take good care of you."

"Hi. I'm Officer Winkindale. Scott," a young man said, and Hope remembered this was the name of the rookie who had impressed Gideon. "If you'll come with me, ma'am."

"Hope. It's Hope," she managed to get out.

"Okay, Hope. Right this way."

Somehow, the policeman took the bag of cash and gave it to someone, getting her into a squad car. By then, she heard the sound of a siren and supposed it was the ambulance coming. She looked out the car's window and saw the place was filled with squad cars and people. She shuddered.

"Here. Let me wrap this around you, Hope. You might be going into shock. Let's make sure you stay warm."

She held the blanket tightly to her, closing her eyes.

She could have died today.

And Gideon would never have known about the baby.

Why had she ended things with him? She had accused him of hiding the fact that he knew she was Dr. Deborah Busby. In truth, she had done the same. She had kept her past a secret from the man she loved. The man she had planned to marry. And she believed her crime was worse than his. She hadn't shared something she should have with him. Once she knew she loved him, she should have been open and told him everything.

It had taken a crisis, but it was all so clear now. Regret filled her.

Would Gideon even want her back? Would he ever feel he could trust her again, much less love her?

At the station, she was given hot coffee. Even though the thought of coffee soured her stomach, she drank it, hoping it would warm her. Others who had been inside the bank appeared in the room where she had been taken, and they hugged one another. The teller who had been waiting on her handed Hope her phone and purse.

"I thought you'd want these, Dr. Keller. You helped save us all by leaving your phone on."

Dr. Rex Carpenter appeared with his wife, Sandy. She had met the couple when they had turned out for the opening of Keller Critter Care. Dr. Carpenter was a local GP, and his wife served as her husband's RN. The couple did quick examinations of all those who had been inside the bank.

"What about the man who was shot?" Hope asked. "Will he be all right?"

"Yes, Dr. Keller," Dr. Carpenter assured her.

After that, she and the others were taken to interview rooms. Gideon had arrived and joined Officer Winkindale, who stood in the corner, and a plainclothes officer who was sitting at the table. She wanted to reach out to him but understood he was in police chief mode now.

"I'm Detective Douglas, Dr. Keller. I'll be leading your interview. We'll record it if you don't have any objections."

"All right," she said quietly, wishing Gideon would come and sit next to her and hold her hand.

She told the detective everything that had happened inside the bank from the time she entered. He had her go through everything twice, and Hope remembered more details the second time around.

"You thought fast on your feet, Dr. Keller," Detective Douglas praised. "If not for your quick thinking—and Chief Ross mobilizing everyone so swiftly—we could have had a very different outcome."

Hope smiled weakly. "I'm glad I could help."

Another man entered the room. "I'm Deputy Chief Pete Blest, Dr. Keller. I was watching your interview from another room." He handed her a card. "If you think of anything else, please give me a call. I'll be heading up the investigation into the attempted robbery and kidnapping."

"Kidnapping?"

"You weren't going willingly out of that bank, were you?"

"No, of course not," she said, and then asked, "Why isn't Chief Ross in charge?"

Blest glanced at Gideon and then back to her. "Chief Ross will be placed on temporary leave for a while."

She realized it was because he had shot and killed a man.

"I'm going to have Officer Winkindale drive you home now," Blest told her.

Hope glanced to Gideon, and he said, "I can't take you. It's my turn to be interviewed."

Blest looked at the two of them. "Two minutes, Chief. Then we'll begin." He glanced to Winkindale. "Officer."

The patrolman followed Blest out of the interview room. Hope stared across the table at Gideon, who crossed the room and took the seat next to her. She reached out her hands, and thankfully, he took them.

"Thank you for saving me. In more ways than one."

His brow furrowed. "What do you mean?"

She squeezed his hands. "Will you come over when you're finished here?"

He looked at her, uncertainty in his eyes. "You want me to?"

"I need you to."

"Okay. It'll be a couple of hours. At least."

Hope swallowed. "I don't care how late it is. We need to talk."

"I'll text you when I leave the station."

She released his hands, and they both stood. Hope wanted to touch him. Hug him. Kiss him. She did none of those things, though. She needed to see if she could mend things between them before she attempted to do anything else.

"I'll see you later," she said.

Gideon opened the door for her, and she saw Officer Winkindale waiting for her.

"Ready, Dr. Keller?"

Hope was more than ready—to set things right with her and Gideon again.

25

_____

Gideon saw that Hope was in good hands with Scott Winkindale. He returned to the interview room, pushing all thoughts of Hope from his head. He had to be totally in cop mode now. Not that his career was on the line. He knew it had been a good shoot. He simply wanted to make sure all the I's were dotted and the T's were crossed.

Pete Blest returned to the room, along with Sergeant Leland Brown.

"Need anything, Chief?" asked his deputy chief.

"Maybe some water," he said, finding his mouth and throat dry.

Brown stood and left the room, returning with a bottled water. He handed it to Gideon, who uncapped it and downed half of it in one, long swig.

"I want to play everything by the book, Chief Ross," Blest said. "Do you consent to this interview being filmed?"

"Yes, I do."

Brown played camera operator as Blest gave the time and date of the interview, stating that he would be asking all the questions, but identifying that Patrol Commander Sergeant Brown was present in the room.

"As you know, Chief, we will have to temporarily relieve you of your command while we complete our investigation into the shooting and death of Roger Mills. Since it's late on a Friday night, I believe it will take the bulk of this weekend, along with Monday and Tuesday, to interview all personnel and witnesses involved and complete our report."

"I understand," he said, his attention returning to Hope. Gideon shook his head to clear her image and again, picked up the water bottle, draining its contents and setting it aside.

"I will tell you from my preliminary discussions with officers on the scene that the shooting seems to be justified, Chief Ross. The perp left the bank with a hostage in hand, gun pointed at her. Dr. Keller was smart enough to get out of the way. That's one woman who thinks quickly on her feet."

He smiled for the first time in hours, if not days. "Yes, Dr. Keller is one amazing woman."

Blest continued with the interview. "The perp—and we have identified him as Roger Mills of Tyler—swung his loaded gun toward you. You were defending not only your life but that of Dr. Keller's. I wanted that on the record as we start."

The deputy chief took Gideon back through the timeline, from when Hope first had dialed his number.

"Because she put her cell phone on speaker," Gideon told the pair. "I was able to ascertain that she and others were in danger and the most likely place the situation was unfolding, based upon comments Mills made, was at First National Bank."

He went on to describe how he had taken over the dispatch controls, having Gladys continue to listen to what was happening in the bank while he did so. He walked Blest through his arrival at First National Bank, being the first officer on the scene, and how in his professional judgment he decided it would be unwise to enter the bank on his own.

"I didn't want to endanger any of the hostages, which I caught a brief glimpse of as I looked into the bank. I didn't want the unsub to see me, which is why I stepped aside and remained close to the exit but out of view. It was apparent that he was very aware of time and was trying to get out within a certain timeframe."

Gideon described how the door opened and Hope first appeared in the doorway, with the two Target bags containing the money she had collected for Mills.

"I don't know if she saw me with her peripheral vision or if she was merely counting on the police to be outside, but Hope—Dr. Keller—fell to the ground unexpectedly. Mills, sensing the threat, swung his gun from where it had been aimed at her to my position. I quickly assessed that he would fire and got off a shot before he could discharge his weapon."

"Thank you, Chief Ross," Blest said. "That was objective and detailed, but you know the routine. Let's walk through it again and see if a second telling jogs anything further from your memory."

He nodded, glad that his deputy chief was sticking to the book. Everything occurring here would be part of the record, and Gideon wanted to make certain nothing was missed or could be questioned. Just because he was the police chief didn't mean any favoritism would be shown.

Once more, he went through his account of the events, leaving nothing out.

When he finished, Blest nodded to Brown, who turned off the camera.

"You have excellent recall, Chief," Blest praised. "I'm honored to be under your command."

For the first time, Gideon chuckled. "It'll be your command for the next several days, Pete."

Without being asked, he pulled out his police ID and badge

and handed it to Blest. He had already handed over his gun at the crime scene.

"You will be put on leave—with pay," Blest continued. "Maybe since you've bought that new house, you can work on moving in during your free time."

Now allowed to leave the station, Gideon went back to his office a moment to collect his thoughts. He logged off his computer and shut it down. Glancing around, he found nothing he needed to take with him.

All he had to do now was get to Hope.

He left the station, which still hummed with activity. Once the investigation was over, he would carefully comb through the official report, from everything the coroner had learned during his autopsy of Mills to what had been discovered about the man he had shot and Mills' motive for attempting to rob the bank.

Texting Hope that he was on his way, he drove to her place, trying to tamp down his swirling emotions. Just because she had broken up with him didn't mean he had stopped loving her. He didn't know what she was going to say to him once they were alone together. Maybe she just wanted to express her gratitude to him for having saved her life.

And maybe it would be something more...

Gideon reached Lizzy Lou's and parked. By now, it was almost eleven o'clock. He climbed the stairs and knocked softly on Hope's door.

She threw it open almost immediately, her eyes large, as she said, "Come in."

He did so, refraining from pulling her into his arms and kissing her. Jake greeted him, and he bent to pet the beagle.

Hope closed the door and said, "Won't you have a seat?"

He went to the sofa he had sat on so many times. Jake jumped up and sat next to him, and Gideon continued to pet the pup as Hope took a seat on the other side of the dog. He caught the scent of vanilla, and longing poured through him.

"I have things that need to be said, Gideon."

He held up a hand. "Stop there, Hope. If you want to tell me you're grateful for me saving your life, I appreciate the sentiment. I was only doing my job. I would have done it for anyone in this town."

"But you did it for *me*," she said softly. "Your ex-fiancée."

His throat grew thick with emotion. "Like I said, anyone. Who knows what would have happened with that guy? You were a hostage—and hostages become expendable at some point."

Gideon hesitated and then added, "Things might not have ended well between us, Hope, but I would always put my life on the line to keep you safe."

She nudged Jake from the couch and slid closer to him, taking his hands in hers. The touch of her. The smell of her. It was all too much for him. Gideon broke the contact and stood.

"I need to get going," he said brusquely, striding toward the door.

"Wait. Please, Gideon."

He turned and walked back to her. Again, she took his hands, standing, and said, "Yes, I'm grateful that you saved me. When trouble hit, you were my first thought. I didn't have time to give you any details, but you were able to figure out where I was. That I needed you. I knew that, Gideon. I knew you would be there when I stepped out that door. I had faith that you would protect me and everyone else at the scene."

Tears misted her sky blue eyes. "But you know what I was thinking of the entire time? What a fool I had been to let you go. Worse, a hypocrite. I chastised you for not telling me what you had learned about my past when I hadn't come clean with you."

She swallowed as a lone tear rolled down her cheek.

"It's a case of the pot calling the kettle black," she continued. "I accused you of not sharing with me what you knew. I said I couldn't trust you, but it's a two-way street. I love you. And I should have trusted you enough to open up to you about my past.

My real name. Why I had come to Sugar Springs. I also lied to you by omission. I'm surprised you didn't call me out on that."

Warmth flooded through him. "I guess we both need to work on our communication skills," he quipped.

He tried not to hope. He tried not to feel as he gazed into her eyes—and it was there he saw her love for him. It was there. It was real.

They moved toward one another at the same time, their arms holding one another as their mouths fused in a kiss. A kiss of apology. A kiss of promise. A kiss which spoke of the unbreakable bond between them.

It was Hope who broke the kiss. "I want to apologize to you, Gideon. More than that, I'm pleading with you to forgive me. To take me back. To start over. To say you love me again."

Tears formed in his own eyes now. "I never stopped loving you, Hope. There's nothing to forgive. You went through hell and back in your life, and you were merely trying to start over here in Sugar Springs. I'm sorry this nosy cop violated your privacy. If I had it to do over again, I wouldn't look into you and your past. I was dishonest as I sought to find out your true identity."

He swallowed. "But you are who you are. The woman I love. The one I want to spend the rest of my life with."

Her tears flowed freely now. "Do you truly mean that, Gideon?"

"I mean every word, Hope. I love you more than life itself, and I wouldn't have a life without you. In fact, I was thinking of leaving Sugar Springs because it was going to be too hard, knowing you lived so close and yet we were alienated from one another."

She pulled him down for a slow, sweet kiss. When she broke it, she said, "Let's always be totally open with one another."

He smiled. "Oh, I believe we've learned our lesson. A painful one. One which kept us apart."

Gideon framed her face with his hands. "I never want to be apart from you a single day, Hope. I love you now and forever and since I'm temporarily suspended from the force, why don't we put that time off to good use and get married?"

Her eyes shone brightly, her love for him obvious. "Well, Chief, we never have gotten around to picking out our wedding bands, much less applying for a marriage license. I suppose we need to go to Tyler and do that before we can say our I do's."

He swept her into his arms and carried her to the bed, undressing her slowly and making thorough love to her.

They lay spent in one another's arms afterward, her head nestled against his beating heart as she toyed with the hair on his chest, playfully tweaking and smoothing it.

"I have something to tell you," she said. "Something I hope you'll be happy to hear."

"Hmm. I'm intrigued. Do tell, Dr. Keller."

She pushed herself up to a sitting position. "I took a test yesterday. A very special kind of test."

He frowned. "Do you have to do some kind of yearly certification to keep your vet license updated?"

"This was a test of a very personal nature," Hope said, a slow smile appearing on her face. "I'll have to go to the doctor to confirm the results—but it was a pregnancy test, Gideon. I think I'm pregnant."

"What?"

Gideon pulled her down and kissed her over and over. He couldn't believe what she had shared. It was amazing. Incredible. He was going to be a father.

"Are you pleased?" she asked.

"I am as happy as I have ever been in my entire life, Dr. Keller," he told her, kissing her again.

Hope smiled. "I hope in our most tender moments that you will always call me Dr. Keller."

He smoothed her hair, smiling at her. "I can do that, Dr. Keller. And all those other moments?

"I'll simply call you mine."

EPILOGUE

TWENTY-FIVE YEARS LATER—SUGAR SPRINGS

Hope finished up on a femoral head ostectomy surgery, repairing the hip dysplasia of a four-year-old Rottweiler. She looked across the table to where her daughter stood, wearing a surgical mask, observing today's procedure as she had many times before.

Cady gave her a thumbs up. "That was amazing, Mom. You have such a deft touch. I don't see how you get your stitches as small as you do."

"Practice?" Hope laughed. "Your stitches are wonderful, honey. You'll get better as time goes on."

"I just wish I would hear from the vet schools. Notifications have started going out this week."

Cady, who was a senior at A&M, had interviewed at three different veterinary schools, starting last October and finishing in January. While her daughter said she would be happy to attend any of the three, Hope knew Cady leaned toward A&M because that's where Hope had gone.

"Let's take Chester into recovery. Why don't you walk me through what needs to be done next?"

She listened as Cady told her in great detail the steps recovery would involve, down to when the dog would need to return for his checkup.

"You know I couldn't be prouder of you, don't you?" she asked.

Cady laughed. "You're my mom. Of course, you're going to say that."

"You are going to make a fine veterinarian, no matter what school you graduate from."

Her daughter had been mad for animals from the time she could crawl after their two dogs and three cats. Hope had called Cady the Animal Whisperer because she had an affinity with animals. Cady could calm them when they were upset. She seemed to know what was wrong instantly. Her daughter had worked summers in the clinic throughout high school and college, easily earning the five hundred hours of recommended pre-veterinary experience. She would graduate in two months with a degree in animal science, with a minor in zoology.

Randy stepped into the surgical room and said, "Why don't you come with me, Cady? We'll get Chester fixed up and comfortable."

Hope removed her surgical gloves and slipped from the operating gown, as well. She went to her office, where she typed notes into the rottweiler's file regarding today's procedure. Then she called Chester's owner, letting her know the surgery had gone well and that they would keep the dog overnight.

"We'll keep an eye on him and if all looks well—no fever developing or sign of infection—I'll give you a call tomorrow morning, and Chester can go home around noon. You'll need to remember to continue administering his pain meds and antibiotics. Christine will give you written directions for his aftercare."

She finished seeing the rest of her appointments, Cady sitting in on each of the examinations. Thankfully, pet owners who came to Keller Critter Care had been used to Cady doing so for years now. Her daughter already knew so much. She would be far ahead of many of her fellow vet students once she started school in the fall.

When it was time to leave, Hope got her purse. She and Cady walked to the car.

"I just called in a pizza order to Romano's, Mom. I texted Will, and he said he would join us at dinner. I texted Dad, and I told him he better *be* at dinner."

Hope was glad she would get to have both her little chicks under their roof, if only for dinner tonight.

Will had joined the Sugar Springs Police Force straight out of college. Gideon had wanted their firstborn to try getting on at a police department in a larger city, but all Will wanted to do was come home to Sugar Springs. He had been on the force for four years now, and Gideon told her that he hoped one day Will might serve as police chief in his hometown.

They stopped at Romano's, and Hope said, "We both better go in. You know Vivi will want to see you since you're home for spring break."

Entering the restaurant, Hope couldn't help but think of the first time she had gone into Romano's all those years ago for pizza. Mr. and Mrs. Romano had turned the pizza parlor over to their daughter many years ago, and Vivi had done amazing things with the menu and décor.

Her friend greeted them and embraced Cady. "I heard you were home for your break. Why didn't you go to the beach with some of your friends? Galveston or Corpus?"

"Because I'd rather spend my time off with Mom at the clinic," Cady replied.

"You and animals," Vivi said, laughing as she shook her head. "Are you dating anyone, Cady?"

Hope was interested in this answer. While she and her daughter were close and they talked about many things, Cady was usually quiet about her love life. She watched the blush spill across Cady's cheeks.

"I have been seeing someone for about eight weeks now."

"And?" Vivi prompted.

"And—that's all you're getting out of me," Cady retorted.

A server brought two large pizza boxes and handed them to Cady.

"Just put it on our tab, Vivi," Hope said.

She and Cady returned to the car and were home within a few minutes. Hope was pleased to see Gideon's SUV already parked in the garage as she pulled in beside it. Glancing in her rearview mirror, she saw Will pulling in behind them.

He got out of his truck and came to meet them, giving his younger sister a bear hug.

"Good to see you, Cady," Will said. "Have you heard from any vet schools yet?"

Hope laughed. "You will feel the earth move when that happens, Will."

He threw an arm around Cady's shoulder. "Wherever you get in is the place you're supposed to be."

"I know. That's what Mom keeps saying. I'm just tired of waiting," Cady complained.

They went into the house and found Gideon setting the table.

"Hey, everyone. The table is ready. What does everyone want to drink?"

Will opted for iced tea like his father, while Cady and Hope asked for sparkling water. The four of them sat at the table, and they opened the pizza boxes.

"Yes!" Will said with enthusiasm, digging into the supreme, which had four meats and five vegetables on it.

"I've missed Romano's pizza so much," Cady declared.

Will looked at her and grinned. "Why do you think I came back to live in Sugar Springs? I needed to work where the best pizza in the world is served."

They caught up with one another, Gideon talking about a string of burglaries which had occurred recently. Will told his sister about how he was now involved in a drug and alcohol education program, giving talks at the high school, answering students' questions.

Then Will cleared his throat. "Since we're all here together, I have something to tell you."

He paused, and Hope had a pretty good idea what was coming.

"I'm going to ask Angie to marry me."

"Yes!" Cady shouted, jumping up and hugging her brother. "It's about time. That's fantastic news."

"Well, she doesn't know I'm planning to do so. That means the three of you better keep quiet about it for twenty-four hours."

"When are you proposing, son?" Gideon asked.

"I'm going to do it tomorrow night." Quickly, Will told them about his plans to surprise Angie. "We've kind of talked about it in general. Nothing specific. I do know neither of us wants a big, fancy wedding."

Gideon slipped his hand around Hope's and squeezed her fingers. "A courthouse wedding was good enough for us. Look how long we've lasted."

"I know we'll talk specifics once I ask Angie to marry me, but I have a feeling she'll want to do it this summer when she's off from school."

Hope thought that Angie would know Will would be popping the question. They had dated almost three years and seemed more in love each time Hope and Gideon saw them.

"We're happy for you, Will," she said. "Angie already feels like family to us."

Cady's phone beeped. She grabbed her phone. "Oh! An email just came through. It's from A&M." She bit her lip. "I'm so nervous. I'm afraid to open it."

Gideon looked at his daughter. "This from the girl who was skiing black routes when she was six? The one who talked her way into riding a rollercoaster at Six Flags when she was still two inches too short? You're brave, Cady. Open it."

"Okay, Dad."

They all watched as she tapped her cell and began reading. Suddenly, a smile appeared.

"I got in! I'm going to stay in College Station!"

Mother and daughter hugged, and then Hope slipped from the kitchen and went to the extra fridge in the laundry room. She removed a bottle of champagne that she'd placed there, wanting to use it to celebrate when Cady found out where she would attend vet school.

She brought it back to the kitchen and handed it to her husband to open while she got glasses for them. Bringing them to the table, Gideon filled them.

Cady was texting like crazy, letting her friends know.

"Pause the fingers, kid," Gideon said, passing the final glass to Cady. He looked to Hope and nodded.

She lifted her glass. "Here's to Cady and all the hard work she's put in. You will be an incredible vet, honey."

Cady beamed. "I may just come back to Sugar Springs and take over your clinic, Mom. I thought I better give you a heads up now."

Hope did the math. She would be sixty-two and Gideon sixty-six by the time Cady graduated from vet school. It would be an honor to turn the clinic over to her daughter and talk Gideon into retiring.

They all stood and raised their glasses as Gideon said, "To Cady."

"To Cady!" Hope and Will echoed.

After they celebrated with the champagne, Will said he had to go. Cady retreated to her room, saying she had someone special she needed to call about her news. Hope wondered if it were the boy her daughter was dating.

That left Hope and Gideon alone. He slipped his arms around

her, and the thrill she always felt being close to him was still present after all these years together.

"Here's to us as parents, Dr. Keller," he said huskily. "We've done a pretty good job."

"We certainly have, Chief," she replied, just before his mouth covered hers.

ALSO BY ALEXA ASTON

Love and the Lawman

Ballad Beauty

SAGEBRUSH BRIDES

A Game of Chance

Written in the Cards

Outlaw Muse

KNIGHTS OF REDEMPTION

A Bit of Heaven on Earth

A Knight for Kallen

SECOND SONS OF LONDON

Educated by the Earl

Debating with the Duke

DUKES DONE WRONG

Discouraging the Duke

Deflecting the Duke

Disrupting the Duke

Delighting the Duke

Destiny with a Duke

DUKES OF DISTINCTION

Duke of Renown

Duke of Charm

Duke of Disrepute

Duke of Arrogance

Duke of Honor

Code of Honor

Journey to Honor

Heart of Honor

Bold in Honor

Love and Honor

Gift of Honor

Path to Honor

Return to Honor

Season of Honor

NOVELLAS

Diana

Derek

Thea

The Lyon's Lady Love

ABOUT THE AUTHOR

A native Texan and former history teacher, award-winning and internationally bestselling author Alexa Aston lives with her husband in a Dallas suburb, where she eats her fair share of dark chocolate and plots out stories while she walks every morning. She enjoys travel, sports, and binge-watching—and never misses an episode of *Survivor*.

Alexa brings her characters to life in steamy historicals, contemporary romances, and romantic suspense novels that resonate with passion, intensity, and heart.

KEEP UP WITH ALEXA
Visit her website
Newsletter Sign-Up

MORE WAYS TO CONNECT WITH ALEXA

www.ingramcontent.com/pod-product-compliance
Lightning Source LLC
Chambersburg PA
CBHW020127120726
47903CB00007B/2144

* 9 7 8 1 6 4 8 3 9 4 7 9 9 *